He was about to i
when she emerged at
Uncertainty flickered
thought she was going
upper floors. But she took a deep breath, squared her
shoulders, and stepped off the landing.

He inhaled a ragged breath at the sight of her. Her dress
accentuated the slight swing of her hips while the tight
bodice molded perfectly to the swell of her breasts. With
each step as she descended, a slow burn heated his blood,
flooding hot desire straight to his groin. She shimmered in
the soft light spilling from the room—a light acting as a
path for her to follow, illuminating her way…to him.

She entered with her head bowed and lowered into a
deep curtsy. "Your Majesty."

He extended his hand and tried to keep his fingers from
twitching in anticipation of her touch. She hesitated, and
had yet to look him in the eyes. But she could not deny
him, not without causing insult, so he waited. His body
trembled when her hand slipped into his.

For the second time today, he couldn't let her go. She
had entered the room on a whisper, but swept across his
senses like a winter storm.

As she looked down, he resisted the urge to brush his
thumb across the soft curve of her lips. She was a feast for
his eyes to devour. He wanted to tell her that she looked
stunning, but his voice failed him and he could only mutter
her name in a gravelly, scrape of sound.

Praise for *CALLER of LIGHT*

"The story is shown through well crafted visual imagery as well as narrative. The heroine is deftly portrayed from the very start."

~Marisa Corvisiero, L. Perkins Agency

"This is classic high fantasy. STELLAR research & world-building. You are a GOOD writer, with super world-building and description. You were MADE to write fantasy."

~Renee Wildes, Fantasy Romance Author

"I was enticed from the beginning! I feel total admiration for Carina. Marek possesses all the qualities required of a stellar hero. The author used all the senses to establish an enchanting 'otherworldliness' of the setting."

~Joelle Walker, Editor, MuseItUp Publishing

"The world building is both fun and different."

~Alicia Condon, Editorial Director, Kensington Books

"This story was remarkable!"

~Dee Carney, Erotic Romance Author

Awards

2012 – Yellow Rose Winter Rose contest WINNER

2012 – Cleveland Rocks contest finalist

2012 – The Sandy contest finalist

2012 – Great Beginnings contest finalist

2012 – Smoky Mountain Laurie contest finalist

2012 – Touch of Magic contest finalist

2011 – Oklahoma Finally a Bride contest WINNER

2011 – Heart of the West contest finalist

2011 – Melody of Love contest finalist

CALLER
OF
LIGHT

....

BY
TJ SHAW

Forgotten Dreams Publishing, LLC
Laveen, AZ

Cover Art by *Debbie Taylor*

Publishing History
Forgotten Dreams Publishing, LLC, 2017
5045 W. Baseline Road, Suite A105-191
Laveen, AZ 85339
Print ISBN 978-1-948175-02-9
Digital ISBNs 978-1-948175-00-5; 978-1-948175-01-2

The Wild Rose Press
PO Box 708
Adams Basin, NY 14410-0708
First Faery Rose Edition, 2012
Previous Print ISBN 978-1-61217-706-9
Previous Digital ISBN 978-1-61217-707-6

Published in the United States of America

Dedication

For my mom,
who always provided encouraging words,
a shoulder to lean on, and a swift kick in the pants
during the times I stopped believing
I could touch the stars.

Acknowledgements

To Debbie Taylor and D.C.A. Graphics, thanks for creating a fabulous cover.

And to the reader who purchased *Caller of Light*, thank you too. I truly hope you enjoy the story.

Don't hesitate to contact me through my website at http://tjshaw.com/. Also, for information and news about upcoming releases, please consider joining my newsletter.

Contents

CHAPTER 1

FIRST LOOK

With a final grunt, Carina McKay scaled the remaining expanse to the top of the stark mountain. She crouched low, scanned the sky, and listened. Looking up at the Dorrado heavens, she gulped cold air into her lungs to calm her heart from the exerting climb. Even from a distance, only a few wispy clouds dotted an otherwise clear day, and aside from the wind whistling across the rocky surface, silence welcomed her. No voices or thunderous roars from angry Critons. No heavy footfalls from hundreds of soldiers running in the valley below, and no stomping hoofs or neighs from excited coursers.

Satisfied no one watched, she stood and rubbed her arms, trying to warm them from the chilly breeze slicing through her thin blouse. She wished she'd brought her long, split tail riding jacket, but it remained tied to Mira's saddle on the warmer, sheltered side of the summit.

Mira, her young winged Criton, perched on a large overhang below, nestled under a strand of wide-leafed trees. Mira whined and stomped her feet, shaking the trees that would shelter her from the inquisitive eyes of animals and men flying overhead.

Squirming at her Criton's noisy commotion, Carina peered over the edge. Knowing the animal could hear her even from the distance separating them, she whispered, "Shhh Mira. They'd see you up here." Carina frowned when Mira thumped her tail against a tree, making the leaves shiver, but the little Criton quieted under the canopy.

Feeling exposed on top of the desolate mountaintop, Carina scouted for a place to hide. The barren peak didn't offer much protection, sporting jagged boulders and deep crevices. With cautious steps, she crossed over the shards of blackened rock to avoid slashing an ankle and spotted a crack underneath a boulder large enough to conceal her from anyone flying overhead. After another glance across the bluff to confirm there was nowhere else to hide, she scrambled into the dark hole, praying nothing lived inside the blackness that would bite or sting. She knelt against the cold rock and tried to get comfortable.

During the last few days she'd ridden Mira to the edge of her father's lands, hoping to get a glimpse of King Duncan and his Criton riders. After finishing her chores, she'd sneak away to soar on the wind currents and calm an unexplainable restlessness building inside her. A rising awareness poked at her mind, needling her with a sense that her life was about to change forever. No matter how hard she tried to quash the sensation, the unease festered and swelled until it lived within her consciousness. The desperation had spiraled into an unbearable ache, her only solace found on the beating wings of her beloved Criton.

A growing burn in her thighs from kneeling forced her to slide down to a seated position and draw her legs up to her chest in the cramped space. If Father discovered her riding Mira, she'd be punished. He never liked her riding Critons because he considered the large, fire-breathing creatures, with rows of sharp teeth, as beasts for war and inappropriate for a noblewoman. Why he even considered her of noble blood made no sense to her anyway because of her mixed heritage.

She learned at a young age that she'd never be a true daughter to her father. The little things hurt the most—the hugs Father offered her half sister Marissa, the gentle teasing to goad Marissa before kissing her cheek in apology, the well-spoken comments about his *only* daughter to visiting royals—just small moments in time that pricked Carina's heart with each occurrence. After twenty-two years of life with a hollow ache in her heart Carina realized Father would never love her.

When Mira's screech pierced the silence of her dark cocoon, Carina jumped and cracked her skull against the roof of her hideout. "Ouch," she stammered, clambering out of the crevice.

"Mira, I told you to be quiet." She probed the top of her head, exploring with her fingers in search of a bloody wound. Satisfied she wouldn't die from blunt trauma, she stomped over to the ledge and murmured in her most authoritative whispering voice. "Be still down there."

Mira wailed and slammed her tail into the trees, peppering the already irritated Criton in a shower of dislodged leaves.

Carina leaned over the rock face, trying to see through the treetops. Something was bothering the usually obedient Criton, but she couldn't determine what was troubling her green friend. She decided to climb down for a closer look when a resounding roar thundered across the sky.

She turned to witness Criton riders flying overhead while squads of men riding their mighty war coursers and fleet-footed soldiers approached in the valley below, flooding her veins with adrenaline. King Duncan and his men stormed toward her, shattering the silence of the countryside with every thud of a hoof, swoosh of leathery wings, and scream from an angry Criton.

****

3

Marek Duncan couldn't find any comfort in the steady beat of FireStrike's wings. Even the impressive display of eleven bonded Criton riders spread out in a wide arc below him didn't lighten his mood. He'd spent the last two weeks traveling hundreds of miles from his home, Stirrlan, to court King McKay's daughter, Marissa. Just the thought of another arranged marriage after the first miserable attempt—or a mistress, for that matter—angered him more.

The crisp air chilled his skin, matching the iciness in his heart. During his twenty-second year, he'd agreed to a marriage union with the daughter of a neighboring king, believing he would have a lifetime to fall in love with Saffron, his new bride. However, the love he'd so hoped for never happened, not even friendship. Five years later, at her request, he released her so she could journey home.

His black leather gloves crackled when his grip tightened on FireStrike's reins. He needed an heir to his throne to protect his lands from Outlanders. Sampson VelMar, his captain and trusted friend, had suggested he either marry another noble or find a mistress. He chose Marissa because rumor suggested she might be the next Caller of Light.

FireStrike jerked his red head sideways to stare at a nearby mountain. "What do you see, boy?" Marek asked, focusing on the peak.

Sampson flew up on Reeza, his dappled grey Criton with silver-tipped accents, and settled into formation behind and to the left of FireStrike. He pointed toward the summit. "Do you see him?"

"Aye," Marek grumbled. A lone man this far out raised some concern. Although the man might just be a lookout for King McKay, he could also be a spy with questionable intentions.

"Do you want to send some men?"

He heard the anticipation in Sampson's voice. They had traveled hard for several days and the monotony of an uneventful trip had drained their spirit. Fighters at heart, journeying to another kingdom without so much as a hint of trouble left everyone restless. He smiled. He too had grown listless and needed to stir things up a bit. "Why don't we all go?"

A wide, toothy grin spread across Sampson's face as both Critons banked in unison, followed by the other riders in a tight formation.

Carina shielded her eyes from the sun to better glimpse the riders and their glorious beasts. The graceful animals soared above the foot soldiers and coursers. They glimmered in the bright light as the sun's rays reflected off the sheen of polished saddles, head gear, and body armor. Flying wingtip to wingtip, they formed a wide V spanning the valley.

Mira squealed, drawing Carina's attention away from the riders. "Mira, shhh."

A shadow descended upon Carina and her breath caught in her throat. She recognized the distinct silhouettes of Criton wings dancing on the black rocks beneath her feet. The riders' flight pattern had changed, blotting out the sun with their approach.

Although in her heart she already knew she'd been spotted, she still hoped otherwise. Maybe they hadn't seen her. Maybe the riders had simply adjusted their course. So, instead of fleeing the summit, she chanced another glimpse at the sky. To her dismay, all the riders bore down on her.

She stared at the magnificent beasts, the beat of their wings moving in a unified, sweeping dance. Although the glare from the sun made it difficult to see, the Alpha Criton looked to be solid red, a rare color.

She would've continued to watch if she hadn't snuck away from home, but another yowl from Mira jolted her into action. She spun and ran, trying not to fall on the uneven ground. The cold wind swirled around her, whipping through her hair and bringing tears to her eyes as she raced across the mountaintop.

Fear rippled down her spine, throwing her heart into a sputtering, flip-flopping rhythm. She resisted the urge to glance over her shoulder to assess the shrinking distance of the approaching riders and summoned the courage to hurtle herself over the edge of the mountain. She landed on her heels with a painful grunt and somehow managed not to tumble headfirst. She tried to maintain control in an almost uncontrollable descent as she dodged rocks and prickly bushes.

As soon as her feet touched the level outcropping, she sprinted toward Mira. Sensing the riders were almost upon her spurred her reckless behavior. Without so much as a quiet greeting to her little Criton, she untied Mira and vaulted into the saddle.

Trees whipped back and forth in the strong currents caused by the powerful beating wings of Critons overhead, forcing Mira to dodge the swinging branches as she navigated through the dense grove. They paused at the cliff overlooking a vast valley below. Mira had to leap away from the mountain and freefall before she could extend her wings to catch a draft. If her little Criton didn't jump out far enough, they'd never clear the rock face and tumble off the steep ledge. Carina squeezed the reins in a death grip and crouched, her body vibrating with fear, anticipating Mira's plunge.

****

As they neared, Marek scowled in confusion. Their quarry's long hair flowed behind him. When Marek saw shapely curves, he realized his mistake. *What in Criton's breath?* The scout was a woman.

He had watched her scurry across the peak, jumping over crevices and skirting around boulders. She had run as if her life had depended on it, like he was the hunter and she the prey. And when she had flung herself over the side of the mountain in one long stride, he had pursued her until she disappeared into a thicket.

He reined FireStrike into an abrupt hover. The Criton's red wings flapped up and down in an effortless rhythm. "Continue with the men," he ordered to Sampson.

"Sire, let me go. It might be a trap."

Marek grinned. "Don't worry, my friend. I'll meet up with you before Brookshire."

Leaning forward in the saddle, he encouraged FireStrike to circle the timbered sanctuary sheltering his prize. She had nowhere to go, except off a very steep embankment she could not traverse by foot. So how did she even get up there? He soon had his answer when he glimpsed a small Criton teetering on the edge of the mountain. The girl hunched low on the beast's back—a Criton rider. His brow furrowed. Except for a very narrow gap, the wide canopied trees covered the entire rock shelf. She had no room to take off.

"No," he yelled. "Stop!" But his words scattered in the wind, going unheeded as the Criton's muscles tensed and she leapt into the air.

Marek gasped as the little animal clamped her wings against her body and plummeted. When the mountainside fell away her wings snapped open, but she continued her rapid descent toward the wooded valley below.

Never taking his eyes off the foolish twosome, he urged FireStrike to shadow them from above. Once animal and rider reached the forest, they'd have to climb to avoid the trees and he'd be waiting. His pulse quickened as he watched them follow the angle of the mountain. The agile beast hugged the uneven terrain, skimming so close to the ground she almost touched it with every downstroke of her wings. They soared to the bottom of the slope,

7

but instead of rising, the pair surprised him when the Criton tucked her wings and disappeared into the woods.

He straightened in the saddle and laughed, shaking his head in astonishment. His mount snorted in frustration, chomping at the bit, eager to follow. "We're too big," he chuckled, petting FireStrike's neck with powerful strokes. "They got the best of us. But in our defense, they know the lay of the land."

With a final pat, he spurred his Criton upward. Since he couldn't follow them into the forested valley, he'd either have to fly over it to catch them on the other side or give up the chase. Even at full speed, he doubted they would find their little lemming. With a regretful sigh and a twinge of remorse, he steered FireStrike toward his men. He would have liked to meet the rider. She had courage. When he reached Brookshire, he would ask King McKay about the girl who rode a Criton with the fearless skill of a battle-trained warrior.

CHAPTER 2

....

FIRESTRIKE

Carina released Mira in one of the Criton cliff dwellings farther away from the castle and raced down the obscure trail snaking along the side of the mountain. She ignored the Critons who screeched as she ran by or groaned in irritation when she pushed them out of the way. When she reached the road leading home, she slowed and veered toward the main stables.

She walked in the shade of a large barn, enjoying the season of the harvest. Warm weather still gripped the afternoon hours, but an unmistakable chill now lingered in the morning. All too soon the leaves would change color and drop, exposing bare branches and abandoned tanagers' nests to the environment as the Mother Source prepared for the season of sleep and rejuvenation. But not today. She smiled and tilted her head to enjoy the sun's warming rays on her face.

As she walked past the barn door, a threatening growl from a Criton inside disturbed her thoughts and she hesitated at the entrance. She peered into the building, but the shadowy darkness hid the occupant. Although she wanted to see who made the sound, she needed to get home to prepare for King Duncan's formal greeting. She bit her lower lip and looked for the Criton's owner, but only spied a stable boy and his yapping warrigal ambling toward an ovine pasture.

She puffed her cheeks out with air before exhaling. Curiosity, always her downfall, overrode better judgment. She entered the vast shelter and paused just inside the double doors so her eyes could adjust to the dim light. The barn smelled of stale straw, aged wood, and worn leather. She ventured deeper and discovered the single tenant in the first stall. An enormous red Criton stared at her.

She stood in front of the great animal within easy reach of his snapping jaws and gazed into his big eyes. His aristocratic head towered above her, yet she didn't fear him. Using the shafts of light filtering in through the small windows spaced along the walls above her, she noted every detail of his defined body with an experienced eye.

His small front claws, located in the bend of his wings, rested on the ground. She admired the shimmer of light reflecting off the thin membrane of skin and muscle connecting the fragile-appearing bones of his powerful wings. His tail tapered down to the classic diamond-shaped flap of skin that enabled him to maneuver with the dexterity necessary to locate the slightest air current.

But his regal head captured her attention. An exceptional specimen, his ruby eyes regarded her with a calm, quiet wisdom. The distinctive red band, darker than his body color, rimmed the bottom of his eyes and trailed down the sides of his face like war paint. A small ridge ran the length of his snout, ending at his nostrils, and a short, blood-red mane covered his neck. Although pitched forward, his small ears could swivel in almost a complete circle.

"Aren't you beautiful."

The Criton lifted his head higher in a definite "I know I am" response, and she smiled. She extended her hand for him to smell. He lowered his massive head, inhaled her scent, and sighed, apparently satisfied she wasn't a threat.

She stroked the soft, downy hair on his thick neck. "I bet you're wonderful to ride."

"He is," boasted a male voice from the doorway.

Startled by the unexpected intrusion, Carina yanked her hand off the Criton like she'd been scalded by boiling water and stared at the straw-littered, dirt floor. "I'm sorry, I didn't mean any harm."

The steady clomp of footsteps approached until a pair of black boots stood in front of her.

"I'm surprised FireStrike let you pet him. He's very particular."

Her courage rose when she didn't detect any anger from the rider for touching his Criton. "He's magnificent." She smiled, venturing an upward glance. Her breath caught as a sudden awareness of the man standing before her warmed her body.

His dark, brown hair, blown into a roguish dishevelment, gave her the impression of a lad coming in from the fields after a hard day playing. But the disarray suited him. He wore all black leather except for a tan shirt with a v-shaped, loosely-tied collar. His duster, a long riding jacket much like her split tail, displayed the Duncan insignia—a red Criton breathing fire. Specks of dust from the journey dotted the duster, adding to his boyish charm. His broad shoulders tapered to a compact waist before flaring down to sturdy legs.

"Aye, he is," the man replied, stroking FireStrike's neck.

"Are you bonded?" The intrusive words tumbled out of her mouth without thought.

"We are. Why aren't you afraid of a Criton you don't know?"

She shrugged. "I've never been afraid of Critons."

11

"Then you are either our next Caller or a fool."

She clamped her teeth together and bit back the choice words burning at the tip of her tongue. How dare he call her a fool. Her spine stiffened. She pinned the rider with a stern glare and balled her hands into fists. "I suggest you watch what you say when speaking to King McKay's daughter."

The man bowed with a slight tilt of his head. "Lady Marissa, forgive my indiscretion."

Carina swallowed the groan threatening to push past her lips. Her eyes traveled down the interior of the barn to stare at the empty stalls, like silent sentinels waiting for occupancy. She reached for her Criton necklace, clutching it for reassurance. The only remaining keepsake that once belonged to her mother, the precious medallion never left her neck. "Marissa is my older half sister."

"I didn't know King McKay had another daughter. May I ask your name?"

"Carina."

"Well, I imagine King McKay has had his hands full with suitors then."

She glanced up to determine if he mocked her, but witnessed a sincere smile and sparkling, green and grey-flecked eyes. Small lines around his eyes, either from laughing or spending hours in the sun, hinted at a maturity beyond his years. His eyes with those alluring specks glimmered down at her and a curious smile played across his mouth. Her lips curved into a small grin.

He chuckled. "Well, Lady Carina, the men are resting in a lower field waiting for instructions. Since I couldn't find anyone to acquaint me with your father's holdings, would you be so kind to offer that courtesy?"

Her heart stumbled. Never in her life had anyone spoken to her in such a kind, respectful manner. "Well...Father would want to escort you himself, but he took Marissa to see Father Augustus for a fertility blessing."

The man's eyes widened. "Is that so?" He laughed.

"Yes, you know, because King Duncan is here to court Marissa." She stared at this brown-haired man with a furrowed brow. As a member of King Duncan's legion, how could he not know the reason his king had traveled here?

"Aye, of course. And we did arrive early, which explains why no one greeted us. I guess that leaves you to guide me." He extended his arm.

After a small pause, she placed her hand on his leather-clad forearm and tried to calm the rabble of danaines dancing in her stomach. His breathtaking smile as a reward for her courage stunned her senses. But the world stopped moving and the air stilled in her lungs when his fingers grazed across the back of her hand before motioning in front of him.

"Where do we go from here, my lady?"

CHAPTER 3

....

WALK

Carina squirmed at the blatant stares from the servants as she guided King Duncan's man around the grounds. She'd never escorted anyone before, let alone a soldier who displayed such courtesy, and his special attention made her jittery. But his casual manner calmed her nerves, and after showing him the castle and main grounds, she felt comfortable enough to ask for his name.

He frowned at her question. Her stomach churned in turmoil thinking she'd been too forward. But he surprised her.

"Call me Marek," he answered with a casual shrug.

She blushed at the familiarity he bestowed upon her and whispered his name under her breath.

As she led him toward the pastures and rockier areas, she pointed to the barracks where Duncan's men would stay. They continued their walk down a narrow roadway until Marek stopped at a fence next to a mountainous outcropping leading to several Criton lairs. Ovine grazed in the field.

Her chest swelled when she noticed his eyes light up at the impressive array of Critons flying overhead or perching on rocky knolls. "Father says we have the largest unbonded nest around."

"I agree. But I'd prefer to see more adults with bonded riders."

She nodded. "I wonder what happened to the Caller."

Marek rested a hand on the top post railing. "No one knows."

"It's a shame Callers cannot Criton-bond."

"I guess a Caller's burden is to only see the tether between rider and Criton."

Although she didn't totally understand the complexity of Criton-bonding, the enormity of the joining still awed her. A hollow ache filled her chest as she stared at the pasture. "I know. But it's kind of sad, don't you think? To have the ability to see the connection between two separated souls and bring them together for the bonding, yet never able to experience it?"

Marek's lips twitched into a soft smile. "I suppose never joining in the communion could be disappointing. Powerful Callers can bond with a lifemate," he added in an encouraging tone.

They slipped into a comfortable silence as a black Criton named Midnight dove from a ledge and grabbed an unsuspecting ovine in his mouth before the herd could scatter. Carina watched the Criton carry the bleating animal back to his den. The ovine kicked and thrashed until Midnight's jaws closed and the animal stilled.

Although ovine served as food, Carina hated to see an animal die and offered a silent prayer to the Gods. When she turned her attention back to Marek, he was staring at her with an intensity that made her uncomfortable. "What?"

He shrugged and continued to eye her. "Most women are too squeamish to observe Critons feeding."

Exactly what did he mean? That something was wrong with her because she didn't swoon at the sight? "Well, how else are they to live?" she snapped with a defiant tilt of her chin. "And I prayed for the ovine, asking that it receive eternal blessings. Did you bestow such a request?"

She jerked her hand off his arm and stood glaring at him through narrowed eyes.

Marek threw his head back and roared with laughter. "I'm humbled by your kindness for the poor animal. Please, forgive my insult for that wasn't my intent."

The warmth in his voice radiated over her, while his smile crinkled the tiny lines around his eyes. Her heart fluttered. A blush heated her cheeks. "And I'm sorry for my outburst." She glanced away to hide her embarrassment.

In an unexpected movement, he cupped her chin with his hand and forced her to look into his intense eyes. "Never apologize for speaking your mind, Lady Carina."

She stopped breathing. Her body blazed as if she'd been seared by the white-hot fire of Criton flame. He smelled like an evergreen forest, sunlight on a spring day, the anticipation before the rain—like freedom. She could drown in those eyes with the interesting grey specks that revealed an undeniable passion, a true pathway to what lay hidden within his soul.

He smiled, breaking the moment, and placed her hand back on his arm.

As they wandered toward the medical barn, she grumbled, "Well, maybe I'd get into less trouble if I didn't speak out so much."

Marek's laugh filled her with unexpected pleasure and she laughed with him.

They had almost reached the barn when her thoughts returned to the Caller. "They say she went searching for her lifemate and looks for him still."

Marek's brows furrowed. "My lady?"

"The Caller. They say her love for all eternity was lost in battle and she went looking for him and won't stop searching in this life or the next until she finds him and their hearts are reunited."

They paused at the double doors as danaines fluttered around them, flitting from flower to flower. The sweet smell of hay drifted on the breeze blowing in off the Arrakan Mountains and rustled the leaves in nearby trees. Even the tanagers were enjoying the day as they jumped from branch to branch, chirping to each other.

"Well, *they* also speak of Critons twice as large as ours, and little blue sprites that once lived in the forests, and that the Caller fell under the spell of the Naiads and jumped into the Locksneed River." Marek shook his head. "No, I think what you speak of is just folklore, an invented tale to explain the unexplainable."

"Even so, I hope she found him and they're together again," Carina mumbled, uncomfortable for revealing a childhood dream.

"Aye, looking for love is by far the best reason to leave the kings of this land struggling to defend their borders."

She stole a quick glance at Marek. His hooded eyes seemed lost in thought. Was he a casualty of lost love? She'd never be such a victim since she'd never marry. She tried to ignore the self-pity that settled in her stomach. At least she had Mira and the other Critons to comfort her.

"We bring our sick or hurt Critons here," she informed him as they entered the airy building. As if on cue, a young Criton stood in a stanchion. Carina's heart constricted. The healer was monitoring her beloved Mira. She released Marek's arm and rushed over to the animal. Mira lowered her head and Carina dutifully scratched behind an ear.

"What's wrong?" Carina asked.

Abbey, King McKay's best healer, finished running her hands along Mira's flank. Abbey spoke in a soothing voice. "Mira grows into her junior years and will transition into adulthood soon. I need to determine when we should place a watch on her."

The healer's long robes tumbled forward as she pulled her brown, velvet-trimmed hood over her head. She placed a gnarled hand on Carina's shoulder and gave it a reassuring squeeze. "Don't worry, your Criton is still a few weeks away from transition."

Abbey turned to Marek and bobbed her head in greeting before leaving.

Marek rubbed Mira's nose. "You seem very fond of this Criton."

"Oh yes." Carina grinned. "Father and some of his men found her orphaned when she was young. Father wanted to leave her, but I convinced him to let me keep her."

"Well, you've done an excellent job raising her." With a final pat, he turned toward the doorway and extended his arm.

She planted a quick kiss on Mira's nose before curling her hand around Marek's bicep. The little Criton snorted in agitation as they walked away, and Carina rolled her eyes. "Mira doesn't like being inside," she muttered, justifying her friend's behavior.

She looked at Marek. He was staring at her again with those piercing eyes, as if trying to penetrate her defenses and spy upon her innermost secrets. Self-conscious, she peered at the ground. She never should have kissed Mira farewell. What an unladylike thing to do.

"Did you know that we spotted a Criton rider at your border when my men and I entered King McKay's territory?"

Her heart hiccupped. She'd get into trouble if Father discovered she'd defied his no Criton riding mandate. She continued to survey her feet, but could sense him probing her. In a weak attempt at deflection, she guided the conversation away from its current direction. "You said *your* men." She glanced up to focus on the waiting eyes of the man accompanying her. "Does that mean you're Captain of the Guard?"

He smiled and his expression softened. "Aye, I guess you could say that."

"Oh my," she whispered and then wanted to kick herself for sounding so childish.

"Now, as for that rider," he continued. "We gave chase, but she eluded us."

She tried not to smile at the frustration coloring his words. She was very proud of escaping King Duncan's men.

"The rider had long, brown hair...much like yours. And the little Criton she rode looks a lot like the one we just left in the barn. Do you know anything about that?"

Her heart thumped in an erratic rhythm as they wandered toward the main house. She inhaled the cool, harvest day air deep into her lungs, struggling to think of an answer that wouldn't incriminate her. Deciding avoidance was her best option, she tucked a loose strand of hair behind an ear and ignored his question altogether. "Mira does fly fast."

Marek stopped and stood in front her. His lively eyes hardened into green ice, the grey flecks like little pokers boring into her. "It's not safe for you to ride alone so close to your father's border. You should never leave without an escort."

She stared into his determined face and her resolve crumbled on a defeated sigh. "But Father doesn't let me ride. He says riding confuses the Critons, so they might not rider-bond." Once she started, the words spilled out. She couldn't stop herself. "I don't know what I'd do if I couldn't fly. I only ride Mira since she's small and no one wants her, I swear."

Her other hand reached out to clutch his arm. "Father says Mira won't amount to anything, and I don't mean any harm by it." Her grip tightened, as if by squeezing harder she could convince him that for a few hours a day riding freed her from a life filled with loneliness and boredom.

"Flying means that much to you?" His voice lowered and his lips pressed together in a firm line. "To cause you to disobey your father and place your life at risk?"

She blinked back tears as her heart tumbled into her stomach, and glanced toward the hunting pastures stretched out in the lower fields. She had displeased this man, and for some unknown reason felt horrible about it. Except for flying, she always obeyed her father. She went out of her way to vie for his attention and gain his acceptance, but nothing she did earned his favor. And now, she'd disappointed the only man who had ever shown her any measure of respect. She chastised herself for even considering a Captain of the Guard would be interested in her anyway.

When he spoke her name, his voice rippled through her like a soothing caress, commanding her with a quiet calmness. "Answer me."

But what could she tell him without sounding like a whining, spoiled noble...or rather, mixed noble? Fortunately, she didn't have to answer as her half sister's high-pitched voice permeated the air. Carina stepped away, waiting for Marissa to take center stage.

"Father, he's over here." Marissa giggled as she sidled up to Marek.

King Regin McKay appeared from behind the barn and strode toward them as fast as his stubby legs could carry him, and with all the spectacle only her father could display. His squinty eyes sliced into her before dismissing her altogether. With a slight incline of his head that served as a bow between royals, Regin's throaty voice rumbled. "King Duncan, I trust your journey was uneventful."

Marek gave a similar nod of respect. "Aye, we had no trouble, even when we traveled through the Bridal Lands."

21

Carina's mind raced. *But Marek was Captain of the Guard, not King Duncan.* Carina's eyes widened when Marissa gathered her flowing, blue satin skirts and performed a deep curtsy.

Marissa's blond curls fell forward to frame her flawlessly powdered face as she dipped her head. "Welcome, Your Majesty. I am pleased to make your acquaintance. May I call you King Marek?" she asked, holding out her gloved hand.

Carina broke into a cold sweat. Her chest seized, squeezing the air from her lungs. King Duncan's first name was *Marek?* Marek Duncan? *King Marek Duncan!* She'd been walking with King Duncan the entire time, acting like a nitwit. She looked at her scuffed boots and dirt-smudged clothes and cringed. She was filthy and needed a bath. Just the thought of what her hair must look like made her wish for a rock big enough to crawl under so she could slam it on top of her rattlebrained head.

Marek reached for Marissa's hand—a hand covered by a pristine, white glove. She balled her own hands into fists and tucked them behind her back.

"Lady Marissa, I would be honored if you call me King Marek."

A spark of jealousy smoldered in her belly as Marissa's dainty hand settled on Marek's arm…the *exact* spot where hers had been moments ago. She fought the urge to push Marissa out of the way and retake her place at his side, but her grubby appearance kept her feet rooted to the ground. How ridiculous she must have appeared, walking arm-in-arm with a king. Unlike her, Marissa looked as though she'd been born to stand at the side of someone as handsome as King Duncan. The jealous ember inside her turned to ash.

Marek reached for Regin's forearm and they shook hands.

Regin's lips curved downward. "I'm sorry no one was here to formally greet you, but we didn't expect you until tomorrow."

"I wanted to stay ahead of a storm rolling over the Arrakans, so we left a day early. And Lady Carina did offer a proper welcome."

Carina bowed her head when Marek's quick look in her direction drew her father's gaze. Again, she wished for that rock, knowing Father noticed every detail of her less than proper appearance. Heat flooded her cheeks. Why couldn't she ever do anything right to please him?

"You have many more Critons nesting here than I thought," Marek said.

"We take very good care of our Critons. And since Marissa is of age, the fact we have so many is a good sign she's our next Caller."

"Oh, Father, please," Marissa gushed.

Regin's voice boomed with authority. "Come, Marek, let us have the honor of presenting our home and surrounding grounds to you before we serve dinner."

"Lady Carina already has done an excellent job of showing me—"

"Carina is a bit unruly. I've tried to teach her to behave like a lady of the court, but she's a mixed blood after all." Regin gave a *'what is a king to do'* shrug that made Carina wish she was anywhere but where she stood. "Carina, bid King Duncan farewell so you can finish your chores."

"Yes, Father." She stepped in front of Marek and dropped into a deep curtsy. "Your Majesty, it was a pleasure to meet you."

Marek reached down and offered his hand. If she could have avoided accepting it without causing insult, she would have, but her flustered mind couldn't think fast enough to find an excuse. With a hesitant reach, she eased her ungloved hand into his. His fingers enclosed and pulled her up. When she tried to remove her hand, he clasped it tighter.

"The pleasure was all mine, Lady Carina." His baritone voice seeped into her pores. "I'll see you at dinner?"

Startled, she gazed into his eyes. Did he really want to see her again? She searched his face for any hint of sarcasm, but saw only sincerity and warmth.

"I doubt she'll be able to wash the Criton smell off her by then," Marissa trilled.

Carina stiffened, trying again to pull free. Marek's grip tightened. With deliberate slowness, he raised her hand to his mouth and brushed his lips across it. "Lady Carina, would you please join me for dinner?"

The ground spun beneath her feet. She struggled to maintain her balance as an energy ripped through her, awakening her body with an acute, almost painful attraction for the man standing before her. She didn't know if the sensations zinging around inside her were ignited by the gentle press of his lips against her hand or the deep timbre of his voice, but they fascinated her. Tongue-tied by her body's inner turmoil, she could only stand there, speechless, staring at the massive chest of the man in front of her.

"Carina!" Marissa's voice held an unmistakable edge. "Don't act like a dolt. Let go of his majesty's hand."

Marek refused to let her go when she tried to withdraw from his grasp. His vivid, grey-flecked eyes pierced her with such intensity, her breath caught in the back of her throat.

"You haven't answered me," he whispered, his eyes sparkling.

"Oh, of course she'll be there," Regin huffed. "But only if she finishes her chores."

She remained silent. If Father knew she'd already finished her chores, he would've found another reason to keep her from attending the formal dinner.

Marek released her hand, straightened to his full height on an over six foot muscular frame, and stared into her eyes. "Very good,

I'll see you at dinner." With a slight pause, as if reluctant to dismiss her, he turned away. "King McKay, you wished to show me your estate?"

"Oh, yes," Marissa exclaimed.

"Then carry on."

Carina stayed behind, listening to the fading drone of her father's voice as he bragged about the castle and grounds. Her eyes followed as Marek's broad back, with Marissa attached to his arm, disappeared around the corner of the medical barn.

The thought of seeing Marek again filled her with excitement as a dormant part of her stirred to life. But her more realistic side dreaded the idea of attending dinner. She'd have to find something to wear, which always caused heartache. But Milly, a household servant who also happened to be an excellent seamstress, could help locate a suitable gown.

With growing anxiety, she stomped toward the main house. Though she'd embarrassed herself with King Duncan, she anticipated that her appearance at dinner would cause Father and Marissa greater distress.

CHAPTER 4

....

GETTING READY

Perched on an old rickety chair, Carina stared into her dressing table mirror. Milly had surreptitiously acquired a gown Marissa no longer wore, and in a flurry of ripping, cutting, and sewing, altered it in time for dinner. Milly had boasted about how she changed it to fit Carina's style—Carina didn't even know she had a style—by making the bottom half stream out in flowing layers instead of billowing out in a hoop skirt. Although Milly had kept the long, snug fitting sleeves, she had cut a large scoop out of the neckline so the gown rested just off Carina's shoulders, accentuating her mother's necklace.

Carina preferred to wear her hair down, but somehow Milly had convinced her to arrange it differently. After much griping about Carina's unruly golden-brown locks, Milly had wrangled it into an elegant affair on her head, but left a few long curls to drape around the swooping neckline in a graceful display.

At last, alone in her small bedroom, Carina studied herself in the mirror. The sweet scent of jasmine filtered in from the open window, filling the room with a flowery aroma. She turned her head to the left and right, admiring Milly's handiwork. To her surprise, with the fancy dress and hair, she almost looked like a full royal.

But even with her sophisticated appearance, her stomach churned at the thought of seeing King Duncan. Her temper flared, flooding hot blood to her cheeks. He must've enjoyed humoring the poor mixed blood girl until the nobles arrived home.

In an attempt to calm her heart, she traced her finger over the two intertwined Criton heads protecting the red jewel in the center of her mother's necklace. Her mother had told her the medallion held the key to her past and future. "Mama, I wish you were here," she murmured.

A soft knock at the door beckoned her. She stood, inspecting her gown with a critical eye. She liked the dark green velvet fabric on the bodice that tapered into lighter, varying shades of green in her multilayered skirt. When she walked, the fabric flowed around her; only the wide swaths of cloth prevented her legs from showing. Very daring.

She straightened her shoulders and stood tall. Although she'd been made to feel foolish, she would not be made the fool. Since she only attended formal dinners on rare occasions, she'd make the most out of tonight. She forced a smile on the person staring back at her in the mirror and brought her Criton necklace to her lips for a quick kiss of courage before slipping out the door.

Her bedroom was located on the top floor of the castle, a floor reserved for servants who held a place of honor in the household, meaning they performed the more important tasks. The lower levels were reserved for Father and Marissa, followed by the main floor. The courage she'd so gallantly summoned melted away when she rounded a bend in the staircase and almost crashed into Marissa.

"Watch out!" Marissa snapped. "I don't want you to wrinkle my new gown."

Marissa stood in front of her in a pink monstrosity consisting of puffy sleeves and large hoops. To her shock, however, the dress lacked the high collar Marissa preferred.

As if reading her mind, Marissa's eyes glittered. "In case he'd like to kiss my neck after dinner when we go for an unchaperoned walk." She clasped her hands together and sighed. "Isn't he the grandest man you've *ever* seen?"

"You'll make a fine couple," Carina muttered.

Marissa's eyes narrowed to slits. "And you didn't even know who he was." Her hand flew to her chest. "Is that my dress? Oh, my goodness, you ruined it." She opened her mouth to say something else, but paused. A sly smile creased her lips. "On second thought, maybe the dress suits you because it's…different."

With a final scrutinizing look, Marissa spun and glided down the hall, her hoop skirt swishing back and forth. After a few steps, her voice echoed in the narrow passage. "Don't be late, sweet half sister."

Carina trailed her hand down the front of her dress and watched the light strips of fabric sway on a gentle breeze. Marissa was right. The dress was too different. Tempted, she almost raced back upstairs to change into something else until she thought of Milly. Although she wouldn't feel as vulnerable in an old dress, Milly had worked so hard. She just didn't have the heart to offend her. So, with reluctant steps, she trudged down the corridor.

CHAPTER 5

....

TALK OF KINGS

Marek strolled into the hosting chamber followed by Sampson. A roaring fire blazed in the stone hearth, but the heat didn't reach his troubled heart. He hated formal occasions. Except for Carina, he would've preferred standing on a biting fire rifa hill to avoid spending an evening with the McKays. Regin and Marissa were just as he expected—all pomp and bluster. But as much as he disliked their arrogance, he did admire Regin's thriving Criton market. With so many unbonded Critons converging on McKay land, the obvious conclusion seemed to be that Marissa, as a true blood royal, was the next Caller of Light.

He ran his fingers through his hair and stared out a window overlooking the gravel driveway leading to the castle entrance. A knot of apprehension curled in his gut. Marissa reminded him of Saffron. How could he take Marissa back to Stirrlan to become his wife and queen when he didn't enjoy being in her company?

"Lady Marissa doesn't even like Critons," he grumbled. "Wouldn't the Caller at least appreciate the companionship of the animals she calls?"

"Sire, there are more unbonded Critons nesting on King McKay's land than I thought possible. Perhaps the attraction doesn't have to be mutual."

Marek stared at his captain. Sampson wore a heavy cotton tunic, quartered in white and red panels, with the Stirrlan crest embroidered on the upper left quadrant. Two dirks, their silver handles gleaming in the light, draped across his chest while his hand casually rested on the hilt of the great sword hanging around his waist.

Marek shook his head, disapproving of his friend's eagerness. If Sampson thought spending what little money Stirrlan had left to journey here and court Marissa was a good idea, he was mistaken.

Sampson shrugged, his curly, black hair bouncing at the movement. "Well, even if she's not the next Caller, you still need an heir."

He threw Sampson a warning look. They'd grown up together as boys—he, a prince to become king, and Sampson, a captain's son to someday run his army. Their friendship allowed Sampson the latitude of free speech, but this time the truth in his words touched a nerve.

Marek scrubbed a hand over his face. "I know Sampson, but have you seen her?"

Sampson's eyebrows drew together. "She's beautiful, no?"

"I suppose," he groused. "But I never knew there could be so much to say about the way one dresses."

"Well, as far as I know, not much talking need occur when conceiving an heir."

He glared at Sampson. "Aye, but really?"

"The burden a king must endure, Sire."

Marek frowned.

Sampson grinned.

Both men burst out laughing.

"I'm delighted to see you enjoying yourselves," Regin bellowed as he entered the room. He sparkled in a burgundy doublet with slashed sleeves displaying the white lining underneath. Gold buttons fastened the bottom of the doublet for a snug fit around his ample waist. Breeches, stockings, and shiny black shoes complemented his royal ensemble.

Marek inclined his head in agreement. "Your house has been most hospitable."

"Outstanding." Regin strutted over to a plush, red chair and plopped his wide body into it. "Marek, please sit here," he said, patting the chair next to him.

As Marek sat in his assigned spot, Sampson moved to a location offering the best strategic vantage point. From Sampson's position, he could now watch the door and the entire room while protecting Marek's back.

Regin's fingers thrummed on the overstuffed armrest, waiting for the servant to pour the drinks. As soon as the servant stepped from the room, Regan sipped his drink and began asking the questions Marek expected, but dreaded just the same.

"How protected are your borders? I don't want my girl going where she'll be in danger."

"My army is strong and my house well guarded."

Regin raised his red, bushy eyebrows. "I hear savage tribes encroach your land?"

Marek kept his face neutral. "Although part of my eastern border butts against the Outlands, my perimeter remains secure."

"And you seek my daughter's hand hoping she's the next Caller?"

"The goal of every king is to strengthen his holdings by having bonded riders protect not only his land, but his most prized possessions, like…" Marek swallowed, forcing the words from his mouth, "…your daughter."

Regin chuckled. "I think she's quite taken with you too."

"I'm honored," Marek answered with an obliged nod.

Regin's wide smile pushed his chubby cheeks upward, squeezing his small eyes into slits. Regin's scrunched look reminded Marek of a stubby-legged, tusked pecari, forcing him to stifle a smile.

Regin swirled the dark liquid in his glass before placing the chalice on a nearby table. "Marissa will bear you fine heirs with strong, royal bloodlines. And, as the next Caller, she'll increase our holdings substantially. By the time I leave this world, both you and Marissa will inherit significant wealth."

Marek nodded. Regin spoke of Marissa as his only daughter. Yet, even a mixed blood could produce an heir if a king wished it so.

At the thought of mixed bloods, Carina filled his mind. His pulse quickened when he remembered chasing after her on FireStrike. She rode with an unwavering courage. Many people feared Critons and would never get close, let alone ride one. But Carina rode with a graceful, natural style.

He'd never encountered a woman with such passion. Although she deferred to Regin and Marissa, he detected an unyielding strength brewing inside her. He clenched his teeth and fought a growing urge to seek her company. She might not have the power to call Critons, but her inquisitive, brown eyes and slender, curvy body called him. He needed to be very careful.

"And your other daughter?" he asked. "What of her?"

Regin's eyes clouded. "Carina is of no consequence."

"She seems very fond of Critons. What happened to her mother?"

"She died of an illness several years ago when Carina was but a child."

Although Regin appeared reluctant to discuss Carina's mother, Marek continued his questioning. "Was she from Brookshire?"

"We found her unconscious and nearly drowned on the bank of the Sassame River. She couldn't remember anything about her prior life including her name, so we called her Sasha. But that didn't stop her from trying to become my mistress by seducing me after supplying me with too much drink." Regin hesitated as if he'd said too much, then frowned. "Why do you ask such questions? Are you interested in Carina as your mistress? Because if so, her cost is the same as that of my Marissa."

Marek bowed his head. "I was merely curious. My intentions haven't changed."

Regin smiled. "Good. Carina takes excellent care of the Critons."

"Father, am I interrupting?"

Marissa descended upon the room like a griffon swooping in for the kill, capturing everyone's attention in the biggest dress Marek had ever seen. He spared Sampson a quick glance before rising from his chair along with Regin. Although Sampson never smiled, he knew his captain well enough to recognize his silent amusement.

Marek walked over to Marissa and kissed her white-gloved hand. "You look beautiful, Lady Marissa."

She batted her eyes and dipped her head. "Thank you, King Marek."

Regin clapped his hands in delight. "Daughter, you look ravishing."

"Oh, Father, please."

Regin edged toward the door. "Shall we move into the dining hall?"

Marek was about to inquire into Carina's whereabouts when she emerged at the top of the stairs. She paused. Uncertainty flickered across her face. For a moment he thought she was going to fade back into the shadows of the upper floors. But she took a deep breath, squared her shoulders, and stepped off the landing.

He inhaled a ragged breath at the sight of her. Her dress accentuated the slight swing of her hips while the tight bodice molded perfectly to the swell of her breasts. With each step as she descended, a slow burn heated his blood, flooding hot desire straight to his groin. She shimmered in the soft light spilling from the room—a light acting as a path for her to follow, illuminating her way…to him.

She entered with her head bowed and lowered into a deep curtsy. "Your Majesty."

He extended his hand and tried to keep his fingers from twitching in anticipation of her touch. She hesitated, and had yet to look him in the eyes. But she could not deny him, not without causing insult, so he waited. His body trembled when her hand slipped into his.

For the second time today, he couldn't let her go. She had entered the room on a whisper, but swept across his senses like a winter storm. She was the calm, silent stillness just before the skies unleashed their wrath to prove yet again the power of the Mother Source. The sweet anticipation of thunder crackling through the air slammed through his defenses, yet her tranquil demeanor kept the sizzling turmoil at bay.

Her hair was arranged in elaborate curls and braids that exposed the delicious contour of her neck. As she continued to look down, her dark eyelashes contrasted against her pale skin. He resisted the urge to brush his thumb across the soft curve of her lips. She was a feast for his eyes to devour. He wanted to tell her that she looked stunning, but his voice failed him and he could only mutter her name in a gravelly, scrape of sound.

She lifted her chin and peered at him. He saw something within her troubled eyes. Confusion? Pain? Had he caused this? Guilt plagued his mind. He should've told her his true identity when he first saw her boldly petting FireStrike. But after he'd accidentally insulted her and she had stood defiant in front of him with her feet planted and hands fisted, her willfulness had struck him like a fire bolt. Her enthusiasm and spirit was a refreshing surprise that threw him off guard. His desire to maintain that brief illusion so he could enjoy her unshielded companionship had hurt her, and he was paying a heavy price for his omission.

Somehow, both of his hands now sandwiched her smaller hand in a possessive hold while he struggled to control his beating heart. He could only stare at her, his eyes focused on the incredible woman now standing before him. But like an oozing wound, Marissa's perfumed scent invaded his senses just before her fingers settled in the nook of his arm, claiming him.

"Half sister, stop embarrassing yourself," Marissa reprimanded.

Carina blushed and dropped her head, pulling free from his grasp.

He had an uncontrollable urge to retake her hand, but Regin slipped between them.

"Yes, Carina," Regin chided. "Remember you're here because of King Marek's generosity."

Carina nodded and stepped away.

"Let's adjourn to the dining hall," Regin announced, and motioned toward the double doors leading from the room.

Marek's blood boiled. Carina might be mixed, but a royal family line also flowed through her veins. She deserved better. Walking away from her took all his willpower. She confused and excited him. But the girl he'd witnessed this afternoon, the one with the flash of mischief in her eyes and an easy laugh, had disappeared, as if Marissa and Regin had transformed her into a submissive inconsequence of the household.

He shook his head, forcing the desire to go to her out of his mind and body. He had to keep the welfare of his land and people in the forefront of his thoughts. If he indulged in his ambition to seek Carina's company, he'd ruin his chance with Marissa.

He tried to justify his decision as Marissa led them toward the double doors, pushing his irrational feelings into the far corners of his mind. Regin showed generosity by not disowning Carina. Her life within the McKay castle was not his concern. He shouldn't worry about her.

But even as he attempted to convince himself, he indulged in a quick glance behind his shoulder to find Carina staring out a window. Her skin glimmered in the soft moonlight filtering in through the panes. As he spied her reflection in the glass, the moonlight danced in her eyes. He followed her gaze and saw two shining eyes staring back at her, piercing the outside darkness. Mira stood in the grass looking up at the window as if beckoning Carina to come outside and play.

In that brief instant before Carina disappeared from his view, she seemed so vulnerable that an overpowering need to protect her surged through him.

"Don't you agree?" Marissa asked, giving his arm a little squeeze.

"I'm sorry, Lady Marissa?"

"The weather has been unusually warm this harvest season." She tilted her head sideways to glance at him.

"Aye, I suppose."

"I haven't been able to wear my best winter outfits yet." She pouted.

"You look lovely."

Marissa twittered with happiness before prattling on about something else. But she was a sandfly buzzing around him, a nuisance that disturbed his thoughts—thoughts that had already traveled back to the girl standing alone in the moonlight by the window.

CHAPTER 6

....

MOONLIGHT

Except for the conversation he had forced out of Carina, dinner had been as Marek expected—dismal. Once again in the hosting chamber, he roved back and forth like a caged animal, rippling the hanging tapestries with his restless stride. In a few minutes, he would discuss his future with Regin and seal his fate with Marissa. He stopped his futile pacing and stared out the same window Carina had peered through earlier.

A growing apprehension slithered through his mind. But the unease gathering inside him like a coiled urutu wasn't caused by his pending arrangements to wed a woman he didn't love because he'd already done that...once. The foreboding felt more ominous, like a storm brewing on the horizon. And if he couldn't navigate his way through it, he'd roam forever lost within the raging tempest.

He leaned against the window frame and inhaled a deep breath. Nothing moved outside, not even leaves rustling in the trees, like the world had gone into hibernation waiting for a signal to reawaken.

His stomach twisted and the beginning of a headache thumped in his right temple. He shook his head trying to clear the confusion encircling his mind. Unlike with Saffron, this time he knew the consequences of his courtship to Marissa. He understood the loneliness he would commit to based on a chance Marissa could call Critons. But a good king made sacrifices for the betterment of his people.

Although he understood the practicality of his decision, his chest constricted and the pounding in his head increased. He couldn't shake a sense that if he wasn't careful, if he failed to discover what he was meant to see, he'd travel down the wrong path—a path doomed to irrevocably alter his life.

He glanced up at the moons, Luna and her son. Bright and full, they exposed the night as if it were day, except with a softer glow.

What am I supposed to see? Tell me. He sent his plea in a silent prayer.

As if by answer, she darted across the grounds, an apparition running toward the Criton lairs, breathing life back into the Mother Source and reviving the world. Her hair spilled behind her in a wave. Although still wearing her evening dress, she ran barefoot through the grass. She extended her stride. The strips of fabric in her skirt glided around her, exposing the muscular curves of her legs. His body stirred at the breathtaking vision illuminated by the moons.

The walls enclosed around him, the air humid and stuffy. He needed to escape the room and the consequences about to occur within it. He rushed toward the door, eager to share the moonlight with the girl who could capture his attention with a simple smile.

He had to talk to her, to ensure any misunderstandings between them were resolved. A thought flickered through his mind about his inappropriate behavior. But for a brief timespan tonight, he would forget to be a king with obligations so he could be a man spending his final moments of freedom with a girl who captivated his mind and soul like no other. Then, he'd walk away from her for the rest of his life.

CHAPTER 7

AWAKENING

Carina whistled and waited. She needed to run her fingers over Mira's smooth skin and let her Criton's unconditional acceptance comfort and reassure her. She was confused, very confused. She didn't know how to behave around Mar…King Duncan. And why had he made her talk during dinner?

With the mother and son moons lighting the sky, she spotted Mira just before the animal tucked her wings and dove. A familiar quiver of excitement caressed Carina's skin as she watched the animal's blistering descent. At the last second, Mira spread her wings and glided to a perfect stop. She snorted a greeting before folding her small wings against her body. Carina smiled and located the sweet spot behind her friend's ear. Mira groaned in pleasure.

The anxiety Carina had tried to ignore since before King Duncan's arrival pulsed within her stronger than ever. Why did she feel this way? Why now?

Her heart fluttered when she remembered catching her first glimpse of King Duncan before dinner. He wore a flowing purple cape and a matching silk velvet knee-length jerkin. Gold brocade adorned the upper third of the jerkin while black leggings and polished knee-high riding boots finished off his formal dress.

She'd been so afraid of tripping on the stairs. And King Duncan had seemed larger than life, commanding the room with a casual confidence that only exacerbated her discomfort. When he had taken her hand and spoken her name, her entire body had trembled like she'd been struck by lightning.

She couldn't concentrate. His presence distracted her. Throughout dinner she would catch herself staring at him and then feel her cheeks burn when his piercing eyes caught and held hers. These strange and bewildering emotions excited her, yet were tempered by the fact he was courting Marissa, not her.

A knot of anger roiled through her stomach. King Duncan and Father were in the hosting chamber finalizing their agreement while Marissa was in her room, packing. Marissa had always been the darling. Although Carina had no aspirations of being the favorite, she longed to be considered part of the family.

She blinked away tears and hugged Mira's neck. "Maybe Father will notice me once Marissa is gone," she whispered to her companion. Mira tossed her head as if in agreement.

"You are fond of that Criton, aren't you?"

Although he spoke in a soft murmur, his voice reverberated through her like a gong. She struggled to maintain what little respect she still possessed and dipped into a quick curtsy. "She's going to be a great Criton one day."

Marek stepped up beside her and stroked Mira's neck. "She seems a bit small."

A nervous spark shot through her body at his nearness, rattling her self-control. She concentrated on keeping her voice level. "She hasn't transitioned yet, that's all."

"Aye, some change drastically after they transition."

****

Her lips twitched into a small smile, but she kept her eyes averted. "They do indeed."

Marek sighed. Carina had no intention of making this easy for him, and deservedly so. Although courteous, she remained reserved. To his surprise, her distance cut him like a blade, creating a hollow, festering wound. He longed to hear her laugh and see her smile, and the more she turned away from him, the greater the ache in his chest.

"Look at me," he commanded quietly.

After a short pause, she raised her head and speared him with her large, brown eyes. Pain reflected back at him, confirming that he had offended her.

"I'm sorry for my behavior earlier. My actions were inexcusable."

She stared at him a moment before her eyes narrowed and her anger bore into him. He squirmed at her stabbing gaze.

"Did you enjoy making me feel foolish?" Her voice trembled and two large tears swelled and bubbled over her lashes. She reached to swipe them away, but he grabbed her hand before she had the chance.

He heard her gasp. They were inappropriately close, but he couldn't help himself. He wrapped her hand within his and held it against his chest. With his other hand, he brushed the tears from her face, letting his fingers linger on her silky skin.

He reacted without thought when he saw her tears. His only aim to somehow right the wrong he'd committed against her and to atone for the embarrassment he had caused. But as soon as he touched her, an unyielding attraction crashed through his body. Her parted lips and the wide-eyed expression dancing across her face enticed him. She didn't pull away or shrink from his touch, which made him want to do what he could not—kiss her.

He inhaled the night air deep into his lungs to cool his heated blood and took a safe step away. Mira bumped his elbow, demanding attention. The Criton's loyalty to Carina was undeniable—a silent guardian protecting Carina's back. He, on the other hand, had betrayed Carina the first moment he saw her. "I didn't tell you because I was selfish," he confessed.

Carina's teary eyes were like red-hot branding irons burning his skin, reinforcing his need for her forgiveness. He couldn't part on bad terms. "I wanted to enjoy your company and our conversation knowing you were with me as a man, not as a king. Will you accept my apology?"

"Of course, Your Majesty," she answered obligingly without emotion.

Marek stared at the stubborn woman who rode a Criton better than most men. His eyes locked onto hers, willing her to feel the desire racing through him that he couldn't share; to hear the words he wanted to say, but remained silent in the back of his throat; and to see the emotion she could elicit from him with a simple blind touch. She blinked and faltered, but held his gaze.

"Will you please forgive me?"

She matched his stare, but he refused to yield until her penetrating glare crumbled and she looked away. After a long exhale, she whispered, "Your Majesty, I forgive you. You wanted to be someone else for a short while. I understand, because I too want that at times."

He grinned as the tension ebbed from his body. But a minor detail needed fixing. "I have one more request."

Her eyebrows raised in question.

"You once called me, Marek. I would ask that you do so again."

Her contagious smile blanketed him like a warm caress. "Very well…Marek." She giggled, then bit her bottom lip and focused on Mira.

He leaned against a pasture fence post so he could watch Carina. She was petting her Criton with an undying vigor, and if not mistaken, blushing. He stifled the smile threatening his lips.

"What do you think Mira will look like after she transitions?"

He glanced over his shoulder to look at the animal whose eyes were closed because of Carina's devoted touch. "Oh, I don't know," he said, settling his gaze on Carina again. "Sometimes the changes are significant and sometimes you can hardly tell."

"I think she'll be very special."

"She already is. She's special to you."

Carina tilted her head as if weighing his comment. "Yes, she is."

A cool breeze whistled through the silent night, swirling the strips of fabric around Carina's legs in an alluring dance. "It's late. I should go inside," she murmured.

He untied his cape and placed it over her shoulders before extending his arm. Her dazzling smile stunned his senses. And when she wrapped her hand around his arm, a sudden rightness swept over him as if she had reached out and soothed the unease troubling his body.

"You're leaving tomorrow?" she asked as they retraced her path across the lawn to the main house.

"The weather is turning faster than I thought and we must cross the Arrakans before the heavy snows begin."

"Oh," she mumbled and glanced away.

He stopped at the large, front door to the castle. Two flickering lanterns hung in metal casings on each side of the fortified entrance throwing dancing shadows against the walls. He reached for her arm, enjoying the soft feel of her velvet dress. She quivered at his touch and his body jerked in response. He also noticed her bicep muscle and smiled. Arms had to be strong to handle a Criton, even a small one like Mira.

"Will you promise me something after I leave?"

Carina pressed her lips together and regarded him with wary eyes. "Tell me what it is."

Marek frowned, knowing that she wouldn't blindly agree, but wishing just the same. "Although I now realize it would be unfair to ask you to stop altogether, I'd like you to avoid riding alone near the border." What he hoped would not happen, happened. Carina's spine stiffened, her chin lifted in a stubborn tilt, and her eyes narrowed.

"I never said I was the rider you chased."

"Nor did I. But if you were to ride Mira one day, remember it's too dangerous for an unattended female to ride by herself so far out." His jaw tightened. "So, promise me."

Carina shook her head. "I cannot," she said with a defiant edge.

"I could tell King McKay what I saw yesterday. Perhaps he'd know who the rider was."

Her eyes widened and her mouth opened before she snapped it shut. She yanked her hand off his arm and spun for the door, but he grabbed her by the wrists and pinned her lithe body against his. She smelled like honeysuckle and the fresh promise of early morning dew. He fought the urge to bury his head in her hair so he could memorize her scent.

"Promise me," he ordered in a rougher tone than intended, but he couldn't leave her knowing she would continue to risk her life. "If you agree, I know you'll not break your vow."

Carina's face crumpled and tears rimmed her eyes. The tremor in her voice tugged at his resolve.

"You might as well ask me to stop breathing."

His gut twisted. He had hoped she wouldn't be so resistant. He loosened his grip and wrapped his arms around her slender waist, comforting her against his chest. "You can ride closer to home," he whispered.

She raised her head and stared at him with sorrowful eyes. "I would get caught flying closer in. Please, don't ask this of me."

"Father, where is he?" Marissa's high-pitched voice floated through the heavy door just before she flung it open, rattling the iron-ring accoutrements decorating the outside wood. Carina pulled out of his grasp, but not fast enough.

Surprise flitted across Marissa's face an instant before her eyes tunneled into Carina. "What are *you* doing?"

"Ahh, King Duncan, there you are." Regin appeared in the doorway, his wide frame blocking the light inside from spilling into the night.

Marek noticed Regin's eyes drift to the cape draped across Carina's shoulders. Although the smile never left his face, Regin's eyes darkened. Marek tensed with regret. Not wanting to get Carina into trouble, he reached for the cloak.

"I was checking on FireStrike when I saw Carina and insisted she take my cape." Marek stood tall, ignoring the stunned expression on Carina's face.

Regin smiled. "That was a kind honor you bestowed. Carina, say thank you and go upstairs."

With a noticeable sigh of relief, Carina curtsied and muttered a quiet thank you before turning toward the door. She paused at the threshold. Her inquisitive eyes swept over him. Pinned by the intensity of her gaze, her sadness drilled a hole through his chest. Just as quickly, she released him and disappeared inside, leaving him cold, alone, and in the dark.

"You too, Marissa, up to bed. King Duncan and I have much to discuss."

"Father, please—" Marissa choked on her words when Regin held up his hand.

"Don't argue, daughter."

Marissa's bottom lip jutted out. "Yes, Father," she grumbled and stomped into the house.

With a sweep of his hand, Regin motioned toward the open door. "Shall we?"

Marek strode past Regin into the castle. "Aye, we've much to discuss."

CHAPTER 8

BREAKFAST NEWS

She surmised he landed on the roof and used a rope to scale down the outside wall to sneak into her room. Exhausted from his midnight escapade, he slept beside her under the thick blanket, his head resting against her shoulder with an arm and leg wrapped over her. His weight comforted her while his body kept her warm.

Following his example, a cooling breeze crept through the now ajar window, stirring the faded curtains in a soft, billowing wave. Except for his boots, he still wore his jerkin and leggings, and smelled like finely cured leather.

They were playing a dangerous game cuddling together, but she couldn't stand the idea of waking him. She stared into his face, his breathing quiet and deliberate. His disheveled hair gave him a boyish appearance, yet he was all man. He looked peaceful, beautiful. With a delicate caress, she laced her fingers through his hair trying to tame those wild curls, but his long, brown eyelashes flew open at her touch. Her breath caught when his emerald eyes latched onto her.

He smiled seductively, wickedly. Like a large cat, his lean body stretched on the narrow bed and his muscular arms tightened around her, pressing her against the steel wall of his chest as he nuzzled her neck. His breath tickled, fanning heated chills up and down her spine.

"You should go," she whispered in a hoarse voice. Her statement lacked conviction because she didn't want him to leave.

"Are you sure?" he murmured before kissing the curve of her neck. "Because my plans would require I stay." He shifted above her and nibbled kisses along her jaw before biting her earlobe.

She whimpered at his touch. Despite herself, she grabbed his waist, securing his body against hers, the thin fabric of her nightgown sandwiched between them. "Maybe you could stay a little longer." She moaned as his hand traveled down the outside of her thigh.

Featherlight kisses brushed over her eyes. His hand cupped her breast and an uncontrollable shudder slammed through her body. She was drowning, losing herself to the sensations crashing around her. She slipped under the surface and relinquished herself to his every touch as he fed a rising ache that throbbed low in her belly.

"Carina, I'll never leave you." Marek's voice rumbled before he plundered her mouth.

A rapid knock on the door woke her with a start, her heart hammering in her chest. "What?" she snapped.

Milly bustled into the room and rushed past her to the small, alder armoire located in the corner, opposite her window. If Milly noticed her flustered state, she blessedly did not say anything as she rifled through the sparse wardrobe.

"Come dear, you need to get out of bed right now."

Carina threw an arm over her face and groaned. "Why are you making such a fuss?"

"The king has demanded you eat with the family this morning. King Duncan dines as well." Milly smiled. "This is your chance to say your farewells."

Carina yawned. "Marissa could care less if I say good-bye. It's cold, just let me sleep."

"No, silly. I'm not talking about Marissa, but *King Duncan*." With her head buried inside the closet, Milly mumbled something unintelligible before pulling out a light blue sundress. "This will have to do."

Carina frowned. She had mixed emotions about seeing Marek again. The daring part of her, treasuring the dream she'd just experienced, *really* wanted to see him. The practical side, however, that remembered the promise he'd wanted her to make last night, thought it best to avoid him. But what she wanted didn't matter. Father had summoned her, so she had to go. She would just avoid being alone with Marek to ensure he couldn't force her into any promises.

She sat up and arched her back with her arms stretched overhead while glancing at the window. A breeze had blown it open because she had forgotten to latch it. Heat flooded her body and a tingly sensation spread through her limbs. She shook her head to clear her mind from the scandalous remnants of her dream and swung her legs off the bed. When her feet touched the floor, she gasped and gathered them back underneath the covers.

"The floor is freezing," she hissed. "And that dress you want me to wear is for summer."

"Well, aside from work or riding clothes, you've nothing befitting a formal meal and I don't have the time to create another masterpiece." Milly stubbornly held out the dress. "Now, hurry up so I can brush your hair and get you downstairs."

****

55

Carina burst into the dining room to find everyone seated. Morning sunshine streamed in through the floor-to-ceiling windows, bathing the grand banquet hall in natural light. There were no shadows or darkened corners where she could hide. No throng of dining revelers that she could lose herself among. Only three other people sat at the end of a large rectangular table covered in white linen and Father's best tableware, waiting for her.

Her throat tightened in embarrassment. She had really hoped to just slide into her chair unnoticed. She grabbed her courage with a forceful hand and stepped into the bright, revealing rays. Marek stood as she entered and grinned, causing her heart to somersault.

"Lady Carina."

His voice tumbled through her like a raging river, which reminded her of the indecent dream she'd just had with the man now seated across the table from her, spurring inappropriate thoughts for the suddenly crowded room and spearheading the blush burning on her cheeks. She hoped no one noticed the telltale sign, but the small smile dancing across Marek's lips indicated otherwise.

"My, sleepyhead, it took you long enough," Marissa quipped, acting as if she always dined with them. Carina also noticed Marissa sat beside Marek today instead of at Father's right hand.

During the meal the men talked about inconsequential matters as servants brought in silver platters containing sausages, egg casseroles, fruit, breads, and drink. At first, she concentrated on what they said, but ultimately lost focus. Instead, she surreptitiously watched Marek. She noticed the gold ring on his right hand with his signet on it. The way his strong hands worked the knife and fork, his enticing lips as he spoke, and his intoxicating voice as it flowed around her. His voice penetrated to her core, prompting the same dull ache from her dream.

"Excellent meal, Regin. Thank you. Now, I must prepare for our departure."

Although Carina had disappeared into her musings, her distraction didn't prevent a wash of remorse from rolling over her at his statement.

"Yes, I understand," Regin replied, sounding uncomfortable.

"Don't worry about me, King Marek. I spent most of last night packing and should be ready within an hour." Marissa beamed, pleased with what she obviously considered a huge accomplishment.

Marek kicked his chair out from underneath him and stood, looking irritated. He stared at Regin in an expectant manner, but Regin seemed very interested in the liquid in his goblet.

"What's wrong?" Marissa asked.

"King McKay," Marek said in a crisp tone.

All eyes focused on the chubby man at the end of the table as he fidgeted in his chair like a schoolboy. After a long sigh, Regin appeared resigned to the consequences he was about to set in motion. "Marissa, my dear one, Marek's intentions have changed."

"To what, Father?" Marissa asked. A slight twitch at the corner of her mouth cracked her otherwise unwavering smile.

"I said his intentions have changed."

Carina cringed. Father was never good at explaining delicate matters and attempts at subtlety usually resulted in frustration.

"Oh." Marissa's simple two-letter word voiced a volume of unspoken concern. She glanced down at her plate before asking, "King Marek, am I to follow you in a few days then?"

"Oh, Criton's breath," Regin muttered. "He's decided to take a mistress. You're going nowhere."

Marissa sucked a long, ragged gasp down her throat as if someone had just kicked her in the stomach. Her hands flew to her chest in a protective gesture while the color drained from her face.

Carina waited for the tantrum, but to her surprise, Marissa composed herself.

In a small voice, Marissa whispered, "Well, since a mistress is beneath my station, I imagine he'd have to choose another."

"Yes, of course dear. I'll contact King Villar Remy who has also asked for the opportunity to court you." Regin returned to his breakfast with the gusto of a starving man.

Carina stared at Marissa as she picked at her food. For someone who had never been denied anything in her life, Marissa seemed to be handling the news extremely well. Carina nibbled on a buttery roll and mulled over what had just happened. Although a little dismayed she'd have to endure Marissa's continued jibes and insults, Carina thought it a worthwhile consequence knowing Marissa would not be accompanying Marek.

She was so intent on watching Marissa that she didn't notice Marek staring at her until the hair on the back of her neck rose. She turned to find him. He stood in a shaft of sunshine. The radiant beam bathed him in brightness as if the Mother Source had chosen him as the perfect example of raw, masculine beauty. The grey flecks in his eyes glimmered in a secretive, knowing way that warmed her body and scared her at the same time. Her heart pounded as she stared at him in helpless amazement, wondering why he hadn't left to prepare for his journey home.

As if she had spoken, Father sputtered with a mouth full of food. "Carina, you best hurry."

"What?" Carina's and Marissa's voices echoed in unison, motivating Regin to glance up from his plate. What chore did father expect of her?

With a wave from the hand holding a half-eaten croissant, Regin motioned to Carina. "You will join Marek as his mistress."

Everything in the room slowed…and…stood… still. Carina gazed at Marek.

A small smile played across his lips and the deepened creases around his eyes indicated his amusement.

After a moment of silence, Marissa screeched and slammed her fists on the table before storming from the room.

At last, the tantrum Carina had been waiting for, but her thoughts turned inward when she realized she'd stopped breathing. She tried to calm her sputtering heart with a deep inhale of air, but could only manage little gasps.

His mistress? How could this be? She had resigned herself to spending her life at Brookshire, striving to please a father who didn't love her.

"Carina!"

Father's shout catapulted the room back into focus, but she viewed her surroundings with confused, unseeing eyes.

"I told you to get moving!"

"Yes, Father," she croaked. Using the table for support, she stood on shaky legs.

After an awkward curtsy, she fled the room and the blinding light that had just revealed her future in stark clarity.

CHAPTER 9

··

LIES AND DECEIT

Marissa stomped through the flower garden trying to subdue the hatred blistering through her veins. But even in her angered state, she stepped with care to avoid brushing against a thorny bush and snagging the beautiful yellow, satin dress she had made especially for King Duncan. With a low cut front and tight waist, it didn't leave much to the imagination, which she had hoped would entice him. Instead, he'd barely noticed her, acting like Carina was the only one in the dining hall in that silly dress. Then of all insults, to endure complete shame when he chose Carina over her pure breeding.

She followed the little stone path through the rose bushes. Normally, their perfumed scent comforted her, but today she didn't appreciate their aroma. No one, not even Father, could humiliate her and get away with it. By now, all the servants must know of her disgrace. If she caught any of them laughing at her, she'd make their miserable lives...well...more miserable.

Across the lawn, she spotted Marek striding toward the barn where his Criton waited. He wore a short sleeve, rust colored shirt that emphasized his muscular arms. Even from the distance, she could see the definition in his biceps, which fueled her desire to chase after him. She could convince him that Carina's misfortune in life was no reason to choose a mixed blood over her.

With a frustrated exhale, she caressed the soft petals of a perfect, red rose. She controlled the fate of the flower cupped in her palm, the velvet petals so delicate and frail. In a calculated, slow movement, she fisted her hand around the fragile bud and watched the crushed petals drift to the ground.

She could make him realize his mistake, but Marissa McKay didn't chase after anyone. She was the one to be sought after, not the other way around. As Marek disappeared into the barn, she had the uncontrollable urge to kick something, anything to ease the anger broiling inside her. No one denied her without facing the consequences.

A sudden, bright thought burned a searing path through the fury in her mind. She giggled as the plan blossomed, its simplicity making the idea brilliant. Her anger dissipated, leaving her body on a quiet exhale. Yes, that's exactly what she'd do. She smoothed the front of her dress and strolled toward the guest barn in search of King Duncan so she could offer him some advice on dear sister's behalf.

CHAPTER 10

....

THE END OF A BEGINNING

Carina sat alone, already packed. She didn't have many clothes and few personal items of importance aside from her mother's necklace. Her sparse room containing only a bed, dresser, and armoire had been her sanctuary for most of her life. She stared at the bare walls and regretted never making it more intimate. The small space appeared as if a guest had lived within its confines for all these years, but maybe that's what she'd always been.

She walked to the room's best feature, a tiny window overlooking the training grounds. A group of young soldiers were sparring under Master Sabian Dupree's watchful eye. Their grunts and groans reverberated off the castle walls while the slash and thrust of their swords caught flashes of sunlight.

She skimmed over the bare chests of the grappling men until her eyes found the aged master trainer. Although not a tall man, Master Dupree's demeanor exuded the confidence of a fierce fighter. And the scar running diagonally from the middle of his forehead across his right eye toward his ear only enhanced his intimidating appearance, ensuring obedience from his young students.

She remembered the day she first met Master Dupree. She'd just watched a group of trainees and snuck into the weapons bunker to play with a small dirk. Since girls were not allowed to fight, she thought she could practice the maneuvers hidden from prying eyes.

She'd been so focused on moving her body as Master Dupree had instructed that she didn't notice him watching from a darkened corner until she turned to lunge and almost drove her blade into his stomach. Scared for being caught and horrified at almost plunging a knife into someone's belly, she dropped the dirk.

Master Dupree's grim look of disapproval as the weapon clattered across the stone floor still haunted her. She tried to fumble out an apology before begging for forgiveness with the promise to never touch a weapon again, but his threatening glare smothered her voice.

As he picked up the small blade and handed it back to her, his scolding words ricocheted throughout the room like dive-bombing fireflies. "Not paying attention to your surroundings was your first mistake. If I was the enemy, you'd be dead. Dropping your weapon was your second."

With an agile spin on his heel that prompted his grey ponytail to swish back and forth like a cat twitching its tail, his gruff voice drifted over his shoulder. "Keep the dirk. If you want to learn how to properly handle the weapons you play with, meet me in the small clearing above the north hunting pasture tomorrow after the trainees. Don't be late," he shouted as the door slammed behind him.

She'd stood motionless for several minutes after Master Dupree's exit, but as his words sank in, a small kernel of excitement had unfurled inside her. The *master trainer* had just bestowed a great honor, one that could get him—and her—into trouble. Self-preservation warned against going to the clearing. But her life had become such drudgery that she couldn't ignore the invitation.

Master Dupree became her sparring partner, pushing her harder than the men. And although her body was often so sore or bruised she could hardly move the next day, she always went back. He taught her how to fight with a sword and dirk, how to grapple, and perfected her skill with the longbow to such an extent that he'd praised her for being better than his other trainees. But most of all, he had become her friend—the best gift he could've given her. She turned away from the window blinking away tears.

A soft knock at the door was her only warning before Milly entered. Never one for formality, Milly always barged into her room without waiting for approval. Carina's eyes widened in surprise when Milly properly addressed her.

"Are you all packed, my lady?" Milly stood at attention.

"Why did you say that?"

"What?" Milly asked with an innocent lift of an eyebrow.

"My lady." Carina rolled her eyes. "You've *never* called me a lady."

"Pshh," Milly scoffed with a wave of her hand, dismissing any pretense. "Because you've never been chosen as a mistress before." A mischievous glint burned in Milly's eye and she laughed with delight. "Oh, Carina, I would've given anything to see Marissa's face."

Carina smiled. A deep sense of satisfaction rippled over her skin knowing Marek had chosen her. She barely knew him, yet for the first time in her life someone had noticed her and her entire body glowed in the warmth of that knowledge.

"Ah, good," Milly said, nodding in approval. "You're packed." She walked over to the bag and tied it. "I've been sent to fetch you."

Fear knotted Carina's stomach at the thought of leaving the only home she'd ever known. She sat at the foot of the small bed and clasped her hands together in her lap. Milly plopped down beside her and placed a comforting arm around her waist.

"Sweetie," Milly whispered. "You know King McKay will never accept you as his daughter."

Carina knifed her hands between her legs and tried to ignore the onslaught of tears. "Why, Milly? Why doesn't he love me?"

"Because dear one, his heart is small and he only has room for two, Marissa and himself." Milly rested her head on Carina's shoulder. "Haven't I always looked after you?"

Carina nodded, splashing tears onto her riding pants.

"Go with King Duncan and be *happy*," she urged. "He seems nice and fair. With him you have a chance at a good life. If you stay here, you'll grow old long before your time."

Carina clutched Milly's calloused hands. "You and Master Dupree are my only friends. What will I do without you?" She choked down a sob as a fresh set of tears tumbled over her lashes.

Milly pulled Carina into a tight hug and rubbed her back while making little *shhh-ing* noises. "You'll do fine, Carina. You're strong and *so* like your mother."

Carina buried her head into Milly's shoulder. "I'll miss you."

"Then honor me by being the brave woman I know you are." Milly squeezed Carina one more time before releasing her. "Meet me downstairs in two minutes." She raised two fingers to stress her point before grabbing Carina's travel bag and disappearing through the door.

Carina stood, and wiped the tears from her face with the back of her hand. After a final glance, she walked out the door knowing she'd never see her little room again.

CHAPTER 11

....

FAREWELLS

Marek, his riders, and twelve Critons fidgeted within the confines of the graveled driveway. Most of Regin's household staff also stood in a line to the left of the front door. Having so many servants present made for a good showing indicating a king's wealth.

Leaning against FireStrike, Marek exhaled a long, slow breath and waited. A whine emanating from the guest barn drew his attention. He followed the noise down the hill to find Mira chained to a hitching post. The agitated Criton had clawed a shallow depression in the ground in an attempt to free herself.

Like a supernova, Carina threw the door open and stood in the doorway, blinding him with her radiance. Her dark eyes scanned the area, absorbing the organized chaos. Her hair draped across her shoulders and framed her face in a sensual beauty. She wore a pair of tan riding pants with a matching long sleeve shirt. Intricate beadwork adorned the top of the blouse while a few short pieces of fringe threaded with beads hung from her shoulders, accentuating her chocolate eyes.

He stepped forward to greet her, but his voice grated across his vocal cords. "Hurry and say your farewells. I want to be at the base of the Arrakans by nightfall."

"Yes, King Duncan," she murmured with a slight frown.

As Carina walked toward King McKay, a twinge of guilt pressed at his mind for his harsh tone. He'd been around vindictive women enough to know that Marissa's claim wasn't necessarily true. And it was his fault for not inquiring into Carina's purity—he'd simply assumed she remained untouched. He swore under his breath for allowing Marissa's words to fester beneath his skin. He'd chosen his path—a path he and Carina would travel together, regardless of the consequences. So, Marissa's accusations shouldn't bother him.

He stroked FireStrike's thick neck, encouraging his restless Criton to stand still amid the milling throng of people and animals as Carina prepared to leave her old life behind. She hugged Regin who patted her awkwardly on the back before she dipped into a small curtsy for Marissa who sniffed and turned her head.

When Carina approached a short, robust servant, the woman pulled her into a huge hug and started crying. Carina moved faster down the line with the other servants until she reached the master trainer. Startled to see him standing there, Marek decided Regin had ordered his presence. But Marek's amusement vanished when Carina threw her arms around the master trainer's neck and the man embraced her in return. Marek inhaled sharply at their contact, and with deliberate effort, kept his hands from fisting as Marissa's words whispered through his mind.

When they stepped apart, the master trainer presented Carina with a wrapped bundle. Even from his vantage point, Marek could tell the deerskin sheath contained a longbow, and from the bulge at one end, a quiver full of arrows. A smaller leather case held what appeared to be a sword. He glanced at Regin, surprised that the king would allow women to train, but smiled at the scowl on Regin's face. The master trainer risked much by giving Carina the weapons. Marek's respect for Carina grew as he wondered what else, aside from riding Critons, she'd kept hidden from her father.

Her eyes were red when she approached him, but she held her head high. A spark of pride surged through him at her courage. "Are you ready?"

She nodded. "I just need to get Mira." She turned for the barn, but Regin stepped forward and held up a hand.

"Wait."

"Yes, Father?"

Regin hooked his thumbs into the pockets of his gold-threaded, red vest and rocked back on his heels. "Where are you going?"

Marek's eyes narrowed as the realization hit Carina like she'd been slapped in the face.

"To release Mira," she whispered.

Marissa snickered and covered her mouth with a gloved hand.

Regin shook his head. "Our arrangement didn't include Mira. The Criton stays."

Carina walked over to Regin and reached out to touch him, but paused. Instead, she turned the palm of her hand up and extended her fingers in an appealing gesture. Her voice quavered. "Please, Father. You don't even think Mira will amount to anything."

Regin spun and returned to Marissa's side. "Mira stays until the Caller bonds her to a rider." He smiled and patted Marissa's hand.

"But I raised her—"

"And you did a fine job, but Critons are not pets."

"To call Mira yours would be selfish," Marissa added with a solemn nod.

Regin's voice lowered. "This conversation is over. That Criton should've been part of the negotiation if you wanted her."

As if Mira knew she was the topic of discussion, the little beast issued a low, plaintive wail before slamming her tail against the metal hitching post.

Marek could only see Carina's profile, but he noticed her cringe when Mira's tail smacked the rail. Although Carina stood tall, the single tear that bubbled over her eyelid and tumbled down her cheek betrayed her. Seeing her pain and McKay's indifference ignited a primitive urge to protect what Marek now considered his. He couldn't explain the irrational feeling coursing through his blood, but it gripped him with a strength he was powerless to resist.

He stepped in close and placed his hand on the small of Carina's back. She jumped at his touch, but held her ground and looked at him with large, sorrowful eyes. With forced restraint, he struggled to maintain a measure of decorum. "King McKay, since Carina is fond of this Criton, maybe we can come to an agreement."

The sparkle in Regin's eyes at the prospect of increasing his wealth at Carina's expense turned Marek's stomach.

"Of course, everything is open to discussion. I'd hate for Carina to leave her precious Criton behind." Regin tapped his finger against his lips in contemplation. "Because Mira hasn't transitioned yet, she still has great potential and deserves a high price."

Of course. Marek thought. Since he'd started the negotiation, he was obliged to continue, but Carina turned and stayed the words in his throat by placing her hand on his chest. Wrapped within his arm, she molded perfectly into his embrace.

With a small, amazing smile, she whispered so only he could hear. "You honor me, but my father enjoys tormenting me in this manner and his offer will be unreasonable." She lifted her chin and squared her shoulders. "Please, let's leave now so he cannot demean me further."

Marek enfolded his hand over hers, keeping both their hands on his chest. Her eyes widened as if she just realized they were touching. "Are you certain?"

Tears loomed, but she blinked them away. "Yes, Marek. Please, take me from this place."

Using his name to make her request whispered through him like a soft wind, but commanded him with the force of a hurricane, and he could not deny her. "Then so shall it be," he murmured.

"Never mind, King McKay. Carina has changed her mind." Marek almost smiled when Regin's mouth dropped open in a momentary lapse of composure.

Marek guided Carina to FireStrike. After securing her newly acquired weapons, he stepped into the stirrup and swung his leg over the saddle. When Carina secured her foot in the stirrup, he pulled her up so she could sit behind him.

"Ready?"

"Yes," she whispered.

With a gentle nudge, FireStrike's muscled hind legs hurtled them off the ground as his powerful wings propelled them upward. FireStrike huffed out a massive roar and his band of Critons answered, jumping into the air to follow their Alpha.

After the bellows subsided, Mira's screams pierced the countryside. Knowing that the animal's pitiful wails were ripping Carina's sensitive heart apart, Marek urged FireStrike into a blistering pace grateful to be leaving King McKay, his horrible daughter, and Mira's shrieking behind.

CHAPTER 12

....

FIRST NIGHT

Marek didn't slow down until they were far beyond McKay's border. Carina remained a silent shadow at his back, her hands resting on his waist the only indication she sat behind him. Her confidence around the large, intimidating Critons fascinated him. He'd never encountered a woman like her—strong and independent, yet vulnerable in many ways.

He scanned his Criton riders as they fanned out behind him and spotted Sampson on Reeza scouting the terrain below. Sampson had avoided him since his announcement that Carina would become his mistress. He'd offered Sampson no explanation and his captain knew not to ask for one, but Sampson's disappointment rode plainly on his face.

Maybe he'd not given Marissa much of a chance, but as soon as he'd settled on Carina, a sense of peace had washed over him, soothing his nerves and energizing him at the same time. While Marissa's fake and artificial demeanor left him cold and hollow, Carina's genuine smile and sincere heart lay open like a book for him to read and enjoy. With Marissa, he had nothing in common.

75

Carina however, not only captivated his attention but did so without realizing her pull.

She was a contradiction, a cool breeze across his face on a warm day. Instead of being an obligation, for the first time in years he looked forward to spending time in the company of a woman. He would consider Carina a gift bestowed by the Gods for him to unravel and discover.

A stab of jealously chased through his gut at the thought of Carina bedding another man. He tried to rationalize her actions by thinking how lonely her life must have been living with a father and half sister who treated her more as a servant than blood relative. Since she couldn't find love and companionship with her family, she would naturally look elsewhere.

But no matter how hard he tried, his temper flared at the idea of someone else touching her. Although unreasonable, he couldn't ignore the possessive emotions hammering through his body. He had no right to be angry over something she might've done before he knew her, yet the thoughts and images persisted, slithering around inside his head like an urutu. Marissa had done her job well by planting seeds of doubt.

FireStrike snorted a greeting as Reeza and Sampson glided into a submissive position. "Sire, it'll be dark in a few hours. If you want a full camp, we need to locate a site large enough to accommodate the tents."

Marek leaned forward and rested his elbows on the pommel, stretching his back. He knew what his captain was asking without saying the words. If he hadn't told Sampson of Marissa's allegation, Carina's tent would've been raised without hesitation. But since her purity now stood in question, Sampson wanted to forgo her tent and have her sleep with the rest of the riders. One less tent meant fewer men would have to stand watch. Looking back, he regretted confiding in Sampson. Although too late to make amends now, he vowed to be more mindful of what he told Sampson in the future.

"A full camp isn't necessary."

Sampson nodded and reined Reeza into a downward spiral.

****

The hair on the back of Carina's neck recognized that a silent message had just passed between the two men. An unheard conversation about her, hidden beneath the words they'd just spoken. She wanted to believe her imagination and insecurities were playing tricks on her, but the uneasy feeling persisted.

When they landed, the sun had just slipped under the horizon relinquishing control to Luna, who hung low in the sky. Son, the smaller moon, wouldn't appear until Luna had fully risen as if she had to rouse her cautious boy into joining her by bathing the world in a soft light.

Marek's well trained men assembled camp with a quick and efficient expediency. Tents rose while others walked the perimeter and scouted the area. Fires were built and food prepared. The Critons were released so they could hunt, flying low over the terrain to flush out small game. She had wanted to go with FireStrike and the other Critons, but Marek's set jaw and firmly pressed lips dashed her hopes. In the end, she stayed out of everyone's way by sitting on a log near the main fire.

As evening shadows danced through the trees, the soldiers with the earliest watch ate first before disappearing into the gathering darkness to their assigned locations. Carina's stomach growled as the smell of roasting meat teased her hunger, but too timid to go stand in line, she remained rooted to her log like a mushroom. The men also seemed uncertain about her and kept their distance. Many wouldn't even look at her, choosing the safest course of action by ignoring her completely. She finally decided to wait for Marek who had disappeared into a tent earlier with Sampson.

In the distance, a dugar howled at the night sky as twilight settled over the camp. The hollow sound ignited a slow shiver up her spine. Dugars were ferocious beasts with long venomous fangs and sharp claws. They traveled in small family groups and were known to prey on weak or aging animals, something she irrationally found dishonorable.

The night sounds and the quiet conversation from the soldiers courageous enough to share her fire lulled her into a peaceful contentment. With her gaze lost in the flickering flames, it took her a moment to realize someone stood beside her. She looked up to see a soldier smiling down at her, holding two plates of food.

"Excuse me, my lady, but I brought you dinner."

Carina brightened and reached for the plate. "Thank you." When he turned to leave, she motioned to her log and blurted, "Would you like to sit?"

The soldier glanced around, unsure.

"There's plenty of room," she added, realizing she'd grown lonely sitting by herself.

"Very well." He smiled again and plopped down, careful not to sit too close.

"My name is Carina McKay."

"I'm Damon Finn. It's a pleasure to meet you." He touched a hand to his chest and bowed his head in greeting. "Now, please eat." He pointed to her food then took a large bite out of the drumstick on his plate. His eyes widened and he moaned in delight before using the back of his hand to wipe away some wayward juice that had dribbled down his chin.

Carina laughed as he tore off another piece with exaggerated eagerness. Although she didn't show as much enthusiasm, she had to admit that the cook had done an excellent job.

When full, she set her plate on the ground at her feet. Growing up in a family that preferred to ignore her had not honed her skills for initiating conversation, but she found this fearless soldier who was brave enough to share her log interesting. He looked older than most of the other men with a generous amount of silver coursing through his short, black hair. His elbows rested on his thighs as he stared into the fire.

"How long have you been a soldier?"

Damon chuckled. "My wife would say too long."

"She worries when you're gone?"

Damon's eyes grew distant. "Aye. But the girls tend to get unruly when I'm away and she misses my help."

"How many children do you have?"

"Three. My eldest just married and my twin girls are much younger than you."

"Really?" She tried to hide her surprise at the age discrepancy between his children, but Damon's grin confirmed he'd picked up on her tone.

"Aye, we're a little old to have young children. For some reason after our first, we were not blessed until later in life, and then with twins." He rolled his eyes. "I think the Gods were bored that day and granted our wish so they could have a good laugh."

She smiled. "Have you always been a soldier in Marek's legion?"

"No, I first received my sword under King Sebastian, Marek's father."

Carina's eyes widened at the thought of how old Damon must be. "Really?"

Damon leaned close. "Aye," he said in mock sternness. "Although I'm an old man, my wife doesn't complain and we have two young children as a result." He winked.

She stared at him until the embarrassing blush rose on her cheeks, forcing her to glance away. She opened her mouth, but snapped it shut. Not knowing what to say, she fumbled out a weak reply. "Umm, I wouldn't know."

Damon's back stiffened. "Of course, my lady. Please, forgive my transgression."

Hearing his discomfort twisted her stomach into a big knot. She'd isolated the only person courageous enough to talk to her. "No, I'm sorry," she rushed. "I guess I'm just naïve about some things," she finished with an awkward shrug.

Damon's eyes narrowed briefly before he relaxed and rubbed a hand over the scruff on his face. "No apologies needed. And don't fret, Lady Carina, things are as they should be."

She didn't understand what he meant, so she remained silent as he picked up her plate.

"King Duncan comes." He nodded in Marek's direction. "I'll bid you a good night."

"Thank you, Damon." She smiled, grateful for his companionship.

"My pleasure, Lady Carina." He bowed.

"Carina. Please, just call me Carina."

"Sleep well, Carina," he said before disappearing into the evening shadows.

From across the fire, Marek strode toward the center of camp. The smoke blurred his form, a wavering ghost-like figure of muscle and leather. His eyes roved over the men until they found her. Even from the distance, he commanded her attention like no other. She couldn't turn away from his piercing gaze. He was the fire wrapping her in an uncontrollable flame. Her heart pounded and her skin felt too tight for her body. Her stomach fluttered, anticipating his approach. Although she had enjoyed Damon's company, the person she'd truly missed marched her way.

Entranced, she followed his movements, his long stride deliberate and determined—the walk of a king with the strength and confidence to support it. He stopped to talk to a group of men before clapping one on the shoulder and turning toward her. With a sudden intake of air, he towered over her, blocking the fire from view. She gazed up at him. He looked tired, but his inquisitive eyes held her captive.

"Have you eaten?"

His voice warmed her from the inside out. She nodded because her words were stuck in the back of her throat.

"Very good." He sat down beside her as the cook handed him a plate. "Ahh, smells delicious."

Her tongue refused to work, lying motionless like a slug in her mouth, thick and heavy. She stared into the dancing flames, afraid to look into the face of the man sitting beside her. Because if she did, she feared his eyes would ensnare her, trapping her in a hold she didn't have the willpower to resist.

She still couldn't believe Marek had picked her—a nobody, chosen by a king. Why? Why her? Just the thought of the duties involved made her jittery. She'd never kissed a man, not even a goodnight kiss for her father. Except for Marissa, Father didn't show affection. Maybe her nerves were fueled by the uncertainty of her sleeping arrangements and a dawning realization something might be expected of her tonight.

Carina's hesitancy troubled him. Not knowing what percolated inside her beautiful head stirred a cauldron of rising doubt. She seemed lost in thought as she stared into the fire, biting her bottom lip from the intensity of her contemplations. He wanted to soothe her mind by brushing his thumb across her troubled lip, and bury his fingers in her jumbled, brown hair, but resisted the impulse.

As evening faded and blackness wrapped them in a thick cloak, the men started telling war stories. Marek discreetly watched Carina as she listened, marveling at her fascination. Although the storytellers exaggerated, to the point he almost didn't recognize the battle, since the tales honored those who died and remembered friends who were missed, he didn't see the harm if they weren't completely accurate.

He'd left Carina alone longer than intended, but had to plot the safest route home. If everything went as planned, they'd enter the Bridal Lands early on the tenth day. The Tiwan Tribe claimed the Bridal Lands as their territory and defended it with a savage viciousness. Although he'd never incurred trouble, he also made it a point not to linger within their border.

The schedule was ambitious, but a growing urge to get Carina to Stirrlan had developed into a nagging distraction. He'd learned long ago to listen to his instincts, even if he couldn't justify the reason yet. Sampson had wanted to take a slower, less direct route so the foot soldiers wouldn't have to endure his grueling pace. Although Sampson hadn't come out and said it, his meaning had been clear—a mixed blood wasn't worth the effort.

As Carina laughed and clapped her hands at the end of another mostly fabricated story, she glanced at him and smiled. The tentative curve of her lips enticed him, her radiance rousing a primitive dominance within him. He shook his head to clear his mind and calm the need surging through his body.

If Carina was pure then sleeping next to him, especially in a tent with other men, would be improper until he claimed her. But Marissa had insinuated otherwise, which Sampson for some reason believed without hesitation. Since he chose to reserve judgment, his decision to have her stay in the tent was a simple selfish desire to keep her at his side.

Whether inside one of the tents or outside under the stars, several men had already found their sleeping mats. Marek had watched Damon slip away earlier. Now, with only a few remaining by the fire, Carina's yawn spurred him into action.

Carina wished the stories didn't have to end, but when Marek rose the men stopped speaking to await direction. Their respect filled her with pride for the man gazing down at her, the firelight dancing in his eyes like shining stars.

"It's time for bed," he whispered and extended his hand.

Her heart jumped at his words and then plummeted into her stomach. Fighting her spineless reaction, she concentrated on the simple task of breathing and slipped her hand into his reassuring touch. He smiled, his eyes glittering.

She stared at his rugged face with a day's worth of stubble, unable to move. But an unexpected tug hauled her up so fast she lost her balance and tumbled into him. Her hand landed on his chest as she struggled to regain her balance. He wore a soft, brown chemise shirt, but the suppleness of the shirt didn't cause her gasping intake of air. It was the span of the chest underneath the shirt that caught her off guard. Unintentionally—or maybe a little more intentionally than she cared to admit—her hand remained, and Marek made no motion to remove it. A delicious desire to drag her fingers across the planes of his chest rose inside her. Her hand twitched in anticipation as if it had a mind of its own.

She moved closer, her body brushing against his. Her heart thumped in her ears as images of what lay beneath the irritatingly thin material that separated her inquisitive fingers from their quest invaded her mind. Her body flared. With effort, she ripped her eyes from his massive chest seeking sanctuary in his face. But to her chagrin, his fiery eyes speared her with a hungered desire that seared a path to her core. Liquid heat flooded her body, a primal want demanding fulfillment. She closed her eyes to block his nearness, and with two drunken, shuffling steps, placed a more respectable distance between them.

Marek was a swirling mass of dark passion. He hadn't meant to pull her up with such force, but didn't regret his action when she stumbled into him. His body tensed when she didn't move away, his arousal instant when her hand splayed across his chest. He remained still so his mistress could touch him, although he wished they were in a more private place so matters could develop further.

He heard her gasp and noticed the wide-eyed expression on her face as her featherlight fingers lingered in a possessive touch. He could almost see her mind struggling with what she should do versus what she wanted to do. In the end, propriety won and he regretfully let her slip out of reach. And while he admired the curiosity she ventured when she touched him, the resulting blush as she stepped away captivated him.

Despite the darkness and surrounding wilderness, Carina walked beside him with a calm self-assuredness. She had a small almost delicate frame, but moved with a coordinated grace that signified an underlying strength. She might appear timid, but he sensed that if backed into a corner, she'd fight with an unforgiving tenacity worthy of admiration.

He led her to a small tent surrounded by large trees fostering privacy. "There's a basin of warm water inside if you want to wash before changing into your dressing gown," he mumbled with an awkward catch in this throat. The thought of water glistening over her skin made his pants uncomfortably tight and her remarkable smile in appreciation for the washbasin did nothing to alleviate his growing discomfort.

He fidgeted outside the tent, trying not to notice her silhouette on the canvas wall as she glided a damp cloth over her arms and legs. Mesmerized by her bathing, his eyes drifted in her direction more than once while he oddly wished he was the towel she held.

Fire burned through his blood when she tiptoed out of the tent. She wore a white nightgown that flowed to her ankles with long sleeves traveling down to her wrists and a high collar covering her neck. Except for small, lace ruffles decorating the ends of her sleeves, the gown was unadorned. But he couldn't take his eyes off her.

She had yet to look at anything but her fur-lined, soft-soled leather boots, and focused her energy on digging a small depression in the hard soil with the tip of her foot. But she was an angel, an enchantress wrapping invisible fingers around him, so he indulged in the luxury of staring unabashedly. Her hair shimmered in the dim firelight and framed her face in soft waves while her skin glowed with a vitality that burned an unforgettable image in his mind. Her pursed lips beckoned him as she concentrated on her fervent excavation. He covered his mouth, concealing the smile he couldn't stifle. Although young, her allure was all woman.

He didn't hide the raspy desire in his voice, but folded his arms across his chest to prevent his fingers from reaching out to trace the curve of her face. "Should I carry you to the tent before you burrow your way into the Great Mother?"

****

At the sound of his low-pitched voice, Carina glanced up to see him struggling, and not successfully, to hide a teasing smile. He had just run a hand through his hair, ruffling it in a charming disarray. His eyes sparkled in the moonlight, and his lingering gaze made it apparent that his chivalrous offer to carry her was anything but gallant. He finally abandoned any pretense at courtesy by dropping his hand to reveal a breathtaking smile that lit his face in a mischievous playfulness.

He'd baited her, a subtle dare in an attempt to goad her into accepting his offer. She stared at his chest and broad shoulders. Her eyes raked down his muscular arms and heat flushed through her body. Normally, her stubborn willfulness would've made it impossible to deny such a challenge, but the idea of being carried by this man put her nerves on edge and her resolve melted into a mass of goo.

She tried to infuse confidence into her voice but even she could hear the breathy whisper. "I'll walk."

Marek leaned forward, his mouth next to her ear. Her heart stumbled. His masculine presence filled her senses.

"Coward," he murmured in a soft burr.

She giggled, not able to deny his accusation. But her laughter faded when he remained close. With a surprising tenderness, his fingers brushed through her hair. He turned into her, his breathing ragged. At least he could breathe. Her lungs had forgotten how to function. Little shivers spiraled down her body. She slanted into him. But with a sudden exhale, he moved away and she scrambled to regain her balance.

"Very well," he muttered before placing a hand on her elbow and guiding her toward the main tent.

When he stopped and held the flap open, she paused. Typically, only the king and his Criton riders slept in the large tent. She thought she'd have her own. But since she didn't wish to offend, she slipped through the opening and stood just inside the door.

Marek entered and stepped to the front. Grabbing her hand, he led her into the dark stillness filled with the whispered snores and soft breathing of the men. A small lantern near the entrance offered sparse lighting, forcing her to cling onto his arm to avoid tripping over anything...or anyone. She kept her eyes glued on his back, trying not to notice the men around her. Aside from Sampson, everyone seemed to be asleep. Even in the dim light, the gleam in Sampson's eyes and the fact he didn't avert his gaze, disturbed her. Although her modest dressing gown covered her entire body, her skin crawled under his slicing stare.

Marek escorted her to a large mat in a corner away from the other men. He removed his belt, sword, and the two dirks strapped across his chest before sitting. Not sure what to do, she watched him place his weapons within arm's reach and remove his boots.

When he looked up, a small smile danced across his lips. His eyes glinted in the lantern light, but not in a way that made her uncomfortable. Although she could sense his desire, it was tempered behind a gentleness that made her heart stutter.

"Come, Carina," he commanded softly, his voice pouring into her. He reached out for her. "Come lie next to your king."

Her sputtering heart skipped beats as she took his hand and let him pull her down onto the mat. She settled into the soft cushion while he threw a wool blanket over them and stretched out beside her, closing his eyes. Lying on his back, one arm cradled his head while the other rested on his stomach.

She could barely breathe. Her nerves zinged with restless energy. Although they were not touching, she vibrated with anxiety at his nearness. Aware of his body, her senses hummed on a hyper-alert frequency attuned to Marek. The rest of the men in the tent disappeared from her mind.

A dull ache, emanating low in her belly, grew into a steady throb, pulsating with an intensity that radiated throughout her. *What was wrong with her?* She kicked off the blanket to cool her overheated body, and shut her eyes to focus on her breathing just like Master Dupree had taught her. She narrowed her senses until only the inhale and exhale of air entering and exiting her lungs consumed her mind. Slowly, she relaxed and the ache dissipated. Although the cold, autumn air chilled her, she ignored the discomfort hoping the breathing exercise would lull her to sleep.

But no matter how hard she tried, her body remained stubbornly aware of Marek's presence. Sleep, her companion for every night throughout her life, eluded her. As if angered by his closeness, it refused to offer her peace.

With a sigh, she rolled onto her side and stared at the tent wall, clenching her teeth in frustration. Realizing dawn would not greet her anytime soon, she struggled to remain still and grew more impatient as the minutes ticked by. She considered sneaking out of the tent to get some fresh air to settle her nerves, and contemplated the logistics of traversing through the sleeping bodies without waking anyone until Marek moved.

Her body froze in a silent panic when his arm pulled her into the hard muscular wall of his chest. He grumbled and fumbled with something behind her before the heavy wool blanket thumped over her again. Draping his arm across her waist, the back of her head rested just under his chin.

"Be still, Carina," he murmured. "All is well."

He smelled of leather, wood smoke, and pine—a combination that threatened to rekindle the fire she'd worked so hard to extinguish. But the steady rise and fall of his chest against her back soothed her.

Marek holding her this way seemed very inappropriate, but sleep—her long lost companion—welcomed her back into its embrace before she could ponder the consequences of their impropriety further.

CHAPTER 13

....

MESSENGER

As promised, Father sent a messenger to the bordering king, Villar Remy, with information of Marissa's newfound availability. To Marissa's delight, King Remy had dispatched a rider stating he would arrive to court her within the week. His prompt reply was the type of response she deserved.

She'd been up in her rooms wondering whether the servants should unpack her bags because if she found King Remy to her liking, they'd just have to pack everything again. Deciding she liked her belongings around her, she'd finally ordered them to unpack. But when they got underfoot, scurrying around like mice emptying her many trunks, she'd opted to flee her comforts for a quiet stroll through the grounds.

Still unseasonably warm during the day, she wore a light pink and white lace dress, and carried the perfect accessory—a small matching umbrella—to protect her delicate skin from the sun.

She followed a cobbled path toward the barns, lost in her contemplations. She hoped King Remy was as fine a masculine specimen as King Duncan. Her stomach clenched at the thought of

King Duncan. She still couldn't comprehend why he chose Carina. At least Carina would never be his queen.

Instead of following the path, she turned right and paralleled a fence to one of the hunting pastures. Carina's Criton had just killed an ovine and was enthusiastically ripping it apart. She turned her head away in disgust. Although she pretended to like Critons for Father's sake, they were dirty creatures, hard and wild, and she wanted nothing to do with them.

Despite herself, she glimpsed over her shoulder to reaffirm her poor opinion of the foul beasts. The mangled, bloody remains were trapped within the animal's small front claws, but the scrawny Criton had stopped eating to stare at her. Blood dripped off its chin. A ripple of fear shot up her spine. For a second, she almost believed an intelligent creature lived within those evil eyes.

She quickened her pace. Just ahead, the trail would veer away from the pasture and take her through a grove of birch trees before looping back toward home. As she reached the bend, she tortured herself with a final glance behind her. The monster still watched her with those eerie, pale green eyes.

"What are you looking at?"

The beast pinned its small ears back and curled its lips to expose bloody fangs. She shivered at the ferocious display before slipping into the trees, grateful to be out of view from the animal's vigilant gaze. What an unappreciative creature. Father should've put that thing out of its misery years ago. But he'd never kill it now so close to transition.

She ambled through the trees. A breeze whispered through the top branches of the multi-trunked champion birches, showering her path in a soft rain of autumn color. She stomped on the fallen leaves and wondered why Carina loved Critons so much. She attributed Carina's common heritage as the reason for her half sister's affinity toward the animals, but couldn't figure out why the disgusting creatures returned Carina's affection.

An unexpected thought wormed inside her mind. It festered and grew as she mulled over the consequences. Tiwans took their responsibility of protecting the world from Dark Callers very seriously. Her plan crystallized and she smiled.

Although King Duncan had a head start, he would be traveling at a slower pace because of his foot soldiers. If she dispatched a lone rider on a fast, strong Criton, with a little luck the rider might reach the Bridal Lands before King Duncan and his men. She could be doing the world a favor by sending a messenger. After all, since Carina couldn't be the Caller of Light, maybe her mixed blood destined her to become a Dark Caller capable of using the negativity within a soul to bind Critons and riders with a dark bond.

She rested a gloved hand on the white-mottled trunk of a sturdy birch, letting her mind run through the possibilities. The Tiwans would probably consider her warning them an obligation. And since she'd only be delivering the message, her conscience would be clear.

The breeze did not filter down from the treetops, so her hair clung to her neck like a wool scarf in the stagnant air. She brushed it off her shoulders, thinking she should've pinned it up as she strolled toward the servant's quarters in search of a messenger.

CHAPTER 14

....

BRIDAL LANDS

Carina grew accustomed to the patterns of traveling with Marek and his men. But the days were long. Even on Critonback, the days stretched on and on. So by the time they found a place to camp for the night, she was exhausted.

Although tired, she wanted to shoulder some of the work and began caring for the Critons. When Marek first saw her in the middle of the large creatures feeding them juma melons, he had pushed his way through the milling animals—who voiced their displeasure at his encroachment—and hauled her out of the throng.

Marek's actions had caused a brief standoff as she held her ground with her arms crossed in front of her, arguing that she just wanted to help. He reluctantly acquiesced only after she reminded him that the Critons were her responsibility back home. And once she began taking care of them, the men relaxed around her.

But even the joy of handling the Critons didn't ease her pain over losing Mira. Looking back, she wished she'd asked Marek to purchase her. But if he had, Mira would've had a difficult time keeping up with the adults and Marek's pace. She could only hope

Father would allow Mira to grow and transition into the amazing animal she knew Mira would become.

Aside from the time she spent with the Critons, Carina enjoyed the nights the most. Now, she welcomed, and even anticipated, sleeping beside Marek. She savored the heavy weight of his arm draped over her as he held her pressed against his chest. Totally improper, but the wicked pleasure was hers to enjoy. She loved his attention and their closeness as they whispered the night away. Often she woke up more tired than rested because of the late hours they spent awake.

By the tenth day, lack of sleep found her leaning against Marek with her head against his shoulder and her arms wrapped around him—sleeping. She awoke with a start as an angry thunderhead rolled across the sky spattering fat raindrops on her.

"Ah, she wakes." Marek joked.

"Maybe *you* shouldn't talk so much at night." She yawned, still tired and grumpy about getting wet.

"Well, we could do other things, but then the men might have a hard time sleeping."

She giggled and punched his shoulder in mock offence.

Marek's laughter spurred FireStrike's roar, which spiraled to the other Critons who voiced their response. Nearby Criton riders glanced at them with curious expressions making her blush and Marek laugh harder.

They landed to don rain slickers then took to the air again. Although most of the storm stayed ahead of them, the heavy rain saturated the ground and slowed the progress of the foot soldiers and coursers. By the early evening hours, they were only halfway across the Bridal Lands.

Sampson flew up beside them. "Do you want to push through?"

Even with her light touch on his waist, she felt his body tense. She knew he wanted to travel through the Bridal Lands in one day, but the rain had made the terrain too treacherous to cross at night.

"No," he grumbled. "Find a clearing, but make sure it's defensible."

Sampson nodded and flew off. She watched Sampson and another rider skim low over the ground until they topped a small rise and disappeared on the other side. Marek followed Sampson's path, but at a slower speed so the foot soldiers stayed within sight.

They were traveling parallel to the breathtaking Karelides, the largest mountain range she'd ever seen. The Karelides were actually two distinct ranges almost butting against each other, except for a valley between them. The valley, also known as the Realm of Light, housed the gateway between her world and Crios where Critons were born.

The stark, intimidating mountains consisted of craggy snowcapped peaks that disappeared into low lying clouds. Ominous and impressive, the Karelides erupted out of a vast expanse of flat lands as if the Gods had deposited them in the middle of nowhere to shield the gateway. She peered over Marek's shoulder to get a better view of the valley, but it disappeared into the depths of the mountains as they passed.

"Have you been through the valley?"

Marek chuckled. "The Valley of Karelides? No, the Tiwan Tribe would never permit it. As far as I know, aside from the Caller, only a few select Tiwans are allowed into Crios."

"Why?" She had heard this too and tried to suppress her disappointment.

Marek shrugged. "To prevent a Dark Caller from entering Crios."

"To avoid another Dark War."

Marek nodded. "No matter how good, all living creatures have some darkness inside them that Dark Callers can bind, dooming to their souls to the black shadows."

Carina shuddered at the thought of Dark Callers. "I hear Tiwans are savages."

Marek's laughter spilled over her. "Although they won't welcome our overnight stay so close to the gateway, they shouldn't bother us as long as we leave tomorrow."

A flaming arrow arcing high into the cloudy sky captured their attention. "There they are," Marek said, guiding FireStrike toward the small clearing Sampson had deemed appropriate.

She grabbed Marek's waist and locked her knees under the hard, leather restraints to stay in the saddle as FireStrike dove at a dizzying pace, the wind whipping over her. When they neared the ground, FireStrike snapped his mighty wings open to stop their rapid descent and hovered before dropping lightly onto the damp soil.

Marek jumped off and grabbed Carina's waist, lifting her down while she held his forearms. She'd grown accustomed to his touch. Although a proper lady wouldn't let him so near, she couldn't force herself to follow the strict requirements custom dictated after experiencing his body lying beside her at night. And if people talked about her as a result, so be it.

Figuring Marek would go find Sampson to discuss defensive positions for the camp, she turned for the forest to stretch her legs, but Marek grabbed her arm. She twisted and melted into his blazing green eyes. The grey flecks sliced through her like tiny arrows implanting invisible marks of ownership.

In a low tone, he commanded. "Stay close to camp, Carina McKay."

The timbre of his voice as he murmured her name resonated deep within her, leaving her breathless and weak-kneed. He refused to release her until she nodded. As he walked away, she watched his long, confident stride. His leather riding pants captured her attention...and imagination. They fit him well, defining him enough to send her mind tumbling, wondering what lay hidden underneath.

She smiled and shook her head before turning toward the woods. She wanted to get a closer look at the Karelides. Her thoughts rambled as she walked through the quiet cover of wide-canopied trees with small leaves that twittered in the gentle breeze above her. Many of the leaves had fallen due to the cooler weather, blanketing the floor in a soft carpet of color.

When the strand ended, she stood at the edge of a grassy meadow spanning as far as she could see to the east and west, but the vast plain was handcuffed to the north because it bumped against the rugged mountains. The majestic Karelides took her breath away. She sat on a jumble of rocks and stared at the mysterious land just beyond her reach. She could hear Marek's men nearby and decided she was close enough to run back to camp at the first sign of trouble.

Her thoughts centered on the untamed land across the meadow. While the mountains mesmerized her, the mysterious valley between them sparked an unyielding curiosity. If she had Mira, the temptation to get a better glimpse of the secluded valley would've been irresistible. Just the idea of being so close to the gateway filled her with a strange sense of anticipation. Lying in the shadow of the mountains, the valley was obscured by a ground covering mist but that didn't stop her from imagining the excitement of traveling through it into Crios. Hundreds of unbonded Critons soaring through the skies would be a breathtaking sight.

Her mind drifted as she stared into the mist that hid the depth of the valley from view. Transfixed by the swirling vapor trapped within the confines of the two towering mountains, she envisioned the wild beauty of the magical realm. Like a living thing, the haze breathed with a life of its own. Even from the distance, the mist beckoned her, tugging with invisible fingers. Her senses dulled and her eyelids grew too heavy to keep open, and she dreamed of walking in the valley.

The smell of dank, spongy loam filled her nostrils. She could only see a few feet around her, but that didn't stop her from disappearing into the white fog. It curled around her, tickling her skin with gentle caresses before enclosing upon her. She glanced behind her, gone was the path from where she'd come, blanketed by the constantly moving cloud. The mist pushed her, encouraging her farther into its shifting embrace.

A tedious nagging pricked at her subconscious and threatened to pierce through her sluggish mind. But she ignored its growing insistence, choosing to let the vapor guide her deeper. A lethargic sense of peace enveloped her. Only the persistent nagging buzz at the back of her mind kept her from slipping into a relaxed listlessness. The oppressive mountains pressed in on her, but she couldn't see the rugged walls since the wispy fog cradled her in total isolation.

With a sudden jab, the nagging stabbed hard enough to force a hole into her consciousness, oozing into her mind like warm honey.

You should be afraid. You have strayed too far.

She shook her head. No, she was still at the edge of the meadow.

Only your body remains, your mind has drifted. She brought you here and pulls you into the valley.

Carina stopped at the mention of being lured into the fog and turned a full circle trying to orient herself. But the undulating vapor protected its secrets, blinding her.

You are not ready. You must go back.

Ready for what? Besides, she was just daydreaming on a rock.

She comes. You can sense her. You must GO.

Carina winced and grabbed her throbbing head. Disoriented and nauseas, a chill rippled through her, a foreboding of something approaching in the mist. The first tendrils of panic crept up the base of her skull.

Marek is looking for you. You must hurry. She is almost upon you.

Carina's sense of urgency escalated. She had to escape, but it proved harder than just retracing her steps. As if expecting her move, the vapor expanded into a thick cloud of billowing haze, cocooning her in a silent tomb that stifled her breathing. This is only a dream, she thought over and over as if repeating her mantra would make it true and she'd wake up.

She is here.

The hair on the back of Carina's neck bristled. Her flesh pebbled as terror settled into her bones. The once soothing mist coated her body in a cold dampness. Something walked in the fog with her. She stood rooted to the ground, frozen with fear.

She cried out and grabbed the side of her head. Another presence pushed at her mind. Strong and forceful, it seeped through her defenses. She doubled over, pressing the palms of her hands into her temples. "Get out," she hissed between clenched teeth.

"Do not fear, my child." The voice boomed inside her, vibrating in multi-toned layers and definitely not human.

She screamed and collapsed to her knees.

"Turn around." The voice encouraged. *"Turn. See your fate."*

She struggled to her feet, panting softly. The warm exhalation of air from the creature's breath peppered her skin. She wanted to run, but she had become stone. Her body refused her commands.

"Dear one, do not be afraid. See me."

Without consent, Carina's head swiveled while the rest of her body stayed immobile. She moved in slow motion, every action exaggerated and beyond her control. She wanted to squeeze her eyes shut so she couldn't witness the monster commanding her. But like a puppet unseen strings forced her compliance, an unwilling participant in a nightmare.

What she saw caught her breath. The scream threatening to burst from her mouth lay paralyzed at the back of her throat. Out of the mist two large amber orbs for eyes stared at her. She'd never seen such eyes, eyes that threatened to consume her.

"Come to me." The voice whispered in her head and reverberated all around her. *"Come, and claim your birthright."*

Her stomach lurched. She was going to be sick. "I'm a mixed blood," she stammered. "I have no birthright."

The soothing voice transformed into a harsh, persistent pounding inside her mind.

"Do not question what is yours to take."

The amber eyes blazed with a brilliant glow forcing Carina to shield her face from the white-hot radiance. Scorching flames obliterated the mist around her leaving the air humid and smelling of sulfur.

A large Criton head unexpectedly loomed overhead. The animal's tawny irises contracted and speared through her barricades like a flimsy piece of paper, absorbing her mind. Lost within those ageless orbs, Carina throbbed with ancient power and wisdom. A gripping sadness enveloped her, foretelling of an old pain, a terrible loss that could never be recovered. How could any creature live with such an unbearable ache?

Flames licked at the corners the Criton's mouth as she lowered her yellow head and peered into Carina's stunned face.

"No mixed blood could have entered the valley and called me," the Criton bellowed.

Carina gasped and pitched backwards. She braced herself for a hard landing, but strong arms caught her.

"And where did you think you were going?"

His voice poured into her, evaporating the image of the Criton and the mist-filled valley. She scrambled to regain her bearings. She sat on her rock with the Karelides looming in the distance, except now Marek's hard wall of a chest pressed against her back and his arms were wrapped around her. She could smell him, his closeness more intimate than riding FireStrike. She reached for him and let his strength calm her.

"I must've been daydreaming."

"Well, I'm glad I found you because you were about to tumble off your perch."

She twisted to look into his face. His eyes sparkled with mischief. She shrugged, still mentally sorting through what just happened. Was it only a dream?

"You don't listen very well."

That caught her attention. "What? But I stayed close, just like you said. I could hear the men."

"Yet, when they called, you didn't answer." His voice lowered and his eyes narrowed. "You're not on home soil anymore. This land is wild and dangerous. You must remain aware of your surroundings."

She bit her lip. "You're right. I'm sorry." Her eyes inadvertently traveled to the valley, and she shivered.

Marek's arms tightened around her, crushing her against his chest. A sense of peace filled her and the experience faded from her mind. Marek would keep her safe.

"Are you cold?"

"Not now." She relaxed into him, enjoying his affection as she stared at the mountains in the vanishing daylight.

"They are beautiful, aren't they?" he murmured, nuzzling her ear.

Any lingering thoughts about the valley dissolved as she focused on the man pressed against her. His breath on her cheek instigated delicious tingles to splinter through her body, warming her from the inside, yet she shivered again.

"I thought you said you weren't cold?" he whispered, his lips brushing down the side of her neck.

"I'm…I'm not."

His chuckle spilled into her. She loved his laugh.

With a sigh, he pulled away. If she had more courage, she would've protested as his muscular arms unwrapped themselves.

"Come Carina, time to get off your rocky throne and walk with me to the safety of our fires."

He held out his hand and she smiled as she reached for it. She smiled again when he continued to hold it as they walked back to camp in the fading light.

CHAPTER 15

....

MISUNDERSTANDINGS

They were up earlier than usual the next day. The sun had yet to rise, but the increasing glow on the horizon marked its imminent appearance. Although Marek didn't expect trouble, he was anxious to get out of the Bridal Lands. He'd posted extra guards overnight, some even in the surrounding forest farther away from camp to settle the disquiet churning his stomach.

He stood at the main fire, eating a cold breakfast consisting of a hard wheat cake and a strip of dried meat when Carina stepped out of the tent. Her hair, a mass of tangled curls, draped around her in a wild array of untamed independence before a brush had yet to reestablish dominance. She raised her arms overhead and stretched, not bothering to stifle a yawn. He smiled. They had talked well into the early morning hours until she fell asleep in mid-sentence.

She pursed her lips and rubbed her arms at the cooler weather before walking toward the creek, her hips swaying back and forth in an alluring invitation.

He ran his fingers through his hair. He could not deny that he was taken with her. She excited and frightened him. Carina was a dilemma, strong and independent, yet vulnerable and naive. Without knowing it, she tantalized and teased him, and drove him crazy. Lying beside her at night had become an exquisite torment. But the thought that he might not be her first plunged his mind into a downward spiral. He clenched his teeth at the idea of another man touching her.

"She's a wonder, isn't she, Sire?"

Marek turned to find Damon standing beside him watching the barren path where Carina's presence had just lingered. Marek's father had made Damon Captain of the Guard during Marek's teen years. Although Sampson was now captain, Damon had never shown any jealousy. The younger men admired the elder warrior and looked to him for direction. Damon had fought in many battles and seen his share of death, but still retained a sense of compassion Marek respected.

"Aye, she is." Although he'd only told Sampson of Marissa's allegation, Marek guessed the rest of the men suspected Carina's taint. He had intended on her staying with him just the first night because of their late start. But somehow, he'd always found an excuse to keep her next to him. He could only blame himself and his selfish reluctance to move her into another tent. He enjoyed lying beside her too much—the warmth of her body, her sweet smell and whispered laughter, the blush on her cheeks when he suggested something inappropriate—such a wonderful agony the Gods were inflicting on him.

"Sire, if I may...?"

Marek cleared his mind. Not known for idle chatter, if Damon wished to discuss something, the man deserved his full attention.

"Of course." Marek crossed his arms and waited.

"You know I have three daughters. The eldest is Carina's age and just recently wed."

"Your daughters are fine, young ladies. You and Serena are raising them well."

Damon shifted from one foot to the other, acting as if he wanted to be anywhere but where he stood. Marek started to prod him, but Damon blurted in one great rush of air.

"I've noticed Carina sleeps with you and the resulting implication."

Marek's shoulders tensed. Damon needed to be very careful with what he said next.

"I'm not sure where you received your information, but I think she's innocent."

Movement caught Marek's eye and he turned to see Carina strolling back from the creek, her hair once again tamed and in place. He almost missed her disheveled, unguarded appearance.

"Why do you say that?" Marek asked, his eyes never leaving her.

"Because I live in a house full of women."

His eyes flicked to Damon before returning to Carina.

"She has the innocence of all my girls, Sire. She's strong and tries to act brave, but in the end, she's just a girl experiencing a man for the first time."

Her eyes roamed the camp until they found and locked him in an invisible hold. Unable to resist her call, he stood motionless as she walked toward him. His eyes devoured every inch of her. The curve of her hips, beckoned him. Her skin glimmering in the sunlight, whispered to him. Her lips parted in a slight smile, tempted him. The hardness of her nipples pressing against her blouse enticed the rising desire in his groin.

By the time she reached him, his overheated body ached with need to claim her. He fisted his hands and restrained his arms across his chest to keep himself from whisking her into the tent.

Struggling to keep the hunger out of his voice, he rasped, "Good morning, Carina."

"Good morning." She smiled, her eyes sparkling in the dawn light.

"Did you sleep well, Lady Carina?" Damon asked.

She hesitated and a blush rose on her cheeks. Fumbling for an answer, she lowered her eyes. "Um…yes. Very well, thank you."

Marek knew the reason for her embarrassment and fought to hide the smile threatening his lips. Their nightly talks had become a wonderful habit. He would wrap her in his arms and hold her close as she fell asleep, enjoying her smell and the feel of her body.

"Excellent," Damon said, acting as though he hadn't noticed her red giveaway. "Now, if you'll excuse me, the others will think I'm shirking my duties." With a slight bow, he left.

Carina refused to look at him, focusing on her riding boots with particular interest as her blush deepened. Marek knew he wasn't helping by staring at her, but couldn't stop himself.

With an exacerbated sigh, she lifted her head and glared at him. She squared her shoulders and clenched her jaw in challenge. He tried to keep his expression neutral, but failed miserably when he burst out laughing. Damon was right. She was innocent, which meant she should be sleeping in her own tent…alone. But after spending these past few nights with her, how was he going to find the strength to let her go?

"What?" she asked, her eyes narrowing. Her simple one word question contained an undercurrent of complex meaning, a defiant edge poised like a sharpened blade warning him to beware.

Another royal might've taken offense at her tone and posture, but he'd grown to expect nothing less. Carina would always stand her ground, and he would have her no other way. Without thinking, he reached out and stroked her cheek with the back of his hand.

Her lips parted in a startled gasp at his unexpected touch. Ignoring what his mind told him, he stepped closer surrendering to the desire driving his body. Her bottom lip trembled. Fascinated, he brushed his thumb across those amazing lips to soothe their quiver. She stayed her ground, her eyes wide. He buried his fingers in her hair, and in a voice that displayed less control than should from a king, whispered, "We need to talk."

"All right."

He noticed her eyes fill with worry. How was he going to tell her that from now on she'd sleep in her own tent, especially when he didn't want to spend a night away from her? He'd made a proper mess of things.

A sudden yell from the forest, shouting for a call to arms immediately transformed his mind and body into a warrior anxious to protect his command and keep those he cared about safe. The camp blurred into a whirlwind of commotion as soldiers grabbed weapons and took up defensive positions or plunged into the forest to help comrades.

He grabbed Carina and pushed her behind him while drawing his sword, a large claymore.

Sampson ran toward him. "We're under attack," he shouted. "From the forest over there."

"Tiwans?"

Sampson nodded.

"Keep a contingent here," Marek ordered. "Get the riders in the sky."

Sampson spun and raced away, bellowing orders.

Marek clutched Carina's hand and rushed for the tent. Only when they were inside did he turn to her. "You must stay here."

His eyes darted to the door when the Critons took to the sky in a deafening roar, followed by FireStrike's angered scream for being left behind, forced to wait for his rider.

Carina's eyes were wide with fear. He didn't want to leave her, but needed to join his men in the battle. He'd have to rely on the contingent to protect her.

He turned to leave, but she gripped his arms with uncompromising strength.

"Marek," she whispered, her voice quavering.

He pulled her into his arms and buried his face in her hair. "I must go." His tone hardened becoming the voice of a king. "Do as I say and stay here. I'll come back for you."

She nodded, her head still hidden in his chest. He pulled away and cupped her chin, forcing her to look at him. Tears threatened to bubble over her eyelashes, but even now her mouth captured his attention. He brushed his lips across hers, a whisper and promise of something still to come, and smiled at her tentative response. They had much yet to share. After a hurried kiss on her forehead, he bolted from the tent.

Leaving her behind did not sit well in his gut. Darkness cooled the blood in his veins, an omen foretelling he'd made the wrong decision. But they were in battle, and the feeling was simply the uncertainty of the pending fight, he rationalized. As he took wing and glanced back at the tent with the men standing guard around it, he had to quell the unease that his soldiers wouldn't be enough to protect her.

CHAPTER 16

....

FLAMES

The pungent odor of smoke drifted through the air as Tiwan warriors burned the camp, while the sounds of clashing swords and men yelling flooded Carina's ears. Marek's soldiers fought with valor, but they were outnumbered. Although she wanted to believe the guards would protect her, she couldn't ignore their screams as they died on her behalf.

A dawning understanding of her bleak situation clouded her mind. If forced to defend herself the confines of the tent would make it difficult to maneuver. She had two choices, ignore what was happening around her and die where she stood, or do something about it.

She scanned her surroundings. Master Dupree had taught her how to fight so she wasn't helpless. She knew the fundamentals of wielding a sword, and shot a longbow with uncompromising accuracy. But training to fight and fighting for her life was different. She bit her bottom lip as mind numbing fear swirled inside her. As a mixed blood, she'd been raised to do as she was told, and Marek had ordered her to stay inside the tent to await his return.

A soft thud from a torch landing against the tent flaps caught her attention. An instant later, with a loud whoosh and crackle, the front of the tent burst into a raging blaze of brilliant red-yellow flames. Her heart skipped beats and adrenaline surged through her. She watched the conflagration in paralyzed horror.

Heat from the spreading inferno radiated around her. Like a live animal, the fire engulfed the tent with an insatiable hunger, sucking up the oxygen with such greed she struggled to inflate her lungs. Smoke filled the air and burned her eyes, but she stood frozen and stared through the haze and flames with a surreal detachment as a large Tiwan wielding a hammer club, crushed the skull of one of Marek's guards.

She'd never been one to give up. Even during Master Dupree's unforgiving training regimens, which left her so sore and tired she could hardly move, she'd never yielded. In a rare moment of companionship, Master Dupree had praised her for having a hidden strength. And if she ever doubted, she just needed to peer inside herself to harness the power lying dormant within her. He had then proceeded to pound her with a wood sword until she was bruised and face down on the cool earth, gasping for air and praying for mercy.

Tears rolled down her face as smoke swelled her eyes to slits. When another soldier fell to the hammer pounding Tiwan, a small seed of anger unfurled in her belly. Their deaths were unnecessary. They were just passing through the Bridal Lands to get home.

With a loud pop, the tent began collapsing around her, jarring her into action. She scrambled to her makeshift bed and snatched the rolled bundle Master Dupree had given her. Reaching inside, she searched for the welcoming feel of the hilt waiting for her. With a practiced hand, she freed the sword and in a smooth downward motion, slashed the back of the tent open. She grabbed her longbow and quiver before racing through the opening and up a hill to the safety of the forest.

Pausing at the tree line, she crouched and glanced around to see if anyone had followed her, but in the turmoil, she'd escaped unnoticed. She unwrapped her longbow and quiver, and with an ease from years of practice, bent the tip of the bow before looping the sinew-fibered bowstring into the nocked grooves of the upper limb. She grabbed the quiver strap and slipped it over her shoulder so the arrows rested against her back, then secured her scabbard and sword around her waist.

Surveying the annihilation of their camp, she saw dozens of bodies, from both sides, amid the burning tents and carnage of battle. A mortally wounded Criton screamed in outrage. Shot in the chest with a harpoon cannon, the animal had crashed to the ground leaving a trail of destruction behind it. Although the Criton belonged to a Tiwan, remorse shot through her as the poor beast flapped a wing in the air before growing still.

Within minutes, the little clearing had transformed from a tranquil respite into a torn up mound of dirt and bloodshed. Smoke hung in the air like a thick blanket as the last of Marek's men perished. The world stopped turning as she watched the final moments of the soldier's life. A large Tiwan approached from behind and before she could belt out a warning, the Tiwan smashed a hammer club into the young man's head with such force it burst like a melon, dispersing blood and brain matter into the wind. The guard folded like a rag doll, never knowing death had come from behind.

Her throat constricted as she silenced the scream threatening to explode from her mouth. The remaining Tiwans cheered their victory, laughing and patting each other on the back for a successful battle. But where was the honor in sneaking up from behind to kill? Her childhood belief that war was the result of honorable men fighting for a worthy cause crumbled around her. As the large Tiwan slammed his club into the fallen guard's chest while his companions shouted their approval, the angry seed inside her burst open like a dam breaking. Those dead men deserved a warrior's respect.

She moved from the safety of the timberline and stood in the open. One of the Tiwans spotted her. Even from the distance, she could see the tattoo covering part of his face. Her impartial mind interested in self-preservation demanded her immediate retreat, but her emotional heart kept her feet planted.

"LEAVE HIM ALONE."

The men glanced at each other before erupting into additional bouts of laughter. Fear rippled down her spine when their expressions darkened and three men began jogging toward her, spreading out to flank her as they approached. The hammer wielding Tiwan took point.

Run! Her rational mind screamed. But her heart controlled her actions and she bladed her body. Her hands shook as she fumbled for an arrow. Keeping her eyes on the men, she noted their long, ground-devouring strides eating up the distance. Panic clawed at her, preying upon her insecurities in an attempt to immobilize her.

She nocked her arrow and using a three finger split hold, drew the bowstring back to her anchor point, aiming for the large Tiwan holding the hammer club. To her surprise, he skidded to a halt and spread his arms wide exposing his chest.

"You better make it count, girl."

He spoke with an unfamiliar accent in a low, gravelly voice that made her skin crawl. "Because if you miss, you'll beg for death before we're done with you." His sneer exposed a mouth full of rotten teeth.

Her arms trembled, shaking the bow. Fear jumbled her mind. She couldn't focus. But somehow all the hours of routine practice took control of her body and when she released the arrow, it struck the man with a thud in the chest. The two smaller men stared at their companion in openmouthed disbelief.

She held her breath, waiting for the Tiwan to fall. But to her chagrin, he laughed—a loud cackle, mocking her. With exaggerated movements, he broke the shaft leaving the barbed broadhead imbedded in his body. The jagged metal tip would stay impaled in his chest until he cut it out. She stared at her adversaries, confused. Why hadn't he fallen? Although a big man, the force of her arrow still should've incapacitated him. Only chainmail would have prevented severe damage. She'd just made a very foolish mistake by not factoring body armor into the equation.

"She's mine," the hammer wielding Tiwan grumbled to the others as they started toward her. She reached for another arrow. Nocking it, she pulled the bowstring back and tried to ignore her heart thumping like a drum her chest. She centered on her mark, but they were moving faster now, and her shaking hands made it impossible to line up a target.

For a splint second, she panicked and almost ran, but Master Dupree's ever patient voice filled her head, encouraging her to concentrate and remain calm. She repeated the fundamentals in her mind—take a deep breath and hold, draw the arrow to the anchor point, silence surrounding distractions and focus on the target. Her vision tunneled down to the large Tiwan, everything else disappeared. With a slow, steady exhale, she released her arrow and followed its trajectory as it whistled through the air to pierce the man's neck. A bone tingling shriek escaped from his mouth and his legs buckled. The other Tiwans stopped to assist, but they could do nothing. He flopped onto his side, flailing for the arrow as his blood pooled underneath him from a severed artery.

She spun and fled into the trees not waiting to see what the others would do. She ran blindly. Holding her bow while her sword slapped against her thigh, she dodged branches and jumped over brambles and fallen logs. Branches she couldn't evade, grabbed and clawed at her, but she fought her way through them. She ran uphill, not knowing her destination, her only goal to escape the mayhem.

She ran until she could run no more. When her legs gave out beneath her, she crumpled onto the carpet of needles blanketing the forest floor. She sat on her knees gasping for air, letting the tears tumble down her face. She'd just killed a man, a man who would have slain her after doing unspeakable things to her first, yet still she cried for him. She cried for the life she took, for the lives of the men who died trying to protect her and whose blood now saturated the ground, and for something she had lost.

She rocked back and forth, folding her arms around her body trying to soothe her soul and calm her racing mind. She was no longer innocent. She could almost taste the metallic, coppery flavor of the Tiwan's blood at the back of her throat.

Her hands shook as adrenaline raced through her body trying to find an outlet. Fear clouded her mind, but not because she had killed. What scared her and sent her mind tumbling was the ease of the kill and the satisfaction in her gut that chased behind her arrow when it sliced his neck open. She savored that precise moment and reveled in watching him collapse as he took his final, strangled gasps of air. Master Dupree would be proud of her, yet what caused her heart to pound was not pride, but the resulting power racing through her veins—knowing death came from her arrow, her hand—and it terrified her.

She surrendered, prostrating herself onto the soft earth, ready to accept whatever punishment the Gods bestowed upon her. The Mother Source welcomed her as she dug her fingers into the needles, grasping to hold something solid and real. How could she take pleasure in what had just happened? She turned her head and curled into a ball, wrapping her arms around her knees. She cried until she could cry no more then lay motionless listening to the forest lull her to sleep.

CHAPTER 17

....

PRECIPICE

Carina awoke to the screams of Critons and the hiss of flames as their fire scorched the unfortunate foot soldiers who couldn't dash to safety in time. Panic chilled her skin as she tried to remember why she was lying on the forest floor until images of the hammer wielding Tiwan flooded her mind. But she didn't have the luxury of reconciling her memories because Marek's booming voice as he flew past on FireStrike kept her anchored in the present.

The thick canopy of trees obscured her view. She scrambled to her feet, grabbed her bow, and ensured her sword remained secure in the scabbard before racing up the hillside. The carpet of needles that had comforted her in sleep now slowed her progress causing her to slip and struggle for purchase up the steep grade. She gasped for breath, and grabbed at branches to pull herself upward while her feet slid beneath her.

Gulping large mouthfuls of air to quench the burning ache in her lungs, her slow momentum drained her desire to the point she almost stopped to rest until clashing metal and shouting men encouraged her to push forward. With a final surge, she burst through the trees and stood on top of a mountain. Large tufts of grassy reeds grew between haphazard boulders on an otherwise flat summit.

Following the noise, she sprinted to the edge. She had climbed the highest peak in a small range of rugged mountains. Although not one to fear heights, she suppressed a sense of vertigo as she peered at a river hundreds of feet below.

Marek and FireStrike, along with several other soldiers and Critons were in the middle of a bloody battle across the river on a lower plateau. She moaned when she realized why FireStrike was earthbound. Although a Criton's scales were as strong as armor, their wings were vulnerable. FireStrike had been forced to land because of the many arrows protruding from his wings at gross angles. With his fire exhausted, he needed time to regenerate. Marek and his men were doing their best to protect the Criton as he pulled arrows out with his mouth, but a grounded king made for an easier target and they were surrounded.

Her stomach tightened as the Tiwans herded Marek and his soldiers into a shrinking semicircle. Her focus narrowed and an unheard sob escaped her lips. Marek fought with valor, his blades a whirl of motion, but how long could he maintain such an exhausting pace? Several Tiwans, either sensing his growing fatigue or knowing his status as king, directed their attack on him while other Tiwans kept FireStrike preoccupied by barraging the wounded Criton with arrows from a safe distance.

She screamed at her helplessness as the battle raged between Criton and rider. But no one noticed the lone figure on top of a mountain, bellowing her frustration into the air.

An unexpected gust whooshed up from behind, rocking her onto her toes. Her heart dropped into her stomach as she flung her arms wide to regain her balance. She would've fallen off the cliff if the blast had been stronger. A sudden idea caught her breath. She glanced across the ravine. Under normal conditions the distance would be too far for her longbow, but maybe she could harness the wind to her advantage. Maybe, if she waited to release her arrow with a gust, the wind would carry it the additional expanse to reach the plateau. She would have to be careful because accuracy would be hard to calculate. And once she let her arrow fly, it would be at the mercy of the fluctuating weather.

Her thoughts solidified into a plan when three Tiwans isolated Marek and began attacking him with an uncompromising zeal. She pulled out her first arrow and prayed to the Gods asking for her aim to be true.

CHAPTER 18

....

ANGEL FROM ABOVE

Marek knew the odds were against them before FireStrike was forced to land. Tiwans were a fierce foe to begin with, but coupled with the fact they were outnumbered and the Tiwans seemed genuinely ticked off, he'd known early that many of his men would die. He had led the fight away from camp, hoping the contingent he left behind would get Carina safely out of the Bridal Lands if they couldn't hold their ground.

Although his men fought with a courage and strength that made him proud, fatigue and the sheer numbers against them were taking a toll. Like an unyielding tide, the Tiwans were pushing his men toward the summit edge. If the Tiwans couldn't kill them by blade, they'd drive them off the mountainside.

Using his two weapons of choice, his claymore and a smaller double-edged dirk whipped around him in a synchronized dance. A Tiwan with multiple tattoos broke through the ranks and charged. Marek saw him approaching, but fought two others. With a powerful downstroke, he splintered one man's collarbone almost cleaving the Tiwan in two. Dark blood flowed from the man's mouth as he scrambled to keep his insides from spilling onto the already stained soil before his body thudded to the ground.

Marek spun as the other Tiwan with a hammer club lunged, forcing Marek to turn his back on the charging tattooed man. The Tiwan blocked his moves with the skill of an experienced fighter. The hair on Marek's neck rose, warning him of impending trouble as his mind calculated the closing distance of the tattooed man. The Tiwan with the club grinned, knowing that if he kept Marek engaged he'd play a crucial role in the king's death.

The battle around Marek slowed and acceptance settled on his shoulders. Although he wouldn't be able to protect his back from the man charging toward him, with a true fighting spirit of a king born during a time of strife, he continued deflecting and defending strikes before returning blows of his own. When the hammer wielding Tiwan slipped on loose rock, he hurtled his dirk without hesitation, slamming the razor sharp knife into the man's eye socket. The man dropped like a stone.

He couldn't enjoy his small victory. Although a useless endeavor, he twisted his body to defend the blind attack looming from behind. But he was out of position, off balance, and exhausted. The tattooed man roared in victory.

As Marek prepared for the Tiwan's final blow, his mind escaped the bloodshed and drifted to Carina like a cool breeze on a summer day. With dawning clarity, he realized that she was meant to be his outcome, his goal and ultimate destination. Ironic, at how the eyes of death exposed such simplicity about life. Sorrow impaled his heart with the understanding he'd have to let her go. After all the years searching, he wouldn't experience the final journey with her.

The Tiwan raised his great sword overhead. His face, streaked in dirt and smeared blood, exaggerated his white-eyed frenzy to kill. He screamed in triumph as the massive sword, requiring two hands to wield, sliced downward. But the Tiwan's body tensed in a spasmodic jerk and his victory cry hiccupped into a gasping gurgle. A confused expression crossed his face.

Thinking Sampson must have attacked from behind, Marek took advantage of the distraction and shoved his sword deep into the man's stomach. The Tiwan seized Marek's shoulders, but his eyes glazed and knees buckled. Marek pulled his claymore from the Tiwan's dead body before letting him fall face forward. He expected to see a gaping sword wound, but discovered an arrow jutting out of the man's back.

Marek looked at the identifying markings on the shaft and his eyes widened in recognition. The arrow bore King McKay's shield and crossing lances with the distinctive fletching consisting of rare ganse feathers. Had King McKay followed them and joined the battle? As if to answer his question, an arrow whizzed through the air and slammed into a Tiwan's chest.

Sampson raced up, his left arm slashed open and bleeding, but he didn't seem to notice. "Do you see the archers?"

Marek searched the flat plain around them. The air was hazy, filled with smoke from Criton flame and dust from the trampled and churned up earth. Shadows from the setting sun danced within the haze making it difficult to see. But after a quick survey, he was confident the archers were not nearby. The plateau offered no cover and from the angle of the arrows, the bowmen had to be at a higher elevation.

The descending sun was about drape them in the shade of the large mountain opposite the river, but pending darkness didn't stop the onslaught as another Tiwan broke through the line. With a raised sword, the man screamed in rage and sprinted toward Marek. Marek angled his body, preparing for the attack but an arrow zipped through the air and impaled in the man's shoulder, staggering him backward. Sampson dispatched the Tiwan before he could recover.

This time Marek saw the arrow's trajectory and scanned the towering mountain behind him. The setting sun offered no mercy as he stared into its final rebellious glow. Even though he couldn't see her face as she stood on the edge with her longbow in hand, his body recognized her. The winds buffeted her, billowing her hair in waves of untamed defiance. She was a warrior, wild and savage, an angel with the devil's hand, and the most incredible sight he'd ever seen as she released another arrow in a high arc to catch the wind.

CHAPTER 19

ATTACK FROM BEHIND

With her supply of arrows dwindling, Carina had to make the remaining ones count. Although excited over the strong currents propelling her arrows across the canyon, the inconsistent bursts were also a curse. The gusts swirled in a constant changing pattern. Some arrows were lost in the shifting gales. Others traveled wildly off target coming too close to Marek's men for comfort, or simply didn't reach the plateau because the wind fizzled.

As a result, she would stand with her arrow nocked, waiting to release at the best opportunity. Holding her pose altered her practiced routine making it difficult to maintain her anchor point, and her body was paying the price. Her arms shook from fatigue, but she refused to give in to her exhaustion. She wouldn't sit back and do nothing while the Tiwans forced Marek and his faithful men off the cliff. With grim determination, she ignored the aching muscles in her back and arms and held her stance, ready to unleash the next arrow.

She stood in such a pose when a twig snapped behind her. Although she remained motionless, her heart jumped into her throat. Adrenaline flooded her veins. She focused behind her, but aside from the wind whirling around her, heard nothing. She wanted to believe no one stalked her on the mountain, but the hair rising on her neck suggested otherwise.

Fear crawled up her spine. If not for the longbow bucking up and down in her arms, she might have frozen and succumbed to the unseen threat.

"Ah, darlin', you gonna release that arrow or just stand there?"

He spoke with the Tiwan accent she now recognized, and estimated his distance to be a few feet behind her left shoulder.

"I have to admit, you're feisty." He said in a pleasant tone as if talking to a friend.

She closed her eyes, visualizing his exact location. If she moved quickly and used what little element of surprise she had, maybe she'd get lucky.

She released her arrow into the air without finding a target and grabbed the upper limb of her bow with both hands before spinning on her heels. Planting her legs, she used her body as leverage to channel all her weight into her swing, smashing her grand longbow into the side of the Tiwan's head.

The bow connected with a loud *thwack*. He yelped in pain and stumbled. To her satisfaction, a large welt appeared, running from his ear to his mouth, and a trail of blood formed at the corner of his lips.

The Tiwan drew his sword. "And to think, I was gonna to be gentle."

She pulled her sword, realizing her victory was far from won.

The Tiwan chuckled. "Of course," he murmured before charging.

The power of his blows vibrated down her sword and ricocheted throughout her body. She staggered as he pursued her. His hard, fast parries kept her actions purely defensive, forcing her backward. He would either drive her off the mountain or she'd miss blocking his attack.

The Tiwan had pushed her to ledge. Bracing against the gusting wind, the loose shale shifted beneath her feet. Her arms tired from his relentless strikes. She clutched her now cumbersome blade with limp hands in a meager attempt to deflect his blows. A flurry of parries knocked the weapon from her grasp and sent it clattering over the rocks. Standing with her arms at her sides, gasping for breath, a ridiculous thought popped into her head at how disappointed Master Dupree would be for losing her steel.

The Tiwan straightened from his crouch. "You fight good," he acknowledged, bowing his head in respect. "I regret having to kill you."

When he lunged, she closed her eyes and dove to the ground in an unknown desire to make herself small. By changing her elevation, the Tiwan had to adjust his charge to compensate for her new ground-hugging position. Evidently, he didn't expect such a cowardly tactic, possibly thinking she would stand proud and face her death following the warrior's code. He tried to stop his forward momentum, but slipped on the loose shale and found himself teetering on the edge. He dropped his sword, swinging his arms in wild desperation, but the wind played no favorites and a forceful gust toppled him off the mountain.

Ignoring the pebbly grit digging into her cheek, she spread her arms wide and rejoiced in being alive. She didn't know how long she lay there as the wind battered her, but it was long after her breathing had returned to normal and the adrenaline had washed out of her. Shouts from the men across the ravine finally roused her.

She staggered to her knees before rocking up onto her feet. Lumbering across the mountaintop, she picked up and sheathed her sword, then grabbed her longbow. She stretched cramped muscles in her back while reaching for another arrow, and angled her body to see down the shaft in search of her next target.

Ignoring her protesting muscles, she drew the bowstring to her anchor point and held her breath. She found her mark and followed his movements with her body and eye, praying for the wind to grant her arrow a true path. But a sharp stab in her shoulder caused her body to jerk and she regretfully released the arrow in another wasted attempt. Her shoulder knotted as a spasm ripped through it. She collapsed to the ground, gasping at the fire blistering down her arm.

With her fingertips, she touched the smooth shaft of an arrow imbedded near her shoulder blade. Her first instinct was to yank it out, but the arrow was just beyond her grasp and she didn't have the energy to undertake the daunting task anyway.

"I'm sorry," murmured a quiet voice.

She turned her head to see a Tiwan astride a black Criton.

"Your discomfort will end soon."

She shuffled to her feet but swayed precariously. Although she wanted to act brave and make Master Dupree proud, the pain radiating outward from her shoulder threatened to break her. Her tongue lay at the bottom of her mouth like a fat slug, but blinding anger refused to keep it still.

"You shot me in the back, you coward."

The rider bobbed his shoulders in a detached shrug. "I understand you might think that. But someone has trained you well, and with what you want to accomplish, you don't deserve an honorable death."

She shook her head, but the fog clouding her mind refused to dissipate. "We're simply passing through your land and because of that, you attack us? How's *that* honorable?"

The Criton shifted beneath his rider, anxious at the smell of blood and death. The rider rested his hand on the beast's neck.

Even as her vision blurred, she noticed the Criton relax. *Great, they're bonded.* She didn't know why that bothered her, except it seemed to be such a waste of a Criton.

"We usually grant Criton riders safe passage through our land, but your quest could not succeed."

She swayed as a burst of wind pushed her, but celebrated in the small success of staying on her feet. "What quest?" Her voice sounded slurred in her ears. What she wouldn't give for a drink of water to soothe the inferno raging in her parched throat.

"To lead unbonded Critons into darkness." The Tiwan spoke with confidence as if he knew a secret.

"You dipped the arrow in poison."

He nodded.

"And you're doing all this…" she hesitated, waving an arm behind her to the men battling across the ravine, "…because you think I'm a Dark Caller?"

"A messenger on Critonback delivered a warning. Without the current Caller of Light, we couldn't take a chance."

A jolt of white-hot fire lanced through her stomach and she doubled over, panting. She clutched her abdomen, gasping to fill her lungs with air that was too illusive to inhale even though she stood on top of a mountain in a windstorm.

She choked on her words. "You started this because…someone sent you a *message*?"

The Tiwan didn't answer, not that she expected him to anyway. Their willingness to kill Marek and his men based on the possibility she could bind Criton and rider with a dark bond was absurd. She groaned as the horror of his words seeped into her clouded mind. The battle fell on her shoulders. The bloodshed was *her* fault. Because the Tiwans believed she was a Dark Caller, Marek's death and the massacre of his men would stain her soul forever.

Her legs folded and she crumbled to her knees. She cradled her stomach and watched giant teardrops splat on the shale in front of her. *Who sent the message, and why?*

"If you wish, my Criton can end your suffering. Death by Criton fire is honorable."

Endless waves of pain knifed through her body. She was burning up from the inside because of a misunderstanding. She threw her head back and screamed, offering up her torment to the heavens. She would not die from Criton fire or curl up and die in front of this man. Forcing one foot then the other beneath her, she staggered to her feet and threw her arms out to steady herself until her legs stopped shaking.

"I'm sorry," she whispered.

"I can't say that I'm sorry for you, Dark Caller. You should've chosen a different path."

The sun crested on the edge of the horizon, presenting her with a brief distraction as she stared beyond the Tiwan and his Criton to admire its brilliance. The radiant, yellow orb streaked the heavens in fantastic shades of red and orange. Under different circumstances, she would've considered it one of the most beautiful endings to a day she'd ever witnessed.

She continued in a flat, resigned voice. "I'm sorry, because you started this for nothing. I'm not a Dark Caller."

"There's no need to deny it."

"Tell me this..." she paused to lean forward, resting her hands on her knees. "If I was a Dark Caller, wouldn't your bonded Criton sense my dark energy and react with hostility?"

She peered up at the Tiwan, but the ground swayed beneath her. As she struggled to regain her balance, her mother's medallion slipped out of her blouse to dangle from her neck. The eye crystal caught the sun's waning rays and cast prisms of light around her.

For an instant, she thought shock then surprise unfolded on the Tiwan's face.

"Who are you?" he asked with a confused expression.

She no longer had the strength to hold her head up, so she let it dip to her chest and laughed, although it sounded more like a raspy gurgle. "Don't you think you should've asked that *before* you attacked?"

She clutched her mother's necklace. Just the act of reaching for the medallion almost sent her sprawling forward, but she righted herself. The necklace had always offered comfort during the darkest times in her life. She prayed to her mother, asking for strength because she would die on her terms.

With a will she didn't know lived inside her, she stiffened her spine and stood tall. She pulled her sword and with trembling hands, held it proudly in front of her. The wind surged around her, swirling her hair in the shifting currents. She gathered her last bit of energy and inhaled a deep breath into her burning lungs before yelling. "I'm Carina McKay, you bloody savage." A small smile played across her lips. "And although I'm no Dark Caller, I did best some of your finest warriors."

The sun had almost slipped beyond the horizon, but a few bold rays burst forth spilling onto her blade. A startled gasp escaped her lips when the glow captured the beautiful design painstakingly etched into the metal. Master Dupree had crafted something special, just for her. It was her medallion. Next to the hilt, Sabian had etched two Critons with their necks intertwined, protecting the encrusted eye jewel.

"Sabian, thank you for being my teacher...and friend," she whispered before taking a wobbly step closer to the edge.

A wave of dizziness swam through her. Tears streamed down her face.

She didn't want to die.

"Carina, move away from the ledge."

At hearing her name, she twisted around and glared at the Tiwan who had dismounted and was approaching her with his hands outstretched. A concerned expression flitted across his face.

"Don't come near me." She wanted to sound forceful, but fear filtered through her words.

"Please, I can help you."

"Like Haden." She tried to raise her sword, but it had grown too heavy as the poison racing through her bloodstream drained her remaining strength.

Mother, guide me home and may the end be peaceful.

She dropped her sword and let the wind carry her over the edge.

....

CHAPTER 20

RISE OF AN ANGEL

Marek spun in time to witness Carina spread her arms like the rays from a morning star and plummet off the mountain as a Tiwan grabbed at the empty space she'd just vacated. The strength drained from his limbs and he dropped to his knees, digging his fingers into the chewed up earth.

He failed her. He'd taken her from the safety of McKay lands. She had trusted him and he failed to protect her. A crushing ache gripped his chest, squeezing the air from his lungs. He would've welcomed a Tiwan slicing him open with a broadsword over the debilitating hollowness sucking away his spirit. What had happened? How had things gone so wrong?

The sounds of his men fighting around him whispered in the background as he stared at the mountaintop where Carina had stood moments before.

"Marek, get up!" Sampson yelled. Sampson and several soldiers had formed a defensive line to protect him from the never-ending assault. His men were loyal and would shield him with their lives.

Marek's eyes zeroed in on the man who had killed Carina, and who now stood with his head buried in his Criton's neck. Was it regret? Was he ashamed to have caused an innocent to jump to her death? Had he wanted her for himself and now cried for his loss? A rage erupted from deep within Marek's soul—a dark hatred that filled the gaping hole in his chest. Marek let the rage devour him, drawing upon its power to soothe him. He would avenge her. The man with the black Criton would beg for death and Marek would deny him. The Tiwan would cry for mercy and Marek would bleed him more.

An ear piercing roar from FireStrike drew his attention. The animal reared onto his massive hind legs and launched into the air. Tiwan soldiers pelted him with arrows, but the swoosh from his powerful wings hurtled him skyward. Marek could've called him back, but why? He considered FireStrike a close friend and companion, a mighty Criton worthy of a king. But with his fire depleted and more arrows impaled in his wings than Marek could count, Marek didn't see the point in making him return. They had bonded years ago and their bond had only strengthened with the passing of time. If FireStrike had the energy to take flight, he'd grant his Criton the chance to escape.

Marek struggled to his feet, his body depleted and sluggish. Dirt and the blood of those he'd killed covered his body. Fighting was never clean. No one wanted to die. Even a mortally wounded man would reach for an inner resolve and fight until all the blood drained from his body.

That strength of will and desire to live forced Marek to stand even though his body protested. Because if he continued to mourn Carina, to let her death overwhelm him, he too would die and lose the chance to avenge her.

His sword felt clumsy in his hand, the hilt sticky from blood and sweat. He hefted it, balancing and testing its weight before turning to face the battle. Surveying the field with an experienced eye, he located the Tiwan causing the most damage. That Tiwan would be the first one he'd kill. He could've chosen someone weaker, but what kind of king would that make him? A good king always sought out the strongest opponent.

He raised his mighty claymore and planned his attack. Adrenaline coursed through his veins, strengthening tired muscles. He would strike hard and fast. He jogged toward the man who had just killed a young soldier named Jonas. Jonas would be the last of his men to die at the hands of that Tiwan.

Another roar filled the air and every Criton on the ground took flight. Even Critons with riders on their backs joined the others in the sky. Critons from both sides flew together, circling overhead. Their unusual behavior halted the battle as puzzled soldiers gazed upward.

Sampson loped over, his curly, black hair plastered to his head from sweat. He struggled to catch his breath. "Sire, have you ever seen this?"

Marek had witnessed something similar during his childhood. The Critons were acting as though a transitioning was about to occur. But that wasn't possible because all the animals on the field were adults, a juvenile would never be taken into battle. He stared at the marvelous spectacle of Critons circling, diving, and infusing the air with their rebellious screams before shaking his head in bewilderment. "They're behaving like it's a transitioning."

"Is that possible?"

As if on cue, FireStrike hovered in the sky and bellowed, his eyes blazing and tail snapping back and forth in agitation. Marek called to FireStrike, but the Criton amazingly ignored his plea. FireStrike squealed again, his attention focused on something in the gorge below.

135

Marek turned to Sampson. "Whatever is bothering them is in the ravine. Let's go." He covered the ground in long strides, but fear for what he would see twisted his gut. He hoped the river had carried Carina's broken body downstream.

He had just reached the edge when Sampson threw him to the ground as another Criton swooped up from the bottom of the canyon, barely missing them with its sudden ascent to soar with the animals above. The Critons formed a protective ring around the newcomer.

"It *is* a transitioning," Sampson whispered.

Since transitionings were a vulnerable time for young Critons, they usually occurred in the early morning hours when darkness provided cover. Marek had never heard of an evening transition, let alone one happening during a battle.

His eyes widened in surprise. He recognized the small Criton female with the undersized wings and dull, mottled green coloring. Mira, Carina's little Criton, had followed them.

"Sire, look! Someone rides upon it."

Marek's pulse quickened. Carina's motionless body lay doubled over Mira's neck. A flood of emotions rushed through him, the strongest being relief. She'd not fallen to her death.

"Can she survive a transitioning?" Sampson asked.

Marek clasped Sampson's shoulder. "Let's hope so."

A sky full of Critons roared in unison drowning out additional conversation. Mira's body shimmered until she lit up the heavens like the sun, forcing Marek to raise his hand to shield his eyes from her brightness. Sparks flew outward from the blazing center and shot into the darkening sky like a beacon as the magic of transition changed Mira into an adult Criton capable of bonding with a rider.

The deafening bellows from the adults subsided until only the steady beat of their leathery wings whispered through the air. The light enveloping Mira and Carina faded and winked out. The other

Critons dispersed, but Mira lingered, hovering in the sky as if testing her new wings. Even from the distance, Marek could tell she'd transitioned into an amazing Criton just as Carina had predicted. Mira's throaty cry pierced the silence before she arched her elegant neck to survey the land.

She belted out another scream then pinned her wings to her body and dove, her large head scanning the ground. She spotted Marek and angled toward him. While those around him scattered, Marek stood his ground as the young Criton landed with a thud, vibrating the ground in front of him with the fury of her descent.

Carina clung onto Mira's neck. He approached with his hand extended. Mira tilted her head and fixed a large, emerald eye on him, her elongated, golden iris contracting. He touched Mira's neck. She twitched, but didn't shy away.

Even though Carina was his goal, he couldn't help but assess—and admire—the beautiful Criton. She radiated in the soft glow of transition, but would settle into a rich, green sheen. Perfectly proportioned legs and wings balanced her long, lean body. Once she filled out and developed her muscle, she would be a fast, agile Criton.

His hand trailed along Mira's neck as he walked toward Carina. When he approached Mira's shoulder, she snorted and turned her head to watch him.

Sampson and the rest of his men circled Mira, but maintained a safe distance. Sampson spoke softly, his voice full of concern. "Sire, she just transitioned. There's still magic coursing through her. She's unpredictable."

At the sound of Sampson's voice, Mira raised her head and curled her lips into a growl but made no sound.

"Sampson, be quiet," Marek hissed. "She won't harm me." His hand roved from Mira's shoulder down her back until he touched Carina. His body trembled when his fingers grazed Carina's knee.

Feeling her body again, the world settled into place. He wouldn't let anything happen to her. Although arrowshot, her wound didn't appear fatal. An oppressive tension that had knotted his shoulders with its unseen weight slipped off him on a quiet exhale. But his solace was short-lived.

"Carina," he whispered. He squeezed her knee. When she didn't respond, he spoke louder. "Carina."

Her motionless body lay slumped over Mira, crouched in a fetal position. He ignored the erratic pounding of his heart. Something was wrong. But he refused to entertain the possibility she could be dead. His mind slammed the door closed to that agonizing avenue of thought.

He stepped closer, his body brushing Carina's leg. Sampson opened his mouth to protest, but Marek stopped him with a threatening glare. Carina's head rested against Mira's neck, her hair obscuring her beautiful face. Her fingers gripped Mira's pale green mane with a white-knuckle, rigor mortis hold. He brushed the hair off her face, pinning it behind an ear, and tried to keep the quaver out of his voice when he again whispered, "Carina."

Agony knocked at the door he'd just dead-bolted shut. He couldn't prevent it from wrapping ice cold tendrils around his heart as it chanted of her death in the far corners of his mind. He choked on his words, his throat too tight to speak.

She's alive, she can't die. His fingertips traced along her cheek. Willing her eyes to open, his fingers tracked down her neck to check for a heartbeat. Before he reached her pulse point, he stopped and fisted his shaking hand. Gritting his teeth, he bit back the urge to shout out his frustration and rising fury to the Gods, condemning them for Carina's senseless sacrifice. She was pure, the light guiding him home in a valley of darkness. She could not be dead, not while he still breathed.

Lowering his voice, he whispered in her ear, demanding her compliance. "Obey me, Carina McKay. Obey your king and open your eyes."

Although her eyes didn't open—her obstinate character would never bow to such a mandate—a quiet moan tumbled from her lips, a faint acknowledgment of her awareness of him.

His eyes misted as relief washed through his veins, flooding him with hope. But her cold body and ashen skin shot warning arrows through his heart as he tugged her hands free from Mira's mane. "Carina, I'm going to help you," he said before placing his arm on her lower back to avoid the arrow.

She whimpered when he slid her off, and her eyes briefly fluttered open before shuttering closed again. He cradled her against his chest and murmured a quiet thank you to Mira.

Mira snorted and stamped a foot before flying the short distance to FireStrike, who had resumed the arduous task of pulling arrows from his tattered wings.

"Sire, they're gone," Sampson whispered.

Marek glanced up from Carina's pallid face to confirm Sampson's observation—the Tiwans had disappeared. "Move the men. We'll make camp in the shelter of the trees and tend to our wounded and dead."

He strode toward the tree line. The plateau was littered with the wreckage of battle, forcing him to step over dead bodies and churned up dirt while trying not to jostle Carina. "Johansen, find the healer," he bellowed.

"Aye, Sire." The blond-haired soldier raced off.

Marek placed Carina on her side underneath a cloister of tall pines. He resisted the urge to remove the arrow, leaving that responsibility for the healer.

Sampson had followed him the short distance and waited until they were alone to speak. "Sire, now is our chance to escape. We should use the cover of darkness to get out of this blasted land."

Dunston, a grizzled veteran, approached with a tattered blanket and some strips of cloth. Marek nodded and took the items. Before draping the blanket over her, he packed the strips of cloth around the arrow shaft to staunch the bleeding in a feeble attempt to ease the helplessness consuming his mind. Satisfied she was as comfortable as he could make her, he straightened to his full height and stood over Sampson. He spoke without emotion. "She'll die if we leave."

Sampson fidgeted, but didn't back down. "Look at her. She's dead already."

"How many men did she save? And you would just abandon her?"

Sampson clasped Marek's shoulder. "I don't understand your affection for this mixed blood, but we won't survive another assault. Everyone will perish *because* of her if we stay and they attack again."

Marek stepped away, forcing Sampson to release his shoulder. "As captain of my men, you disappoint me." He folded his arms across his chest. "Instead of preparing for our defense, you would refuse me and run?"

Sampson shook his head. "No, I would never disobey you. I'm just trying—"

Marek cut Sampson off with a wave of his hand. "I've spoken. Either do as I say or I'll find someone who will."

Although Sampson's words were unwelcome, they were true. His men were too few and could not withstand the overwhelming numbers in the Tiwan Tribe. The strategically sound maneuver would be to escape, but doing so would guarantee Carina's death.

In the end, tactics didn't really matter because the vestiges of rational thought had slipped from his mind. Carina and her wellbeing had become his sole purpose. Because when he saw her fall, a chasm had ripped through him searing every nerve ending in his body. Although only minutes had lapsed from Carina's plummet to her rise on Mira's back, the bone breaking despair he'd endured during those brief moments would last forever.

The Gods had issued their warning—he now knew what life would be like without her. Grateful for a second chance, he would heed the Gods' admonition and give her every opportunity to live. Helping her was the least he could do. And since he understood what his life would be like without her, it was the least he could do for himself. No matter how irrational his decision, they would stay, fight, and die trying to save her.

He knelt beside her and brushed the hair from her face. Her pale skin and shallow breathing scared him. He could feel her slipping away, the strength draining from his body the closer she came to death.

Aware Sampson stood behind him, his frayed nerves flared in anger. Sampson should've left to ready their defense. About to lash out, Marek stilled his tongue when he noticed Sampson's expression. A range of emotions danced across Sampson's face, but hurt seemed to be the one that settled into place, causing Marek to regret his harsh words.

"Forgive me, Sampson, for I misspoke."

Sampson shook his head. "No, 'tis I should beg forgiveness. You gave an order. It's my duty to obey, not to question. I'm sorry. I'll organize the men."

Sampson turned and almost plowed into the healer before disappearing into the forest, barking orders.

The healer looked like a man who'd never missed a meal in his life. His round, red cheeks were flushed from the exertion of hurrying across the uneven ground. With a small groan, and using a tree for support, he eased his large frame down beside Carina. His chubby fingers performed a cursory exam before he acknowledged Marek.

"Sire," he managed, but went silent again as he monitored Carina. After a moment, he sat back on his heels and fixed a pointed eye on Marek before speaking. "Tiwans lace their arrows with poison. Although her wound isn't fatal, I've no cure for the poison. We should leave her, so I can tend to the other wounded."

Marek did not appreciate being told what he already knew. "Healer, Tiwan poison works quickly. Carina should've been dead long ago, yet she still breathes."

The healer rubbed his double chin. "Hmmm, that is true."

Marek continued. "Since she transitioned with the Criton maybe she absorbed some of that life energy."

The healer glanced at Carina again as if looking at her for the first time. "I suppose the magic of transition could've lessened or absorbed the effects of the poison. I could remove the arrow and give her the remedies I use for other poisons."

"Do it," Marek ordered.

The healer nodded. "I'll need a fire."

CHAPTER 21

HOPE

T he men set up Carina's tent, the only one to survive the destruction of their camp since it had never been raised. Marek carried Carina inside and stayed with her as the healer removed the arrow, sewed up the wound, and applied a salve. Once bandaged, the healer slipped Carina's undershirt back in place.

Marek didn't appreciate the grim look on the healer's face, and to his surprise, even resented him touching her. Although foolish, Marek couldn't curb the jealousy that had flared when the healer had untied her undergarment and tugged it off her shoulder to get to the wound.

"She's not responding to the medicines I've given her," the healer muttered as he checked her pulse. "And her fever is dangerously high to the point if she does recover, I'm not sure she'll be whole."

"But she's lived so long." Marek could hear the desperation in his voice. "No one has ever survived Tiwan poisoning for any length of time."

"I'm afraid the transition only slowed the inevitable. This woman won't last the night."

"There must be something you can do."

The healer shook his head and stared at Carina's lifeless body.

Her breathing had slowed to such shallow, labored gasps that Marek could barely see the rise and fall of her chest.

"I'm very sorry, my king."

Marek scrubbed his hands across his face. This couldn't be happening. They were missing something—something they had not tried yet. He hadn't come this far and endured so many hurtles just to lose her now. His intense feelings for Carina were unreasonable and they frightened him more than the slash of any foe's blade.

A shout from a guard warning of an incoming rider diverted his attention. "Stay with her," he ordered before storming from the tent. When he stepped outside several men stood with their swords pointed at a Tiwan who had landed his Criton in the clearing and walked the rest of the way into camp alone.

Although Marek couldn't identify the rider, he recognized the black Criton and rage consumed him. He drew his sword and lifted it chest high. The corner of his mouth ticked into a sneer. He'd find solace watching the coward's blood saturate the ground. A quicker death than he wanted, but Carina required his attention.

Marek strode toward the Tiwan who had raised his hands in a pleading gesture, but Sampson stepped between them before he could drive his blade into the man's chest. Marek's anger blinded him to everything but one goal, gutting the Tiwan. With clenched teeth, he commanded Sampson out of the way.

Sampson pressed his hand into Marek's shoulder, restraining him. "Sire, he claims to have the antidote."

Marek shook his head to clear the fury from his mind so he could absorb Sampson's words. But even after a moment, his hatred refused to loosen its hold. "What?"

"He says shooting Carina was a terrible mistake and wishes to give you the means to save her," Sampson whispered in his ear.

Marek frowned. "Release me."

Sampson moved away, but remained nearby.

Marek sheathed his sword and stepped forward until the Tiwan stood within striking distance. The Tiwan bowed. The Criton tattoo on the man's face marked him as part of an elite squadron of Criton riders, protectors of the Light Realm. The tattoo encircled the Tiwan's left eye with the Criton's tail curling under the lower lid and the head resting above his eyebrow. A gaping mouth shot flames halfway across his forehead indicating he'd traveled to Crios. This Tiwan held a place of honor within the tribe.

"Is what you say true?"

"Aye, Sire." The Tiwan spoke with an air of regret. "A messenger falsely accused your mistress of being a Dark Caller."

A dry, incredulous chuckle escaped Marek's lips. "So, instead of verifying the information, you chose bloodshed?"

"We thought it best to attack without warning since you were moving quickly through our land and the strength of your men is well known." The Tiwan shrugged, looking helpless. "The Elders felt losses to both sides were a worthwhile sacrifice if it meant saving the world from another Dark Caller."

"She's not a Dark Caller."

"As evidenced by the fact a young Criton saved her, then transitioned with her."

Marek could hear the awe laced within the Tiwan's words. "And now you've realized your mistake and wish to make amends?" He didn't bother hiding his disbelief.

145

"We think she's special and feel her death would be unfortunate."

Marek snorted, and crossed his arms.

Sampson stepped in close. "Let me kill him. Then we'll take the antidote."

The Tiwan shook his head. "The cure contains Criton venom. I must monitor her treatment and alter the doses depending on how she responds. Your shaman wouldn't know how to adjust the mixture." The Tiwan leveled his eyes on Marek. "If you kill me, you kill her."

Marek hesitated. Although he hated to admit it, the healer was correct. Carina was dying. The reprieve she'd received from Mira's transition only slowed her death, it didn't cure her. He could kill the Tiwan then watch Carina die, or let the Tiwan administer the supposed antidote, which could just as easily hasten her death.

He pinched the bridge of his nose. What choice did he really have?

"She's in the tent." He stepped aside so the Tiwan could pass.

The man bowed before moving toward the opening. As he walked by, Marek grabbed his arm, stopping him in midstride. "If she dies, your death will soon follow."

The Tiwan inclined his head, never looking at Marek. "As it should be since it was my arrow. Now, if you'll release me, for the sooner I begin treatment the better chance I have at saving both our lives."

Marek let the man go and watched him disappear inside. Conflicting emotions bombarded his mind, and Sampson didn't offer any reassurances.

"That's it?" Sampson asked, pointing toward the tent. "You're just going let him do it?"

"What else can I do? She's dying."

Sampson inhaled a long, frustrated breath. "We'll watch him, but won't know if he's helping her."

Marek nodded. "That's all I ask. Make sure he doesn't walk the camp. Tie him up and isolate him when he's not with Carina."

"Very well," Sampson muttered, and entered the tent.

CHAPTER 22

···

ANTIDOTE

Although the early morning hours lay upon the land, the cold grip of darkness still held the Mother Source in a firm embrace. Lanterns flickering inside the tent threw off just enough light in the confined space for Marek to see Carina's face. The pallor of her skin and motionless body disturbed him, but her breathing whispered in and out of her lungs in a steady rhythm.

To the Tiwan's credit, whom he learned was named Caden, the antidote appeared to be working. Caden had spent hours hovering over Carina, forcing a foul smelling liquid down her throat. In a show of good faith, the Tiwan had answered all the healer's questions. By relinquishing so much information, the healer could now recreate the cure. But Caden had issued a stern warning—too little, or too much, would result in death. The powerful antidote teetered on the edge, a delicate balance between life in this world or rebirth in the next.

The healer stood and stretched his back before edging toward the tent flap. "She's improving, Sire. I believe the worst is over. Now, if you'll excuse me, I have others to check on."

Marek smiled and clasped the large man's shoulder before the healer lumbered outside.

Caden also rose. "She's resting so I'd like to stretch my legs until the next dose."

Marek glanced at the two soldiers standing just inside the entrance and they stepped forward.

"Thank you," Caden said, and grabbed his cloak with the distinctive orange and black coloring of the Tiwan Tribe.

Marek called to the Tiwan just before he stepped from the tent.

"Yes, Sire?"

Standing over Carina, Marek watched the lantern light cast her face in a soft glow. Her parted lips beckoned him. Even sick, her allure commanded his attention. "What did you mean when you said she was special?"

Caden shrugged, and tied the cloak around his neck. "That young Criton risked her life to save Lady Carina. Behavior like that from an unbonded Criton by itself is unusual, but to then transition with Lady Carina on her back is remarkable. Lady Carina must have a special destiny to be so connected to an unbonded Criton."

"She's mixed," Marek replied flatly.

Caden raised his eyebrows. "Really? On the mountain, she acted with the bravery of a purebred royal."

Marek clenched his teeth. "Was that before or after you shot her in the back?"

Caden's blue eyes flickered. "A mistake I'll regret for the rest of my life. But you don't need me to tell you she's special."

"What?"

Caden pulled the tent flap aside and paused at the entrance. "Because you chose her above her true blood sister," he murmured before slipping through the opening followed by the soldiers.

Marek sat beside Carina, extending his legs alongside her body. Seeing her resting filled him with peace. He hadn't realized how anxious he'd been until the healer had spoken of her recovery, lifting a weight off his chest so he could finally draw a full breath of air.

He ran the back of his hand down her cheek, marveling at the softness of her skin. She muttered something unintelligible at his touch.

"Sleep, Carina," he whispered. "Sleep, and get well."

CHAPTER 23

....

CONFUSION

Carina swam to the surface of consciousness. She hesitated when she touched the brink of wakefulness because once she crossed the threshold she would fully perceive the pain pounding in her shoulder. But cold, thirst, and most of all, fear drove her upward. Shadowing the ache, she allowed it to wake her. Although she braced herself, she still awoke with a gasp.

A soft burning lantern dispersed odd dancing images of light across the sides and roof of the tent. She shouldn't have been cold covered in all the blankets, but a chill gripped her body. Thoughts assailed her, squeezing her chest in a rising panic. Where was Marek? Why was she alone? Did he know the Tiwans attacked because they believed she was a Dark Caller? A whimper tumbled out of her.

She listened, but only the quiet stillness of the night welcomed her. Another notion rattled her brain. Maybe he'd left her. The idea strangled objective reasoning from her mind and she wrangled herself out of the blankets.

In her undergarments, the icy air sliced through her skin. She rolled onto the shoulder without the bandages and pushed herself to a seated position. Nausea threatened to overcome her, but the feeling subsided after inhaling crisp air into her lungs.

She stood on shaky legs and with chattering teeth, padded across the floor. Her bare feet left small imprints in the dirt marking her path to the tent flap door. Pushing it aside, she held her breath and peeked though the slanted opening. Relief washed through her when she saw the camp—she hadn't been abandoned.

She spotted Marek sitting beside the main fire. Sampson sat with him, but Marek seemed miles away, lost in thought. She groaned. He looked so sad and she was the reason for his pain. Because of her several of his men were dead. How would he ever forgive her? How would she ever forgive herself?

Tears plummeted down her face to freeze on the ground. He'd suffered enough. She didn't want to be a burden or painful memory of the men lost. Clinging onto the tent flap for support, she realized that although she couldn't bring back the men who had died, she could ease the suffering of those still living.

Unguarded tears cascaded over her eyelashes, tracing cold tracks down her cheeks, but she didn't brush them away. She stole one more glance at the king who now sat alone by the fire to burn his image into her mind. When he buried his face in his hands, an unbearable sorrow tore through her chest as if the Tiwan's arrow had pierced her heart instead of her shoulder. She'd caused him such misery.

"I'm sorry," she sobbed. "I'll make it right." With a shaky hand, she let go of the tent and lurched forward. A wave of dizziness blurred her vision. Staggering into a tree, she grabbed it to keep from falling and catch her breath. The bark scraped her cheek as she hugged it like a long lost friend, and waited for the pounding in her head to subside. But even her throbbing head didn't compare to her thirst. Every breath raked across her throat like a wasteland craving water.

Not sure which way to go, she picked a direction opposite the camp and shuffled off. Her shoulder, the only hot part of her body, pulsed in a constant rhythm. The biting cold desensitized her feet so she no longer felt the sting of twigs or rocks as she hobbled through the darkness. Other than finding water, she hadn't thought about where she'd go, or what she would do for clothes, or the simple truth she'd probably freeze to death if she didn't find shelter. Her driving force was to ease her thirst and free Marek from the burden she'd become.

She'd only trudged a few steps into the forest when a snort caused her to jump. Turning toward the noise, a pair of shiny, red eyes stared back at her. Fear traveled down her spine. Just her luck, a demon forged from Haden to finish her off.

CHAPTER 24

....

SEARCH

Marek had spent the last three days at Carina's side, rarely leaving her tent. He would still be with her if the healer hadn't insisted he get some fresh air and something to eat. Sitting beside a fire that offered no warmth, he forced the tasteless food down his throat.

A numbness cloaked his body as if he'd gone dormant, waiting for Carina to awake. When not with her, he slept-walked through the days, trying to support his men by encouraging the wounded to get well, helping to bury the dead, and ensuring their defenses were fortified. But his actions were a shallow attempt at being a good king. Emptiness plagued him, a companion to the guilt eating his mind.

Over the past few days, he'd spent countless hours running through the events leading up to the attack, yet struggled to find where he'd gone wrong. What had he missed? What sign hadn't he seen? Who even knew he'd taken Carina as his mistress and traveled through the Bridal Lands? No matter what avenues his mind explored, the paths eventually converged into two possibilities...Marissa and King McKay. Since Regin seemed to be motivated by wealth, sending a messenger to kill an asset didn't make for a fiscally sound decision. By default that left Marissa. According to Caden, the messenger hadn't worn any colors to identify whose authority he rode under, but the more Marek mulled over the possibilities the more convinced he was of Marissa's betrayal.

Thinking of Carina rekindled the ache in his chest, a dull, persistent beating thrum acting as a reminder that she'd almost been killed because of his arrogance. Somehow the attack was his fault, his responsibility. He'd been too complacent and self-assured, and several good men were dead as a result. The weight of their deaths pressed down on his shoulders, a burden he would live with forever. He should've been more diligent, should have seen the signs. Because in addition to his men, he'd almost lost the only person who excited and intrigued him—who encouraged him to see the world as if it were new again.

He stared into the fire. A growing discomfort wrapped cold fingers around his heart. He'd been away from her for too long. The now familiar disquiet would build into a crescendo and finally drive him back to her side just so he could trace his fingers through her hair and find reassurance in the steady cadence of her breathing.

Looking back, he should've never allowed Marissa's accusations to sway the way he had treated Carina. He'd used Marissa's words as an excuse to keep Carina beside him at night, letting his selfishness guide his actions. He should've been stronger and showed Carina the respect she deserved as a person, and warranted as his mistress.

He shut out the world around him by dropping his head into his hands. The Gods had given him a second chance and he would not fail her again. An odd idea sprang into his mind echoing Caden's earlier comment. Just why had he chosen her? He closed his eyes, remembering dinner at McKay's castle—Carina standing alone at the window and his overwhelming desire to go to her. Had he actually chosen Carina? Or had *he* been chosen for *her*? He shook his head, trying to clear the thoughts muddling his mind, but they persisted. Was he destined to find her?

When the healer had spoken of Carina's recovery, a glimmer of hope had sprung from his heart that maybe he could make amends, because ultimately the questions badgering him were unimportant. The only question requiring an answer was whether she'd forgive him.

Sampson interrupted his thoughts by plopping down on the log beside him. Sampson stared into the fire a few moments before speaking so quietly that only he could hear. "Sire, I don't mean to discuss relations with you, but I think this mixed blood is clouding your judgment."

Although Marek welcomed Sampson's honesty, this time his captain had stepped on a gaping wound, sparking his anger. "What in Criton's breath are you saying?" He grunted in satisfaction when Sampson's eyes widened.

Sampson stared at his boots, but spoke after a resigned exhale. "The only way you'll know for sure whether she's pure is when you first enter her. Maybe the guilt you feel is unjustified."

Marek fisted his hands and tamped down the wave of anger threatening to burst into a hurricane. No matter how close they were as boys, Sampson had gone way beyond the boundaries of friendship.

"I've noticed you treat her differently. Is that because of what I told you?"

Sampson shrugged. "I'm not sure a mixed breed is worthy of you in the first place, but she definitely doesn't deserve the life you offer if she's impure."

Marek spoke through clenched teeth, and willed his hands not to clobber the man sitting beside him. "I should've never told you. Leave me."

Sampson disappeared into the darkness and once again he sat alone with just his thoughts to pester him.

Talbrec, a young soldier assigned to Carina's tent, rushed into the firelight. Seeing the boy's ashen face and panicked eyes stopped his heart.

"Sire, she's gone." Talbrec moaned. "I went to relieve myself and saw the tent open when I returned. I checked inside and—"

Marek pushed Talbrec out of the way and raced for the tent, followed by those who had overheard the boy's confession.

When Marek stepped inside and noticed Carina's empty mat, the air rushed from his lungs. He turned to the soldiers standing outside. "Wake the men, grab torches. She couldn't have gone far, unless someone took her." His eyes drilled into Talbrec. The boy's entire body shook with fear. Instead of grabbing the lad by the throat and strangling him until he breathed no more, Marek somehow retained some self-control.

"Bring Caden to me. I want to know if he had anything to do with this."

"There's no need to find me," Caden answered as he approached with his two guards. "And, no, I didn't take her. What fool left her unattended?"

"How dare you." Sampson stormed past Marek, his hand reaching for the hilt of his sword. "I'll teach you a lesson on respect."

"Sampson, stay your blade," Marek commanded. "Carina is our first priority. Once she's found then you two can see who pisses the farthest."

The men trampled any evidence of Carina's track forcing them to organize a search pattern. Because of the late hour, Luna had already coaxed her son into the sky, illuminating the land in an eerie, blue-white light.

Marek assessed his options. Where would she go? The men dispersed into the woods, their torches bobbing up and down like mystical fairy globes. With everyone scouring the forest, he decided to search the clearing and exposed areas.

He hurried toward the grove of trees where the Critons were bedded knowing he could cover more ground on Critonback. But when he reached the animals a threatening growl brought him to an abrupt halt. FireStrike stood with his teeth bared, head low, and ears pinned back in a challenging posture.

"Easy FireStrike," he soothed. Although FireStrike relaxed at the sound of his voice, Marek approached the Criton with caution. Why had FireStrike reacted so strangely? He spied his answer when he drew close enough to identify the huddled mass his Criton protected. Curled up in a tight ball with her arms wrapped around her body in a feeble attempt to keep warm, lay his precious Carina.

He ran his hand down FireStrike's neck to reassure the animal before kneeling beside her. The moonlight bathed her in a deathly glow like she'd already slipped from this world to the next. He clamped his mouth shut to prevent a moan from slipping past his lips, and held his breath for an agonizing moment until his hand acknowledged the faint pulse thumping in her neck. At his touch, her eyes fluttered open and widened in panic.

His grip tightened when she tried to pull away. "Carina, it's me," he soothed. She stilled at his voice and started to cry.

"I'm here," he whispered, taking off his duster and wrapping it around her before gathering her in his arms. He hissed at her chilled body. "What were you thinking?" he reprimanded softly knowing now was not the time, but so grateful at finding her, he couldn't help himself.

Her teeth chattered nonstop as he nestled her against his chest. "I'm ssorrry," she slurred. "Sooo, ssorrry."

Her crying tore at his heart. "Shh," he murmured. Mindful of her wound, he carried her back toward camp. Talbrec met him halfway and held a torch overhead, providing light to traverse through the brambles and exposed roots beneath the closely clumped trees.

He entered the tent and lowered her onto the mat before piling blankets on top of her. "Find the healer," he commanded, hoping the anxiety in his voice had gone unnoticed. Her blue lips and the tremors racking her body filled him with apprehension. And by the time the healer entered, he could no longer wake her.

"Move," the healer ordered, pushing Marek out of the way. Lifting the blankets, he checked her wound before glancing at Marek.

"She's unharmed, but her temperature is too low."

Desperation flooded his body. "I'll send for more blankets."

The healer shook his head. "She needs more than blankets. Take off your clothes and lie beside her."

"What?" He couldn't believe his ears. He'd just vowed to treat Carina following the mandates dictated by protocol and now the healer wanted him to break that promise.

"If we're lucky, your body heat combined with the blankets will warm her."

Marek could see the resignation on the healer's face. After everything she'd been through, even his healer didn't believe she would live.

"Get out," he snapped.

The healer disappeared through the tent flap.

He pushed his mat beside hers and stripped out of his leathers. Keeping his lower half clothed, he pulled off his shirt before slipping underneath the blankets. He pressed the entire length of his body against hers. Ignoring the shiver that traveled up his spine when his body touched her icy skin, he wrapped an arm around her and pulled her into his chest.

"You will not die," he muttered, trusting that the pile of blankets and his body heat would warm her. "I won't allow it."

CHAPTER 25

....

BRINK OF DEATH

Carina remembered the searing cold. Looking back, she realized leaving the tent in just her undergarments wasn't one of her brightest moments. But at the time, her only motivation was to get away so she wouldn't hurt Marek anymore. Nothing else could penetrate the bitter numbness that had enveloped her mind. Shuffling through the trees, her body had felt like she'd fallen into a glacier fed creek, the dark water deadening her nerves and lulling her into a false sense of security.

She stumbled through the forest, indifferent to the small rocks and sharp pine needles pricking her feet, viewing each tree she clutched as a small personal victory before hobbling to the next. Focusing on her slow progress, she had noticed nothing around her until the glow of FireStrike's eyes stabbed her in the darkness.

She stopped to offer FireStrike a small farewell, thinking it'd almost be like saying good-bye to Marek, but didn't take into account her legs would buckle or how wonderful the frozen ground would feel after her collapse. Deciding to rest a few minutes before moving on was her last memory of being outside.

Her feet, especially her toes, throbbed painfully. But other than that, she basked in a warm cocoon. She nuzzled into the warmth and sighed, enjoying the weight of his arm draped over her.

To her regret, she must have awakened him because he called out her name, his velvet voice cascading over her. Instead of answering, she burrowed against his neck. He responded by unfurling his body from around her, and she groaned in disapproval.

"Carina," he murmured again, his voice soft but demanding.

Irritated at the change in her sleeping arrangement, she rolled onto her back and refused to open her eyes. He shifted and leaned over her. His hand settled on her stomach and gently shook her.

"Wake up."

She kept her eyes shut, but her lips curved upward in a traitorous smile.

His breath along her neck caused her heart to thump in an erratic rhythm. "Obey me, Carina McKay."

His baritone voice seeped into her skin, commanding a response. She opened her eyes to view the most handsome man she'd ever seen, staring at her. When he smiled, he stole her breath away.

"Thank the Gods," he sighed, resting his forehead against hers. "How do you feel?"

She considered his question. "I was sleeping." Her voice sounded raspy from disuse.

"Except for your unexpected journey into the woods last night, you've been asleep for the last few days. The sun has just set again."

"You woke me."

His lips tipped into a soft smile as he brushed the hair from her face. "Etiquette would prevent me from lying beside you."

Seeing the concern in his eyes, she pressed her hand against his cheek. "Since when have we followed etiquette?"

He reached for her hand and kissed it. Mesmerized, she watched his lips whisper against her palm, spurring uncontrollable shivers within her.

"Please, tell me you're all right."

"I'm tired and sore, but fine."

Her smile faltered when his face hardened and the grey flecks speckled throughout his brilliant, green eyes bore into her. "Then tell me why in the name of the Gods you left this tent last night."

Although her body remained still, inside she squirmed. What could she say? She considered a cowardly maneuver by overplaying her exhaustion and asking they talk later, but from his firm expression knew her ploy would be useless.

Like a bandage best removed with a fast tug, she spoke in one long, rushed breath. "The Tiwans attacked because they believe I'm a Dark Caller. I thought if I left they'd go after me and you'd be able to get away without losing more men." Although she couldn't muster the courage to look into his eyes, relief washed through her for confessing her burden.

An uncomfortable silence engulfed the tent in an impenetrable bubble, not even the night sounds erupting from the forest outside could break through the thick stillness. Marek shadowed above her, his hand once again covering her stomach. She cringed, knowing he must despise her now that he knew the truth.

She stared at the tent wall, watching the flickering lantern light cast specters against the canvas, waiting for the biting lash of his words. Instead, like warm molasses on a cold day, his voice soothed the danaines fluttering in her stomach. "You left to protect the men…and me?"

She nodded, not trusting her voice.

Her heart sputtered when he nuzzled her neck and grumbled in her ear. "You foolish girl." His hand clenched into a fist, gathering her shirt within his grasp.

She reached for him, wrapping her fingers around the corded muscle in his forearm. Exhaustion pulled at her body. Even her aching shoulder couldn't sway the desire to fall asleep. Her eyelids grew too heavy to keep open, but Marek's body pressing against her was an undeniable force. She welcomed his closeness, safely tucked underneath him as they snuggled within the blankets.

Although sleep lapped at the edge of her consciousness, she remained aware of his movements when he raised and kissed her forehead.

"Carina."

Her mouth wouldn't work anymore. "Hmmm?"

"Look at me."

How could she do that when her eyelids had been sewn shut? Using all the strength she could rally, she opened them in small slits. But even that was a battle she'd soon lose.

The fine lines around his eyes were more pronounced from lack of sleep as if the weight of the world sat stoically on his shoulders. She wanted to smooth away the worry from his face, then pull his head down to her uninjured shoulder and run her fingers through his hair until he fell asleep, but her body defied her and she could only clutch his arm.

"It's not safe for you to be here with me," she mumbled.

****

Marek couldn't believe Carina had almost frozen to death because of some scatterbrained idea. He smiled as she struggled to keep her beautiful, brown eyes open. He'd grown very fond of those expressive eyes. Her rosy skin tone was returning, washing away the pallor of sickness. There were matters they needed to discuss—Caden, their sleeping arrangement, his suspicions about

Marissa—but all that could wait, except for two misunderstandings he had to correct before he'd let her sleep.

"The attack was not your fault. Do you understand?"

She fidgeted beneath him, apparently not willing to relinquish her guilt.

"Listen to me." He kept his voice gentle, but his tone demanded compliance. "Someone told the Tiwans you were a Dark Caller and they foolishly reacted. You can't take the blame for the actions of others. Do you hear me?"

Her eyes slipped closed, but she nodded.

"And you *won't* leave this tent again without me knowing it. Is that clear?"

Her lips puckered at his mandate, and he smiled. She was stubborn. He would have to remember that tendency about her because if he pressed too hard, she'd rebel. If pushed, an inner resistance would always rise within her, but that obstinate trait probably saved her life.

"I won't argue about this, and if necessary, I'll place guards around this tent to ensure your compliance." He conveniently left out the part that guards were already posted. "Do we have an understanding?"

"Yes, Marek," she answered in such a quiet puff of air that he wouldn't have heard her if he hadn't been so close. He sighed and opened his fist, splaying his hand across her flat stomach. She moaned and turned toward him. Satisfied she wouldn't do something so foolish again, he relaxed. Like floodgates opening, the tension he'd experienced the last few days washed out of his system, leaving him drained and worn out.

Carina's hand still held him. He could've easily wrapped his body around hers and fallen asleep. But he'd vowed to behave according to protocol and now that she would recover, he had no excuse for remaining.

When he tried to remove his arm, her grip tightened and her eyes flew open.

"Where are you going?" The peacefulness of sleep had vanished from her face and borderline panic anchored in the harbor of her eyes.

"Shh," he whispered. "I'll be right outside if you need me, but it'd be improper for me to stay," he finished with a lame shrug.

She snorted. "You'll sleep with me like the other nights."

He raised an eyebrow at her forcefulness. Her eyes had slipped closed, but her hand clasped his arm with unyielding firmness.

"Carina," he mumbled with a helpless sigh.

"You will stay," she commanded in a sleepy drawl.

He smiled. Maybe her stubborn nature wasn't such a bad thing. And maybe even a bit endearing, he decided as he curled up beside her and buried his head in the crook of her neck, grateful she was alive.

CHAPTER 26

....

FIRST FLIGHT

Carina hobbled out of the tent into fresh air and bright sunshine. Although they had agreed to leave today, Marek had let her sleep late and now her cheeks burned as she noticed the camp packed and soldiers milling about tending to minor last minute details.

Marek had slipped away from her sometime during the early morning hours. She remembered the chill when his warm body disappeared, but had been too tired to get up. Now, she chastised herself for being selfish and forcing everyone to wait.

Muscles, stiff from disuse, tried to remember their fluidity— each step a disjointed, awkward movement as she strolled through camp working kinks out of her sore body. Two soldiers hurried past her, nodding in greeting. Although she didn't turn to look, she suspected they would break down her tent, the last item to be packed.

She couldn't find Marek but smiled at the sight of FireStrike near a small tree. Saddled and waiting, his crimson wings folded against his body glittered in the sunlight. Where FireStrike stood

Marek would soon follow, and with nowhere else to go the Criton was the best place to be.

Although weak, walking forced stagnant blood to pump through her veins, revitalizing her. She inhaled the cool air deep into her lungs, enjoying the sweet smell of pine and wildflowers. Her shoulder throbbed softly as a reminder of the past few days, but other than that, a sense of peace settled over her for what she had done to stay alive and to protect those she cared about.

Her path toward FireStrike was leading her into a group of soldiers, many with bandaged wounds. They stopped talking and stared at her. She hesitated, wondering if she should give them a wider berth. Even though Marek held her blameless for the attack, she couldn't ignore the heavy hand of guilt as it crept up and squeezed her shoulder.

Misplacing her courage, she decided to alter her course until Damon broke away from the other men and headed her way. A white dressing covered his right bicep. Unable to meet his gaze, she waited to hear what he had to say, expecting the worst.

"Carina," he mumbled in a gruff voice filled with emotion. "One of your arrows protected my back. For that, I owe you a life."

Stunned, she gazed at this grizzled warrior who had just offered her a great gift. Restraining unexpected tears, she spoke quietly. "But, I'm the reason for the ambush."

Damon's eyes narrowed. "Not true," he countered. "The Tiwans attacked because someone wanted you dead. You can't blame yourself for what happened."

Overwhelmed by Damon's acceptance of her, she could only manage a small smile.

"And now that we know you've been targeted, we'll be ready."

Her brow creased. "I don't want any of you to put yourselves in danger because of me."

Damon's voice hardened. "That's not your decision to make. Our king has chosen you as his mistress. We're honor bound to protect you with our lives."

Humbled by his words, she hoped this hardened soldier didn't notice the quaver in her voice. "Thank you for this honor. I'll strive to prove myself worthy."

Damon stared at her for a long moment. "You're special Carina McKay. Our king saw it and I see it. As for being worthy, you've already proven your worth."

Damon palmed the hilt of his broadsword in a loving way. "I look forward to traveling beside you as your future unfolds, and for the blood we'll spill as a result." He smiled, his eyes crinkling.

Carina smiled back, although she found the thought of someone's blood spilling on her behalf troubling. "Thank you, Master Finn."

"No, 'tis I who thanks you," he declared with a low bow.

To her surprise the other soldiers standing nearby also bowed. A rush of blood raced up her neck and slammed into her cheeks. Not sure what to do, she peered at her feet and mumbled, "If you'll excuse me."

"Of course, my lady." Damon chuckled, moving out of the way.

Suddenly self-conscious, her heightened awareness now noticed the eyes of the soldiers following her through camp like stalwart beacons, assessing her movements and judging her with newfound respect. Many stopped to stare, or if she met their eyes, nod their heads in greeting as she walked the remaining distance to FireStrike.

The unexpected attention liberated old insecurities she kept locked away in the recesses of her mind. A mixed blood didn't deserve their respect, especially since she was the reason for the assault. If anything, the men should loathe her.

She sighed in relief when FireStrike welcomed her with a small snort. Critons always calmed her troubled heart. They didn't judge or care about her heritage. Their pure souls and steadfast loyalty washed away negative thoughts and left her thankful for being in their presence.

She stroked FireStrike's neck. He lowered his head and bumped her hand with his nose. She knew what he wanted and scratched behind an ear. Her lips curved upward when he grunted in contentment.

"Some big, tough Criton you are," she whispered when his head dropped against her chest.

"Are you making fun of my Criton?"

Her heart skipped beats as Marek's intoxicating voice poured over her in a warm caress. She gazed into his face, her smile wavering. The grey flecks in his eyes sparkled. Dressed in black riding leathers with his moniker emblazoned on his right shoulder, he dominated her vision. He exuded confidence and power, tempered with enough compassion to avoid arrogance, which only made him stronger. No wonder his men were immensely loyal.

"I would never make fun of one so noble," she replied in her most solemn tone.

"Good," he answered with mock sternness, stepping up beside her. He brushed her hair off her shoulder before sliding his hand down her arm to pause at her elbow. She impressed herself by remaining composed on the outside while every facet inside her quaked.

His lips pressed in a line as worry replaced his amazing smile. "How do you feel?"

"Better, but you should have woken me," she chided. "Now everyone is waiting."

Marek shrugged, indifferent to her concern. "You needed the rest, the men could wait. We have a long journey ahead and I want you as strong as possible."

The sincerity in his voice for her wellbeing opened a door in her heart that had always remained locked and filled the emptiness with a light that cast rays of tenderness throughout her. She could only stare at him with an odd sense of fascination. A bemused smile played across his lips causing her to wonder what lay hidden within the emerald depths of his animated eyes. They were like hypnotic twin pools and if she relinquished control, succumbing to their spell, she'd lose herself inside them forever.

"Then we should go," she whispered a little breathlessly.

Marek's face lit up with a child's delight, but the man who captivated her interest had stopped being a boy a long time ago.

"Aye, Carina, let's go." His lopsided grin lightened her heart. He stepped into the stirrup and swung onto FireStrike with a grace perfected by years of practice, then slid behind the saddle and extended his hand.

She faltered and hoped the shock didn't show on her face. Marek offering her the saddle was more than a simple gesture of kindness. It marked a change in their relationship, both for them, as well as for Marek's men and any other man. Marek had just staked an official claim, his claim on her. She was off limits to anyone else. He would protect and defend her with his life, exposing his back to enemy arrows by shielding her with his body.

Her jittery stomach marched in rhythm with her shaking hands. She didn't deserve such distinction. Her mixed blood destined her to a life as either a servant or a mistress of a lesser noble, not fit for a king. She still couldn't fathom why he wanted her. Really, what was he thinking? She dropped her head to hide her eyes and glanced left and right to see if anyone had witnessed his act.

"Carina," he whispered, drawing her attention back to the man sitting astride an amazing red Criton. Her breath caught at the intensity of his gaze while the timbre of his voice rolled over her like a wave. When she remained flat-footed, his body shifted and uncertainty crept into his face. Did he mistake her hesitancy as a refusal of what he offered?

Warmth spread through her as Marek leaned forward in the saddle with his hand outstretched, waiting for her. His leather gleamed in the sunlight transforming him into a shining vision of masculine dominance. A slight breeze ruffled his hair and whispered in her ear, encouraging her to accept his hand. She smiled as an unshakable pride for this man who would claim her and whose simple gift of the saddle would elevate her to a position of dignity, stunned and embarrassed her. After spending her entire life yearning for acceptance and a small measure of respect, his simple act meant more than he'd ever know.

Marek wiggled his fingers. "Come with me," he murmured.

She couldn't ignore the slight undercurrent of disquiet threaded within his voice. Not wishing to cause him discomfort, she raised her hand and welcomed his fingers enclosing around her. She glanced up into his ruggedly handsome face and his dazzling smile stopped her heart—her warrior, her king, the man who would be…hers. Unable to resist, she smiled in return.

FireStrike was taller than Mira so she struggled to get her foot into the stirrup, but once secured, Marek pulled her up with ease. Grateful for his help, she tried to relax, but every nerve in her body flared to life in acknowledgment of the man whose legs now straddled hers. Although careful not to touch her, his strong arms cradled her as one hand held the reins and the other rested on the saddle horn. They'd broken almost every rule regarding decorum, yet years of training kept her back stiff to avoid any further appearance of impropriety.

Sampson on Reeza loped up from behind. Although he covered it well, his eyes narrowed at her new position.

"Sire, the men are ready. We just need to deal with Caden. Should we dispatch him now?"

The gasp slipped out of her mouth before she could swallow it, and Marek's sudden rigid posture confirmed he'd heard it. Although Caden's arrow had almost killed her, in the end Caden did save her and killing him now after they'd been through so much seemed like such a waste. She wanted to ask Marek for leniency, but didn't have the courage to speak on the Tiwan's behalf.

Instead she gripped the pommel with both hands, anticipating Marek's answer. FireStrike shifted beneath her, sensing the unease twisting a knot in her stomach. Marek flexed his fingers and inhaled a deep breath. She knew he had the safety of his men to think about. Caden might have supplied the antidote, but the Tiwan Tribe had killed several of his men. Marek had every right to order Caden's execution, yet she prayed he'd show mercy.

She gazed into the clearing surrounded by tall pines that had served as their home for the last few days. Except for the fire pits, all evidence of their stay would soon disappear as the Mother Source reabsorbed the meadow back into her care.

The sun had just topped the trees spilling light onto the Critons and riders who waited for the order to finish their journey home. White seed pods from the lion's tooth flower floated in the air giving the clearing a fairytale quality as the puffs played in the breeze, a final dance around the animals and men before settling into the soil and going dormant until the season of rebirth.

Mira disturbed the tranquility of their secluded spot by landing with a thud amidst several Critons. Using her head as a battering ram, she bumped DarkStar in the shoulder trying to get him to chase her. He snorted and whipped his head sideways to nip at her, but she skittered out of reach. Carina smiled at her young friend until Marek's commanding voice reminded her of Caden's pending fate.

"Bind him. Have him ride another Criton while his follows."

She noticed the almost imperceptible rise in Sampson's eyebrows, but any reservations remained unvoiced. Sampson nodded and retreated to follow orders.

Her heart fluttered in happiness for her king who would show an adversary kindness. She tilted her head to look into his face. His lips were clamped tight, and worry danced in the shadows of his eyes as if second-guessing his decision. Wishing to ease his concern, she brushed her thumb across his troubled brow. His eyes brightened at her touch.

"You ready, Carina?"

Her breath quickened at the anticipation in his voice. Oh, how she loved Criton riding. Just the excitement of flying seemed to lessen the pain in her shoulder.

"Yes," she whispered.

Without any noticeable movement from Marek, FireStrike pushed with his powerful hind legs and beat his wings to propel them forward. She glanced down to watch the spectacle below as the other Critons jumped into the air, their strong wings pumping furiously to catch their Alpha and chase down the foot soldiers and coursers who were already running through the forest toward the border.

Another Criton swooped in from FireStrike's right flank and settled into formation behind them. Carina laughed when she realized it was Mira. Her little Criton had transformed into a beautiful animal. Her perfectly proportioned translucent green wings swept up and down in a steady rhythm keeping pace with the others.

"Your Criton seems to think she is FireStrike's second-in-command," Marek mused.

"FireStrike doesn't seem to mind."

"Nor have the others showed any signs of challenging her. I guess they don't want to pick a fight with a female who has made up her mind." Marek chuckled.

Carina scowled, knowing Marek's comment wasn't intended solely for Mira.

"Or, she might consider herself your Criton and is flying beside you," he added. "She did save you after all."

"Yes, she did." Carina grinned. After spending years defending Mira's size, Carina savored the kernel of pride that swelled in her chest as she observed her beloved Criton. The effortless beat of Mira's wings as she matched FireStrike's tempo and the elegant arch of her neck as she pressed forward into the wind, filled Carina with joy.

But, at the same time, Mira's transformation meant she would be a much sought after Criton. Someday Mira would bond with a rider, and no matter how much Carina wished it so, in her heart she knew it wouldn't be her.

Carina couldn't explain the special connection she had with Mira. They were like kindred spirits, growing up alone in a large world with only each other to love. Marek's men believed Mira saving her was a miracle, but she knew better. True friends would always be there for each other. Mira had simply acted like a loyal friend.

Carina grimaced. She'd made a grave mistake by leaving Mira behind. With a silent vow, Carina promised never to abandon her companion again until she bonded with her rider.

"Look Carina!" Marek's enthusiasm as he pointed at a meadow nudged the sad thoughts of eventually losing Mira from her mind.

She followed Marek's gaze to view a herd of pronghorned gambels jumping across a grassy flatland as they raced for the safety of the trees.

"The Critons have startled them," he said conversationally. "If we weren't in such a hurry, I'd let them feed. But they'll have to wait until we cross the border."

They traveled hard and fast and the strain of riding weighed on her. The steady throb in her shoulder influenced a growing headache. She was tired yet couldn't relax because she had to keep her back straight to avoid touching Marek. But even her discomfort and aching body didn't prevent the cadence of FireStrike's wings from lulling her. More than once she jolted awake after drifting to sleep. When she slipped forward again and reached out to grasp the pommel to catch herself, the sudden motion pulled at her stitches and she yelped at the stabbing pain.

"Come here," Marek murmured, and wrapped an arm around her waist encouraging her to lean back.

Her body melted, molding against his chest and arms as if remembering a lost memory. The powerful beat of FireStrike's wings soothed her, placing her in a trance-like state as she relaxed into Marek's warmth.

"But this isn't proper," she grumbled, her mind floating away on the rise and plunge of FireStrike's gentle rhythm.

Marek chuckled, and dropped his chin onto her shoulder in a small, intimate gesture before whispering, "You said so yourself that we've never followed etiquette. Why start now?"

If she wasn't so tired, she might've focused on the vibrations coursing through her from Marek's voice rumbling in her ear. Instead, she wrapped her arms around the arm that encircled her and yielded to the comfort and safety of his body.

CHAPTER 27

....

STIRRLAN

Two full days of riding found them flying over a small mountain range into a wide valley following the path of a shallow stream. Tall, wispy grass waving in the wind filled the valley with endless motion.

After the first poor attempt at protocol, Carina abandoned the endeavor altogether, thriving in the strength of Marek's arms and the wind in her face until she could no longer hold her eyes open and fell asleep. Marek didn't seem to mind their closeness and simply made it a habit of keeping her fixed against his chest.

She woke to the downward motion as they glided into the valley. She wasn't sure how long she had slept, but from her body's stiffened position, decided it had been for awhile. She stretched and arched her back in an attempt to ease some of the kinks.

"How are you feeling?"

She twisted to sit askew in the saddle, leaning her shoulder against Marek's chest to look into his face. Even with her wound and other healing bruises, she loved riding with Marek.

"Better. Where are we?"

"We just flew over the Esquaine Mountain Range, which marks the beginning of my northern border. We're on home soil now." Marek's voice was a soft, soothing ripple of sound, his posture relaxed.

"Are you eager to get home?"

He grinned. "Aye, it'll be good to have you safe." He paused from scouting the terrain to fix her with a pointed stare. "I also grow tired of only lying beside you at night, Carina McKay."

The blush began in her toes and rose to burn on her cheeks. Marek's laugh as he squeezed her and buried his head in her neck confirmed he witnessed the giveaway color.

His voice lowered to a raspy whisper and sparked tiny pinpricks of energy to arc through her body. "Of course, now I'll have to wait until your shoulder heals," he grumbled.

Her reaction to him was powerful, uncontrollable...and totally exciting. But his wicked smile and the gleam in his eyes kept her mouth closed in embarrassment until he released her from his piercing gaze and began showing her different landmarks as they flew by. Anticipation bubbled just beneath his voice as he spoke about his homeland.

He pointed to a stark, rocky mountain riddled with large caves where unbonded Critons lived. As they soared past the jagged peak, a few of the young animals peered out of their lairs and roared at the intruders flying through their claimed territory. FireStrike and the other Critons ignored them, seemingly unperturbed by the youngsters' impetuous behavior.

Marek's eyes glittered as he scanned the rocks below. "Hopefully, once they transition my soldiers will find a bond-match."

She watched him concentrate on the young Critons living amid the caves on his land. With his windblown hair and a day's worth of beard, he appeared wild and untamed like an uncontrollable storm threatening on the horizon. But to her, he looked stunning. At this moment as she sat astride a spectacular Criton flying through the air, she'd never been happier and more appreciative for being alive.

She wasn't sure if Marek sensed her studying him, but with a sudden shift in focus, his gaze speared her. The sunlight bouncing off the grey flecks in his eyes seared through her defenses leaving her exposed and vulnerable. Her lungs constricted. She couldn't inhale a full breath of air. Her body quivered, anticipating his touch.

His head bent toward her and she didn't shy away. Maybe it was everything she had just been through. Or that she'd grown accustomed to his presence, riding next to him during the day and sleeping beside him at night. Or maybe his excitement at being home or enjoying the wind currents on Critonback fueled her boldness. Probably a combination of everything fostered her unexpected self-assuredness. She grabbed onto that courage, letting it support and strengthen her.

In her most daring move yet, she stroked his face with her fingertips and traced her thumb over an eyebrow in an attempt to soothe the passion smoldering in his eyes. Once she started, curiosity took control of her actions. With the back of her fingers, she caressed his cheek before skimming them along his jaw. His teeth clenched as she unfurled her hand in his thick hair. Marek consumed her vision, the rest of the world withered away. The cooling wind on her back couldn't stem a liquid heat building within her from an ache that had only grown in intensity the more she touched him. With effort, she tore her eyes from his penetrating stare to marvel at his mouth. She trembled when she remembered the soft sweep of his lips against her neck.

He secured her unruly hair behind an ear before sliding his hand to the back of her neck. "Carina," he murmured.

He spoke softly, but the need interlaced within his tone crashed through her body catapulting her pulse into overdrive. Her eyes widened as he leaned toward her. Her heart pounded in her ears. She ducked her head in a sudden spurt of panic, but his quick reflexes anticipated her move. His hand curled into a fist and grabbed her hair, forcing her face upward. The setting sun backlit him, but his eyes blazed with hunger. He released her hair and pressed his hand along her jaw, his thumb stroking her cheek as his lips brushed her forehead. His mouth whispered down her face, stopping to deposit a featherlight kiss near her temple before roving down her cheek.

Somewhere during Marek's journey as his mouth set her body on fire, a longing that had lived dormant within her, stirred and stretched. Her breath came in short, panting gasps. Everywhere his lips touched amplified the longing within her. She wrapped her arms around his waist, clutching him to her. Motionless, she smiled as his lips teased the corner of her mouth, fueling the flames within her.

He leaned back and cupped her face with both hands, his eyes hypnotizing her. "You're beautiful," his velvet voice rumbled before his lips touched hers.

The world evaporated and her mind splintered as a jolt of desire shot through every nerve ending in her body. His mouth encouraged and tantalized, and the longing burst to life with a voracious appetite. As one arm encircled her, locking her against his hard chest, his free hand traveled up her thigh. She gasped and his tongue slipped inside her mouth, exploring and tasting.

What was happening? Her body was edgy, aching for something she'd never experienced, but instinctively craved. A passion ingrained from the beginning of time that the longing knew…and wanted, blistered through her veins. She opened her mouth wider supplying Marek and his talented tongue unhindered access to the heat within her. Her hand skimmed up his broad back and gripped his shoulder. He surrounded her—his smell, his body—the very essence of him burned her, but she needed him closer.

The fractured bits of her mind were attempting to piece together a way to crawl inside this man to satiate the longing and ease the primitive ache pulsing in her very core when a deafening roar from FireStrike, which his band echoed, shattered the heavens. A sudden realization of her present location and what they were doing slammed into the forefront of her mind and she jerked away. Gasping for breath, she snatched her hands back into her lap and stared at her fingers, trying to gather her thoughts and slow her racing heart.

Marek groaned and ran a hand through his wind-tossed hair. "You best watch what you do Carina McKay because my control isn't what it should be around you."

The need in Marek's husky voice encouraged the longing within her. But she grabbed the desire beating at her and locked it in a safe place within her heart where only one man had the key. As she stared into his starved eyes and noticed his jaw clenched in restraint, guilt pounded her. She should've recognized the possible consequences when she started touching him. After all, Marek was no boy experiencing passion for the first time. Disappointed for pushing him to the edge, she gathered her wits enough to stammer out an apology, but he stilled her with a simple sweep of his thumb across her lips.

"Don't apologize for an action that is your right to take as my mistress. But…" he hesitated and his eyes narrowed. "The next time you show such abandon, let's make sure we're in a more private place, dear one."

From the faint heartbeat throbbing in her cheeks, she felt confident her blush couldn't get any redder. And for once, silence seemed her best option, especially since she couldn't process coherent thought yet.

Marek's wistful smile and eyes that only spoke of acceptance, reassured her. And after a quick hug the longing retreated so she could focus on what he was pointing at below.

In a triumphant voice, he exclaimed, "Stirrlan. We're home, Carina."

She gasped at the magnificent, white castle glittering in the fading sunlight. Unlike Brookshire, this stark fortress was built as a strategic stronghold with turrets jutting upward into the sky and a drawbridge with iron gates protecting the entrance. Her father considered Marek a smaller king. In her father's terms that meant Marek owned less land, possessed less wealth, and, as a result, fewer people lived under his domain and protection.

But to see Stirrlan, she could only discern its beauty. Majestic towers stood over a six foot wide rampart surrounding the castle. Guards on the rampart and in the towers waved to welcome the return of their king. Even from the closing distance, she noticed a scuttle of activity inside the walls as people rushed about finalizing last minute homecoming arrangements.

The castle sat on a low-lying hill overlooking a bustling city. The city sprawled beside a broad, slow-moving river that flowed east and west for as long as she could view before disappearing around a mountain.

"That's the Carnagie River," Marek supplied. "If you follow the river westward, it'll take you to the sea. And notice the mountain behind the castle. We have a fortress built within it. So, if Stirrlan ever falls during an attack, we can take the underground passages to the safety of the fortress. The fortress has never fallen."

The entire valley was nothing like Brookshire. She had grown up in a colder, rainy climate with a tendency for cloudy, dreary days. But Stirrlan breathed with life, thriving in the sun and warmer weather. Late fall wildflowers still covered the sweeping plain, dabbing the yellowing grass in vibrant blue and violet colors. A strand of poppy trees with brown-speckled, white trunks and round leaves, swayed in the breeze. With the help of his two warrigals, a boy herded ovine out of the grasslands and down the main road toward the city to bed them somewhere safe for the night.

But even with the dazzling color, the castle captured her attention, a beacon standing on a hill calling to her. Carina never realized that the color white could be so beautiful, but the castle literally sparkled in the diminishing sunlight.

She squeezed Marek's arm in excitement. "It's amazing."

"Aye, it is." He grinned.

"How do you get the walls so white?"

"It's a special stone our masons pull out of a nearby quarry. The stone is particularly strong and resistant to cannon fire."

"It's so pretty."

"Pretty?"

Carina looked back to discover Marek staring at her. His eyes were filled with amusement as she bobbed her head up and down.

Marek's shoulders shook with his laughter. "I don't think anyone has ever called my Stirrlan *pretty*," he crooned in her ear.

"Well, it is." She sniffed, trying to ignore the little spirals of pleasure bouncing around inside her from his breath warming her neck.

"Well, I'm glad you think so." He smiled and straightened in the saddle. They were approaching Stirrlan. FireStrike extended his wings to slow their descent before landing inside the walls with the other Critons. Although a large drive for carriages and a grassy area for Critons spanned the courtyard, the animals still had to cluster together in the confined space.

187

Marek jumped off FireStrike and reached for her. She'd never needed assistance dismounting before, but enjoyed the attention he lavished on her as she grabbed his forearms while he supported her by the waist and lifted her down.

Her feet had barely touched the ground when a female's voice buffeted her from behind. "Your Majesty."

Marek's back stiffened before he turned to face the woman. Her dress billowed out in a wide circle around her as she dipped into a curtsy. An elegant braid, interwoven with pearls, kept her silver hair in a pristine arrangement.

Marek acknowledged her. "Mother."

She rose in a smooth, seamless motion and spoke directly to Marek. "Your journey was without incident?"

After years growing up in her father's house, Carina didn't mind that the queen mother was treating her like a servant, but the cold reception made her acutely aware of Marek's arm around her waist. Knowing their closeness would be frowned upon, she attempted to step away, but his grip tightened in an effortless display of strength keeping her at his side.

"Not without some trouble."

"I'm sorry, son." The queen mother nodded, speaking the words with little inflection like she truly didn't care about the men who had died in the Bridal Lands. As if determining Carina's presence had lingered unspoken long enough, she fixed Carina with a hard stare.

"And who is this?"

Marek released Carina for a formal introduction. "Mother, may I present Lady Carina McKay, daughter of King Regin McKay. Carina, this is my mother, Lady Nareen Duncan. Mother returned from our southern estate to manage the household after Saffron left."

Carina dropped into a deep curtsy. "It's an honor to meet you, Queen Mother."

"Of course, my dear."

Carina rose, her heart thumping uncomfortably in her chest. The queen mother's cold greeting was an indication of her future treatment and of her approval—or lack thereof—within the royal hierarchy.

Nareen's eyes refastened on Marek. "I must have misunderstood. I thought Marissa McKay would be attending you?"

Marek shrugged, seemingly indifferent to Nareen's interest. "Carina and Marissa are half sisters. I made my choice. The reasons do not matter."

Nareen gasped as she read between Marek's words. "She's not pure royal? Marek, how will that look?"

"Mother, I really don't care. I suggest you waste less energy on what others think as well."

Nareen frowned, but inclined her head toward Carina. "Forgive my indiscretion, Lady McKay."

Carina knew better than to believe Nareen's act of remorse. She might've had a chance if she had been a true blood, but as a mixed she'd never be suitable. Still, she wanted to be accepted.

"Queen Mother, please just call me Carina. Otherwise I'll think you're talking about my sister."

As soon as Carina said it, she cringed as the correction, *half sister*, blistered across Nareen's face. Instead, Nareen tipped her head. "Very well."

Marek's hand settled on the small of her back. "Come Carina, I want to show you Stirrlan." His comforting touch soothed her jumbled nerves.

She smiled at Marek as he guided her through the front doors leaving Nareen and the rest of the court behind.

CHAPTER 28

ACCUSATIONS

Carina woke up alone...again, and ignored the hollow emptiness clawing at her. She leaned against her intricately carved headboard and surveyed her new living arrangements. Her room, on the top floor next to Marek's chambers, was easily three times the size of her old one. Fine mahogany furniture replaced her old scratched pieces, and a large four-poster bed with a down mattress made her wonder how she'd ever fallen asleep on her lumpy cushion. Large picture windows overlooking the castle entrance and town farther below allowed natural light to stream into the room when the heavy linen drapes were not pulled for privacy.

She had every reason to be happy, yet without Marek, her acquired luxury seemed shallow and colorless. Except for brief, rushed moments, she'd hardly spent any time with him during the five days they'd been at Stirrlan. Dignitaries from Dalia, a small town along his eastern border, had arrived to discuss Criton rider protection because Outlanders were attacking their village. Although he had tried to make time for her, the dignitaries and catching up on what he'd missed while away had demanded most of his time.

She had stayed close in case he beckoned her, but after exploring the castle from top to bottom, boredom scratched at the edge of her mind. Since her shoulder didn't hurt so much anymore, she decided to venture a little farther away from the central grounds today.

A new wardrobe came with her room and she slipped into a pair of tan pants and a blue, cotton blouse before darting out the door and down the winding staircase to the main floor. Although a spineless maneuver, she stepped into the servant's corridor to avoid bumping into Nareen. But she vowed to find her backbone and work on garnering the queen mother's favor once she settled into the patterns of Stirrlan life.

The wonderful aroma of baking bread greeted her before she pushed open the swinging door into the kitchen. The overheated room was a bustle of activity as servants scurried about preparing food for the day. Ovens with roasting meats and stoves containing pots of steaming sauces blended with the rich aroma filtering throughout the room, spurring the grumbling in her stomach.

The chef in charge of the organized mayhem was a robust woman named Rosie who had adopted her the first day she'd accidentally blundered into the cookery. Rosie had her back to the door but turned when she heard it swish open.

"Ah, there you are my sweet lemming." She smiled, nodding toward Carina's usual seat at the end of a large, block table used for preparing foods. "Take your seat," she ordered.

Carina knew better than to disobey Rosie's command and sat on the stool. A plate filled with an egg and meat dish, along with a warm roll and various cut up fruits, appeared in front of her. With an almost unladylike eagerness, she spooned down large helpings to ease her hunger.

"So, what are your plans today?" Rosie asked, speaking over her shoulder while peeling potatoes faster than Carina believed possible. Carina watched in fascination as Rosie, armed with a small knife, made quick handiwork of another potato.

"I'd like to get acquainted with the surrounding area," Carina mumbled with a mouth full of bread. "Do you know of a place?"

Rosie paused, her knife poised over another soon-to-be skinned potato. "If you go out the gate and follow the road a ways, you'll find a grand lake. It's a great place for tanager watching."

"Sounds wonderful." Carina pushed her now empty plate away. "You can't keep feeding me like this," she complained with a hand on her belly.

Rosie waggled her eyebrows. "Oh pishposh. A man likes a woman with a little meat on her bones. Just remember to stay on the path to the left when the road turns right."

A small smile spread across Carina's lips. A peaceful lake seemed like the perfect place to gather her thoughts. She jumped off the stool, thanked Rosie for the meal, and made her way outside. Aside from the guards standing at the door to the main house and posted at the entry points, no one noticed her stroll through the gate and beyond the protective Stirrlan wall.

She followed a well maintained avenue wide enough to accommodate two carriages side by side. Ovine grazed on either side of the road as two boys chaperoned them from under a shade tree while their brown warrigals prevented the animals from straying. One boy raised his hand to her and she waved back.

Perspiration soon beaded across her forehead from the warm day. She wiped the sweat away with the back of her hand as the heat lulled her mind. The road narrowed when she reached a wooded glade. To her relief, the tall trees shielded her from the blazing sun.

Just as Rosie had said, the main thoroughfare angled to the right while a less maintained road, which rapidly dwindled into nothing more than a furrowed path, veered to the left. She turned left.

At first, she enjoyed the soft chattering of the tanagers as they flitted through the branches, and the way the sun's rays filtered through the leaves, dotting the path in patches of shade and sunlight. But, without an occasional breeze to offer respite, the air trapped within the canopy thickened, growing heavy and still. Trying to ignore the stifling humidity, she focused on her goal—dipping her feet into the cool lake water.

After several additional minutes of trudging along the dirt trail, she spied a glint of sunlight bouncing off water. She increased her pace and rounded a small copse of aspens to discover a serene lake sheltered by trees.

The path ended at the water, next to a patch of grass and some boulders. She plopped down on the largest of the smooth stones, which was partially hidden behind a wide shrub, and pulled her tired feet out of her shoes and socks before lowering her legs into the sparkling coldness.

She peered at her dangling feet as she swooshed them around, watching tiny waves radiate out and away from her legs. The lake floor dropped off quickly, but she could still see the sandy bottom. She leaned back and stared at the cloudless sky. Her rock lay in full view of the hot sun. If only she could jump into the lake then let the warming rays dry her as she stretched out on her rock.

A rebellious smile crept across her lips. She glanced around and listened. Aside from tanagers and the incessant buzzing from insects, she heard nothing. No voices, no feet crunching along the gravel path, nothing.

On impulse, she unbuttoned her blouse and threw it down before sliding out of her pants to stand in her white undergarments. After one last fleeting look, she jumped into the waist deep water.

She gasped as the chilly water sloshed on her sensitive belly. Ignoring an uneasy feeling encouraging her to get out, she dunked her head and swam into deeper water. She floated on her back and spread her arms wide, closing her eyes to savor the contradicting sensations as the heat from the sun warmed her face and the lake chilled her body. *Glorious.*

The water lapped around her in a soothing caress until her instincts jarred her into action. She dove and swam back to shore, popping her head out with a splash. Careful to reach with her unhurt shoulder, she grabbed a low hanging branch and hauled herself up. Flopping her feet back into the lake, she lay on her back and let the sun's rays dry the droplets from her skin. The prickly sensation as the water evaporated comforted her and she fell asleep to the sounds of nature.

****

A snort from a Criton jerked Carina awake. Her pulse pounded. She glanced around disoriented until she remembered her location. From the sun hanging low on the horizon and her dry clothes, she had slept much longer than intended. At the sound of approaching voices, panic crawled up her spine because of her half-dressed condition. She shimmied into her pants and threw on her shirt before stuffing her feet into dirty socks and cramming them into her shoes. Without a moment to spare, she stumbled out of the bushes in time to witness Sampson, Damon, and two other soldiers land their Critons in the small openings between the trees.

Sampson jumped off Reeza and stormed toward her with cold, black eyes and flared nostrils. From his agitated demeanor, she resisted the urge to back away. He surveyed her from head to toe and his face reddened in anger. He bunched his fists. For an instant, she thought he might hit her.

She raised her hands in a calming gesture. "I fell asleep. I'm sorry."

Sampson's jaw clenched. "Where is he?"

Her brows furrowed. She glanced at the other men for answers, but their eyes remained averted. Aside from Sampson, only Damon had dismounted while the other two fidgeted on their Critons.

She shook her head. "As far as I know no one else is here. Who are you looking for?"

Sampson turned to the men. "Find him," he ordered before his eyes latched onto her like a gyrfalcon zeroing in on its prey. His rage pounded her in waves of hostile emotion. The two soldiers took to the air without hesitation, but Damon lingered.

"Sir, would you like me to stay?"

Sampson whirled on Damon. His voice dripped with sarcasm. "Why? Because you don't think I can handle this woman?"

Damon stood at attention, his eyes staring into the empty space just beyond his captain. "You're more than capable. I was simply offering to protect your back while you question her."

Sampson shook his head. "That's not necessary. The coward is trying to escape. I need your eyes in the sky. Now go," he muttered with a dismissive wave of his hand.

Damon's eyes flickered her way before he jumped onto DarkStar.

Fear flooded her veins when Damon leapt into the air. She considered running, but Sampson would interpret her action as a confession to some perceived wrongdoing. Her best defense was to tell the truth. After all, she hadn't done anything wrong, except maybe oversleep.

She lifted her chin and squared her shoulders. "Look around, there's no one here. I would never betray Marek, and I'm shocked you think I would." She had hoped that the mention of Marek's name would somehow soothe Sampson's anger, but instead, she'd just tossed kindling onto a blazing inferno.

With two giant steps, he stood in front of her. Although only a few inches taller, his fury and adrenaline-filled body made him seem like a giant. His eyes roved down her body and lingered. Self-conscious, she followed his gaze. In her haste to get dressed, she'd missed a button on her blouse. An empty eyelet lay exposed at the bottom, evidence of her guilt. She inhaled a breath, fighting the rising panic threatening to close her airway. When she looked up, her heart stumbled. Sampson's face was twisted into a snarl, the frenzied look of a crazed man.

Now, she backed away. Blood filled her cheeks, but blushing wouldn't help her. "Sampson, I went for a swim…nothing more." She tried to infuse confidence in her voice, but even she could hear the quaver in her words.

Sampson pursued her. "Marek should've chosen the other one once he discovered you were tainted."

She backpedaled, keeping space between them. "Sampson, please. I don't know what you're talking about."

Icy tendrils crept through her mind, igniting inner alarms and warning her of the terrible danger surrounding her. Sampson's eyes glazed and his face slackened as his thoughts tunneled inward. Nausea tied her stomach in knots from a growing awareness that she would soon experience the brunt of what he was reliving if she didn't find a way out of her situation.

"I've been with *no one*. I assure you, I'm pure."

"But once again, he wouldn't listen to *me*." Sampson slammed a white-knuckle fist against his chest, not hearing a word she'd spoken.

Her mind spun in a wild attempt to process Sampson's words. Who would've accused her? Why hadn't Marek talked to her about these allegations? And how in Haden was she going to escape this raving madman?

She continued her shuffling, backward steps. Once she reached the water, she would either have to defend herself or try to get away by jumping into the lake. "Sampson, this is a horrible misunderstanding. Let's go find Marek and figure things out."

Sampson frowned, and then nodded. She stopped retreating, grateful her pleading had breached his enraged mind. Clasping her hands together to control their shaking, she wondered if Marek knew about Sampson's temper.

Sampson turned, but with a quick shift of his body, whirled and cuffed her ear.

Her head exploded as she catapulted to the ground. She landed on her back with a thud, splashing into the shallow water. Waves of pain throbbed inside her head, but the cold water kept her from passing out. She lay momentarily paralyzed from the force of the blow as the water supported her head while the rest of her body settled on the shallow bottom floor.

Sampson stood over her, watching and waiting. His face contorted into a mask of contempt. He glowered at her from the shore with fisted hands as his body shifted into a bladed stance, ready to pounce. Even with the pain bouncing around like a ball inside her, she could identify the telltale signs screaming for her to get up. On the ground at his feet, she was too vulnerable and at his mercy.

Scraping together her strength, she pushed up into a seated position and forced down the bile rising in her throat when the throbbing intensified to the point she almost fainted.

"Where is your man now?" Sampson sneered, glancing around the small clearing. "Evidently, he has no honor either."

When the pounding in her head diminished to a dull heartbeat, she rolled onto her knees and dug her fingers into the gritty sand before gathering herself. Once standing on unsteady legs, she thanked the Gods for her minor accomplishment.

Staying quiet had never been a character trait, even when she knew opening her mouth could have devastating results. Someone had accused her of being impure and Sampson had just attacked her because of those falsehoods. Her wrath would have no bounds when she discovered who was spreading such lies. But first she had to save herself from the devil.

She swiped the hair out of her face and straightened to her full height. In a low voice, she whispered, "Marek entrusted you with my safety." She raised her chin, letting anger fuel her words. "And my honor is still intact because unlike you, I haven't betrayed him."

Sampson grimaced. "You Haden spawn," he condemned, the vehemence in his voice blasting a bone-chilling tremor down her spine.

When he raised his fist to strike her, she lunged and rammed her knee in his groin. He howled in pain and collapsed, drawing his legs into his stomach in a fetal position.

She sidestepped, but underestimated his tenacity when he grabbed and twisted her foot, knocking her to the ground. She spun onto her back intent on kicking him, but he jumped on top of her before she could react.

His oppressive weight threatened to crush the air from her lungs. She lost all sense, morphing into a wild animal, punching his face and screaming. He pinned one of her hands over her head, but not before she clawed long, bloody scratches down his cheek. When he finally had her restrained, he paused to catch his breath, panting against her neck.

She clenched her teeth, struggling to control her anger. "Get...off...me."

"Not until you confess your taint." Satisfaction bubbled in his throat.

"I'm not going to confess to something that isn't true."

"Very well. I'll find out for myself."

The menace in his voice terrified her. She stared at the man sprawled on top of her. Hatred burned in his black eyes, but something else flickered inside them, a sinister darkness that scared her more than his anger as a growing hardness pressed against her belly.

No! She was not going to let this happen. When Sampson tried to adjust his grip, she channeled all her strength to wrench a hand loose and jabbed her thumb in his eye.

His agonized scream pierced the air as he released her to cradle his gouged eye. She pushed him off, but he jerked her back to the ground, trapping her with his body. No matter how hard she fought, his large hand pinned her arms overhead.

"You'll pay for your disrespect," he hissed, spittle flying from his lips like a rabid dugar.

He groped her left breast. Panic consumed her. She cried out. Fighting with a new sense of urgency, she bucked and wriggled beneath him until she yanked a hand free and punched his face, throwing all her energy into her blows.

Sampson recaptured her hand and while crouched on top of her, lifted her upper body off the ground. She stared into the eyes of an insane man, his delirium transforming him into a monster—the beast nightmares were made of.

"You will obey me!" he shrieked, striking her hard across the face. Pain reverberated through her head. Her vision blurred and blood filled her mouth.

"Now, confess and end this nonsense." He pulled her close, his face inches from hers. From the lust burning in his eyes, she knew that even if she did confess he'd take her anyway. So, she could withdraw into herself as he took her body or continue to fight. Her stomach churned at the thought of relinquishing herself, but she was mentally and physically beaten, and struggling only excited him more.

She summoned her courage and used it as a buffer to build an insurmountable wall inside herself where she could hide from the injustice about to happen. But before retreating, she glared into Sampson's shiny eyes, gleaming with excitement. She spoke with an unshakable resolve. "I'll *never* confess to that of which I'm innocent." She punctuated her statement by spitting blood in his face.

Narrowed eyes and a clenched jaw were her only warning signs before Sampson struck her so hard that the force of his blow slammed her body to the ground. He emphasized his disapproval by punching her in the ribs—two short, quick stabbing jabs. The breath rushed from her lungs and her world went dark.

****

Carina woke to Sampson's bumbling hands trying to unbutton her pants. Her shirt had been pushed up to expose her belly. She wanted to shove him off, but her strength was gone. She turned her head to look at her arm. It floated in the water, drifting back and forth in the ripples Sampson created as he attempted to slide her pants off her hips.

The late afternoon sun pounded her with a merciless intensity. Her dry, cracked lips burned from the thirst seizing her body. Surrounded by water, yet she was unable to wet her lips and rinse the blood from her mouth. She watched her arm with a disconnected, slow motion objectivity, twisting her hand so that her palm faced up. She could move her fingers, yet her arm wouldn't do her bidding.

A cloud floated overhead, blocking the unforgiving sun. She closed her eyes, relishing the short reprieve. To her surprise, the cloud spoke.

"Sir, we found no one."

Sampson growled. "Keep looking. He must be out there."

The cloud shuddered back and forth. She opened her eyes to the awed realization that her cloud was Damon shaking his head. Damon's back to the sun threw his face in shadow.

"DarkStar is an excellent tracker. If he didn't find anyone, there's no one to find."

"It doesn't matter. I'm going to prove her taint. Now leave us."

Damon's feet stayed fixed in place.

"Didn't you hear me?" Sampson bristled, his breath hot on her bare stomach.

Damon spoke in a neutral voice. "Aye, but you'll need a witness to prove she's impure when she doesn't bleed. I'll stand as witness."

Sampson's mouth dropped open. "*What?*"

"You've made a claim, but Carina has insisted otherwise. When such a discrepancy occurs, there must be a witness." Damon shrugged. "Although I'm curious King Duncan isn't the one determining validity, I guess he gave you that authority as his captain."

Carina listened with a strange, detached wonder. She never knew such matters involved a witness. If she was not in such pain, she might have found the whole concept fascinating...or funny. She wasn't sure how to react.

Sampson cursed under his breath before grabbing her breasts and pushing off her, his last demeaning act to inflict. She hardly reacted to the additional discomfort as it blurred with the ache already pulsing throughout her body.

Sampson stood over her and adjusted himself. He seemed uncomfortable with the bulge in his pants. The toe of his boot pressed against her side. She waited for the kick that would break her ribs. He cocked his foot, but hesitated and glanced at Damon, his heavy-soled shoe dangling in midair. With an exasperated grunt, he slammed his foot to the ground splashing muddy water in her face. "Bring her," he ordered, stomping onto shore—the torturer leaving the tortured behind.

Sampson disappeared from view. She lay motionless as the water caressed her battered body, struggling to figure out how this day had gone so awry. Why had Marek chosen her? As a mixed blood any heir she produced would be considered a half-breed. So, *why*? Why would Marek bring another mixed child into the world to be treated with such disdain?

She had forgotten about Damon until he knelt beside her. No longer shielding her from the sun, she squinted at the glaring brightness. He reached for her. "We must go. Let me help you."

She shrank away from his hand, turning from him. Her entire body throbbed and the pounding in her head made it difficult to think. But even in her foggy state, she would not let anyone touch her. Somehow, she crawled onto her hands and knees and paused in the water to catch her breath. She waited until the hammering in her head faded before undertaking one of the hardest tasks she'd ever asked of herself—standing.

It wasn't pretty. There was no grace involved as she pushed her hands off the ground to rest on her knees before forcing one foot at a time underneath her. She swayed precariously as the blood rushed from her head leaving her lightheaded, the delicate balance with the ground and gravity in jeopardy. Damon moved to catch her, but she steadied herself without his support.

She walked stiff-legged out of the water, each step slow and calculated as she concentrated on placing one foot in front of the other. Damon matched her snail pace, providing himself as a crutch if necessary.

They walked past the small beach that had been so appealing just a short while ago and onto the path where Sampson and the other two waited. From somewhere inside her, she dredged up the nerve to meet Sampson's gaze. His bitter stare dismissed her like a bug. Her eyes traveled to the soldiers who squirmed in their saddles and noticed everything around them to avoid looking at her.

Damon mounted DarkStar then slid behind the saddle and removed his foot from the stirrup. With an open hand, he leaned forward offering assistance. Walking the short distance to the Critons had consumed all her strength, so climbing onto DarkStar without help seemed insurmountable. She placed her foot in the stirrup and accepted Damon's hand as he lifted her beat-up body into the saddle.

Although amazed by accomplishing such an impossible feat, she impressed herself further by keeping her back ramrod straight to avoid touching Damon. And except for occasionally brushing against her with his arm as he guided DarkStar into the air, Damon honored her silent request by maintaining his distance as they made the short jump back to Stirrlan where her fate awaited.

CHAPTER 29

....

BETRAYAL

Carina spotted Marek as they descended. He was leaning against one of the stone pillars that fortified the front entrance to the castle and staring at the setting sun. Damon landed in the rectangular courtyard inside the protective walls just as Marek pushed away from the column and strode her way. A broad, lopsided grin spread across his face as the diminishing sunlight danced in his bright eyes.

He wore a white shirt with an elaborate cross-stitched pattern on the open collar and tan pants. A broadsword was strapped around his waist and a single dirk rested in a sling across his chest, opposite his sword. He looked breathtaking with his hair almost dry from bathing and having just shaved. His appearance made Carina acutely aware of her pitiful state.

"Ah, good, where did you find..." Marek's smile faded. "By the Gods. Carina, what happened?" His arms stretched up for her.

Not knowing what to do, she let him grab her waist as she swung her leg over DarkStar. Gripping his shoulders, she slid into his arms, which promptly folded and pressed her against his chest. From the safety of his possessive hold, the shock shielding her from the brunt of what had happened slipped away. Uncontrollable tremors racked her body. Tears welled and tumbled down her face. She clung to his shirt and leaned into him to remain standing on rubbery legs. She ignored the surrounding stimuli bombarding her senses by burying her head in his shoulder, but still cringed when Sampson approached.

"What happened," Marek hissed.

She'd never heard such venom in Marek's voice. An undercurrent of promised vengeance swam within his tone, and instead of frightening her, she welcomed it. Marek would make things right, Sampson would pay.

"Sire, I have terrible news. Carina betrayed you by bedding another man."

Marek's body stiffened. "What?"

"The coward ran when he heard us approach. And when Carina stumbled out of the bushes, her hair was a mess and she'd missed buttons on her shirt in a poor attempt at covering up."

Marek's muscular arms unwrapped themselves and her solid wall of safety disappeared as he gently pushed her away. She watched with helpless despair as his eyes traveled down her, and swallowed a moan when his thumb touched the empty button hole at the bottom of her shirt.

She wanted to defend herself, but the anguish in his eyes silenced her. Her heart twisted as a pain worse than anything Sampson had just ravaged on her body shot through her core, ripping her in two. Marek believed *him*. Her alleged betrayal splashed across his face in an agonizing, vulnerable openness. How could Marek believe *him*?

Her eyes pleaded, willing Marek to see the truth, but he turned away and gripped Sampson's shoulder, acknowledging a deed well done. "Thank you, my friend," he said in a clipped tone.

She crumbled inside, standing alone in her wet, filthy clothes—bruised and broken. She glanced at Damon and the two soldiers. The soldiers still refused to look at her, but Damon's brown, shrewd eyes saw her. She focused on Damon. He had saved her from an indescribable horror. Although she should've been grateful, she couldn't draw any comfort from his noble act that would quell the hollow ache devouring her. A cold numbness enveloped her, buffering her against the devastating pain Marek had just inflicted without ever raising his hand.

Marek spoke, but in her ears his voice floated in the distance. "We'll have to expand the search area," he snapped. "We must find him, Sampson."

Sampson nodded. "We will."

She peered at her muddy shoes. Without doubt, she knew Sampson would scour up some poor soul to be her lover to complete his charade. She closed her eyes and exhaled a ragged breath. Except for her battered pride, she had nothing left. She gathered up her wounded soul, and although it hurt to do so, stood tall. She looked at Damon. He did save her, after all. But when she nodded in thanks, he glanced away. She'd been branded, a mistress who had sacrificed her virtue for a lover.

With Damon's dismissal, she decided to leave. She'd been accused and found guilty. Now, she just awaited final judgment. With shuffling footsteps, she turned for the castle. She felt their eyes slicing into her back as if stripping the flesh from her body. She used every ounce of courage to keep her posture straight and stride measured. Only when the thick, redwood timbered door was latched behind her did she allow the tears to fall as she struggled up the stairs to the sanctuary of her room.

****

When Marek first glimpsed Carina's tear-streaked face and torn clothing, insuppressible rage tore through his gut, flooding every muscle in his body with adrenaline. Like a chain reaction, power surged inside him and hardened his mind to the task at hand—annihilating the person who had dared touch her. The rage overloaded and suffocated his mind from rational thought. But when she crumpled into his body, a sudden need to protect her curbed the pounding anger.

Her body melted into him. He wanted to hold her and tell her she was safe. But guilt weighed heavy on his shoulders as her every tremble crashed through him, every hot tear scorched him, and every whimpered breath ripped apart his soul—piece by agonizing piece.

He shouldn't have left her alone for so long, but matters of his kingdom had been very demanding. Even though he hadn't spent much time with her since returning, she filled his mind during those rare, quiet moments when no one required his attention. So, after dispatching Criton riders to Dalia, he'd decided to focus on what he wanted…Carina. Knowing her propensity for adventure, he hadn't been concerned that she was away from the castle until Sampson had returned and told him of the betrayal—shattering his world.

At first, he refused to believe Sampson's claim. But when he saw the ripped blouse and disheveled hair bespeaking of an overanxious lover, his anger had turned inward. Marissa had warned him, but he chose not to listen. He had found himself wanting and hoping when in reality, he'd been a fool.

Carina's treachery seared his heart, shriveling it into a charred, non-beating organ. With Carina, he'd been willing to reveal himself, to share and expose his concerns as a king, desires as a man, and hopes for a family. How could he have been so blind?

Justice controlled his heart now, filling the terrible black void. He had to calm down. But every time he thought of another man touching Carina, his rage exploded into a twisted mass of darkness.

The rage blurred his vision, turning everything into drab shades of grey, and pumped hot blood through his body, fueling his need for revenge.

Carina's lover would die for his indiscretion. The traitor could run, but Marek would find him. He could hide, but no inn, house, or stable would shelter him from Marek's wrath. The coward had forfeited his life the moment he'd laid hands on Carina, and Marek would personally send the bastard on his journey to Haden.

Marek inhaled a deep breath and ran his fingers through his hair. After Carina had disappeared into the castle, Stirrlan's protective walls had become too confining. Storming through the main entrance, he'd left the gatehouse and everything behind and now stood at a pasture fence where coursers grazed. A stable boy would soon drive them inside the walls for the night.

He placed a boot on the bottom rail and crossed his arms over the top bar, gazing at the sun as it kissed the horizon in the distance. Sampson had gone to ready FireStrike. They'd only have a short search window before sunset, but he needed to be in the air. He hoped the cooling wind in his face would loosen the vice-grip hold of the unseen hand constricting his chest so he could breathe again.

"Excuse me, Sire." Damon's voice interrupted his thoughts.

Marek forced the pain into a corner of his heart and stepped away from the fence. "What is it?"

"Sire, DarkStar and I searched the area at Sampson's request and found nothing."

He frowned. DarkStar and Damon were his best trackers and if they found nothing, it usually meant there was nothing to find. "Sampson said—"

"Aye, I heard him. But I can assure you, *we* found no one. DarkStar didn't even pick up a scent. Nothing."

Marek stared at Damon as he processed this new information. Why would Sampson accuse Carina of such treachery? And why did she look like she'd been through a tornado? His mind whirled. If she wasn't with an overzealous lover, then what had happened?

Damon stood at attention, refusing to look him in the eyes. "You should also know I offered to stand as witness."

Marek shook his head. "What in Criton's breath are you talking about?"

"Carina denied Sampson's accusation that she betrayed you, even after Sampson struck her. He was going to prove her denial a falsehood, so I agreed to determine who was…correct."

Marek glanced toward the castle, his eyes skimming over the curtain wall and traveling to Carina's window. Her room remained dark, a black eye in a house full of light. Although Sampson had been disappointed when he chose Carina, even hotheaded Sampson wouldn't commit such an act against him…would he? No, Damon's words couldn't be true. Sampson was captain of his army, a bonded Criton rider…his best friend. Sampson would never dishonor him in such a manner.

"Damon, why do you make such allegations against your captain?"

For the first time since speaking, Damon's unflinching eyes locked onto his. "Sire, I've pledged my life to you as my king. My wife and girls live within the protection of your walls. I haven't made any allegations, only spoken the truth. But if you feel I've lied, then take my sword because a warrior you cannot trust shouldn't remain within your service."

Damon reached for his sword, but Marek stayed the blade by placing a hand on Damon's shoulder. Marek scanned Carina's window as conflicting emotions raced through him. "Why didn't she say something when Sampson spoke against her?"

"Sire, if I may…as a man whose house is filled with women?"

Marek nodded.

"Sometimes a woman speaks without words. You have to learn to hear what she doesn't say to truly understand her."

When he remained silent, Damon continued. "What did her body tell you when you held her?"

Marek pressed his lips into a firm line and strode toward the main gate and castle door.

CHAPTER 30

EXPLANATION

Marek tapped on Carina's door then knocked again when she didn't answer. Deciding she had ample warning, he opened the door and entered. The last resilient rays from the setting sun bathed the room in a fading light.

Still in her torn clothes, she huddled in a bow window with her arms wrapped around her knees. An onset of nerves forced him to light a lantern on the dressing table and another near the bed before he could approach her. He sat on the narrow ledge beside her. Tear tracks trailed down her cheeks, the only evidence that she'd been crying. He clenched his teeth at the purpling bruise on the side of her face near her hairline. His eyes roved over her, absorbing every detail. Although coated in dirt and mud, the defensive bruises and scratches on her arms were still noticeable.

His chest tightened at the forlorn expression on her face. He needed to touch her and take the pain from her eyes, but she shrank away when he reached for her. She had never shied from him before, and watching her press herself into the corner of the window to avoid his touch ripped through him like a blade slicing into his stomach. Not sure what to do, he dropped his hand as the imaginary knife in his gut twisted.

"Carina, I'm going to leave and send a servant to attend you. Once she's finished, I'll return and you will talk to me. Do you understand?"

She bobbed her head.

He would've been satisfied with that minor acknowledgment, except for her defeated manner. Eyes that once captivated him with exuberant life, stared out the window, dull and empty...and it terrified him. He resisted the urge to grab her and hold her close, to provide the comfort he should've given when she dismounted DarkStar.

Guilt rifled through him like a rat scavenging for food, leaving devastation in its wake and carrying a rising rage that refused to be tempered. The rage encouraged him to confront Sampson, but he had to make things right with Carina first. He scrubbed his hands over his face. She didn't react when he stood. Like a fragile doll, motionless with her lips slightly parted, she gazed out the window. Yet despite her tattered appearance, he couldn't stop looking at her.

Walking out of Carina's room took every ounce of willpower he possessed, but waiting in the main hall was a true testament of his patience. More than once he had to stop himself from bounding back upstairs until the servant appeared to inform him of Lady Carina's readiness.

He entered to the glow of lanterns filling the room with soft light. Carina sat in the middle of her bed in a clean, white dressing gown. Her hair, still damp from bathing, draped over her shoulders. And her hands, which were folded in her lap, must have been particularly intriguing because she wouldn't look at him.

Marek sighed, knowing this would not be easy for either of them, but he needed to know the truth. He sat on the edge of the bed while she twisted and tangled her fingers in a nervous dance.

"Carina," he murmured. "Look at me."

Her heart sputtered and tumbled into her stomach. His velvet voice wreaked havoc with her inner resolve. How could she stay safely tucked away within herself when his mere presence beckoned her to drop her carefully constructed defenses? Summoning all her courage, she raised her head and peered into his penetrating green eyes—eyes that infiltrated her every safeguard, that exposed too much of her, and could condemn her in a blink of dismissal. To her surprise, anger didn't greet her. Instead, concern plagued his face. She gasped when his hand clasped hers to stop their fidgeting.

"You must tell me." Marek hesitated as if it pained him to continue. "Tell me what happened. No matter the truth or who it might hurt. Will you please…tell me?"

She glanced down. Marek's hand covered both of hers. Mesmerized, she watched his thumb caress her, rubbing back and forth.

The truth? How could she tell him the truth when it would vilify his captain and best friend? Sampson would say she was lying and Marek would be forced to choose between them. In the end, he would side with Sampson since they'd grown up together.

She should just accept her fate. She was a mixed blood after all and undeserving of the honor he had bestowed upon her. Why had she even allowed herself to hope? That's what hurt the most, to believe she could've achieved something beyond her station in life. He should just send her home. But the thought of leaving Stirrlan and Marek to go back to her old life caused an ache to spiderweb throughout her body, choking the air from her lungs and constricting her already struggling heart. She knew he waited for

215

an answer, but could only stare at his thumb stroking her hand, her voice failing her.

Marek's tone dropped, a king demanding an answer. "Were you with another man today?"

Her head jerked up and her eyes glistened with tears. Anger and frustration filled her chest. How could he ask such a question? Her voice quavered, although she didn't know if it was from anger or the pain of his question, but it definitely wasn't out of guilt or shame.

"I'm *yours*. You chose *me*. There is no other and never has been." She spat out the words with a bitterness she couldn't hold inside anymore.

Exhaustion pulled at her body leaving her irritable. But she refused to remain silent while others accused her, and she wouldn't continue justifying her actions when she'd done nothing wrong. "If you don't believe me, or if you intend on questioning me every time I go for a walk, then you should return me to my father."

Marek's back straightened and his grip tightened. "I'm *not* sending you back."

Her heart stammered at the possessiveness in his voice. She glared at him unwavering, but his all-seeing eyes were too powerful and her bravery evaporated on a silent exhale. "Then you must trust me," she whispered with lowered eyes.

He sighed. "I know, Carina. And I do, but from now on you must promise me one thing."

She glanced up with an arched eyebrow.

"You must speak out the next time I travel down the wrong path."

The corners of her lips twitched.

"What?" he asked.

"I've never been accused of not speaking my mind."

He smiled. "Well, I'm forewarned. Do you promise?"

"I promise." She smiled softly.

"Good."

Her smile faded when she noticed his eyes darken. He reached out to touch her face. Fear squeezed her heart and her protective defenses slammed into place. She scooted away until her back hit the headboard.

His hand paused in midair. She could hear the reassurance layered in his voice. "Carina, you ask that I trust you, so you also must trust me. Know that I will never hurt you. But I need to see the injuries Sampson inflicted on you, so I *will* touch you."

Tears rimmed her eyes, but she nodded.

He edged closer and leaned forward, imbedding his fingers in her hair before brushing the wet strands off her shoulder. He could smell her—wild roses and the sweet, dazzling expectation just before a winter storm. Their closeness would've aroused him if not for the growing bruise traveling from her jaw to her temple.

Rage consumed him, blistering hot in his veins. "Where else?" he asked in a voice he barely recognized.

Carina frowned before answering. "I guess along here." She motioned down her side.

"*What?*"

"That's where he punched me," she said with a halfhearted shrug, refusing to look at him.

He splayed his fingers the length of her ribcage. His hand was a hairsbreadth away from the beautiful swell of her breast. He tried to be careful as he probed, but she shivered at his touch.

"I'm sorry," he murmured. "Did I hurt you?"

She shook her head as a blush rose in her cheeks. "No, just startled me...that's all."

Under different circumstances, his fingers traveling over her body would be driving him insane with desire. Instead, the rage pounded him and crashed into the bars of the cage he kept it locked behind as images of Carina curled up on the ground while Sampson beat her, invaded his mind.

"Did he…" Marek inhaled a deep breath. He struggled to keep his hands from shaking.

She stared at him with innocent eyes.

"Did Sampson…did he…"

"No," she answered quietly. "He would have, if Damon hadn't been there."

He strained to hear as Carina's voice trailed off to an almost inaudible whisper.

"If Sampson had persisted, I think Damon would've stopped him."

He traced the bruise running along her jaw, trailing his fingers to her temple before resting his palm against her cheekbone. His chest labored in a feeble attempt to draw sufficient air into his lungs.

How could he have believed Sampson? How would she ever forgive him? He cupped her bruised face and closed his eyes. He was so undeserving of her, but had to try to make amends. With a ragged exhale, he spoke. "Forgive me for doubting you…and for not being there to protect you."

She touched his face, smoothing his creased brow with her thumb. "There's nothing to forgive because what happened isn't your fault. You can't be with me every moment of the day." Her lips curved upward in a soft smile.

Her words were meant to comfort, but he could not be so self-forgiving. Although strong and independent, Carina was his responsibility. No other man had the right to touch her, let alone hurt her. The desire to protect her thrummed within his very being. He couldn't control the overpowering compulsion to shield her from all harm. And Sampson would pay for his insurrection with his life.

Although he savored her caress, he reached for her hand and kissed her palm. Did she shudder at his kiss? He longed to explore that idea. But Sampson burned in the forefront of his mind, so he released her and stood.

Confusion spread across her beautiful face. "Where are you going?"

"I have to find Sampson. He must be punished."

****

Carina nodded. But the thought of being left alone another night, especially after what had just happened, filled her with despair. Suddenly, she felt exposed wearing only a nightgown. She gathered her legs to her chest and wrapped her arms around them. With a resigned inhale, she dropped her chin to her knees and stared out the window.

The moonlight bathed the landscape in a calm, welcoming radiance. If she wasn't so sore and mentally beaten, she would've slipped outside to soak the moonbeams into her skin. She loved the moons. People tended to fear the night, but Luna and her son lived after sundown. So, instead of dreading the dark, she embraced it. While the sun was bright and harsh, the moons were gentle and soothing, and offered a place to hide when the events of the day were too traumatic.

She'd just experienced a horrible assault, worse than being arrowshot because the arrow was part of battle and impersonal in a way. But Sampson's attack was very personal, meant to demean and hurt her. How she wished she could run outside and disappear into the shadowed safety of the blue-white luminescence.

"Carina?"

She turned from the window and tumbled into Marek's troubled eyes. He was sitting on the bed again, his forehead creased with worry. He brushed the tears off her face that she didn't know had fallen.

219

"Tell me," he whispered.

She closed her eyes, resting her cheek in his hand. His throaty voice spoke to her in a way she couldn't describe, rolling over her senses and seeping into her skin. It warmed her from the inside, draping her in a peaceful comfort, yet energized her with a promise of something more.

His other hand slid up and down her arm in a soothing manner. His touch was meant to reassure, but instead his slow caress fanned a flame deep within her, igniting a different kind of ache. Her heart thumped as she realized they were sitting on her bed, alone.

She'd never completely trusted someone before. To trust meant a willingness to share her innermost dreams, which went against every protective instinct in her body. But Marek had just asked her to trust him, and maybe for him—and for her—it was time to take a chance, to jump off the cliff and rely on his faithful arms catching her. Maybe, he believed in her after all. Although it went against her internal screens, she stared into his concerned eyes and asked for what she desired most.

"Must you go?"

****

Her unwavering gaze penetrated his defenses with ease, as if she had walked through the front door to his heart. Her eyes held him transfixed, binding him in a powerful hold that surprisingly didn't frighten him. She had wrapped herself into a ball, but when she pinned him with those dark eyes, willing him to stay, her lure was overwhelming.

His warrior instinct demanded revenge. Normally, the urge to spill blood would've been impossible to ignore until Carina's eyes ensnared him and encouraged him to disappear within the tender depth of the woman whose smile lifted his soul.

He shook his head. Damon was right. There was much he needed to learn about women, or rather, this woman. As king, he'd become so used to people with hidden motives, who wanted something from him, or simply liked him because of his status that he'd grown suspicious. Could she be true? Someone who liked him for who he was just as a man and not because of his crown or what he represented?

Her long lashes shielded her eyes as she dipped her head to hide her face. Amid the flutter of lantern light, she looked like an angel surrounded by pillows in her white, lace gown with her hair falling about her face in soft waves. He was completely taken with her.

"You want me to stay?" He spoke in a rough whisper, lacking the control of a king, displaying the needs of a man.

"At least until I fall asleep." She glanced up, hopeful.

He didn't have the strength to deny her and could only manage a brief nod to show his consent. Her resulting smile blinded him. She unfurled herself and placed her head on a pillow, then watched with inquisitive eyes as he kicked off his boots and lay beside her. If not for the bruising to act as a reminder, he would've had a hard time controlling his need for her.

She smiled again, bathing his heart in the warmth of her light. She touched his face, caressing his stubbly jaw with her fingers until her cheeks flamed. If possible, her blush deepened when she realized that he'd noticed her crimson giveaway, and she turned away from him.

Relief flooded his body. His Carina, the one he'd grown so fond of, was gradually peeking out of the safe place she'd retreated to—Sampson hadn't broken her spirit.

Unwilling to let her slip out of reach, he squeezed his arm underneath her pillow and moved in close until the delicious length of her pressed against his body. Thoughts of revenge vanished in the wake of lustier wants. Afraid to hurt her bruised ribs, he rested his hand on her hip and fought the impulse to let his fingers roam.

221

She trembled at his touch. He clenched his teeth and quelled the urge to kiss the long curve of her exposed neck.

With a heavy sigh, he dropped his head on the pillow knowing that lying beside her would be an exquisite torture testing his restraint, and one he would welcome the entire night.

CHAPTER 31

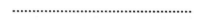

NEW BEGINNINGS

Carina awoke to an awareness that her protective wall of muscle had slipped out of the covers. She had slept soundly knowing he held her, keeping the nightmares about Sampson at bay. She could hear him dressing and her body warmed at the thought of him. With a tentative stretch to assess her sore body and a loud yawn, she turned to find him. Her smile disappeared when she noticed the bleak look in his eyes as he strapped on his sword and two dirks.

"What's wrong?" she asked, her voice shaky with concern.

He sat on the bed and reached for her hand. Morning light streamed in from the window, bathing him in a soft glow. Although he tried to hide his anger, she could hear the undercurrent in his voice.

"I must find Sampson."

"What are you going to do?" she whispered, lowering her eyes to watch his hand holding hers.

"What he deserves."

He spoke with a quiet, unquestionable resolve. Without a doubt, she knew Sampson was about to depart this world. A ripple of approval flowed through her veins, but a flood of guilt chased behind it. Sampson and Marek had grown up together. How could she live with herself knowing Marek had killed his best friend in order to defend her reputation? Kernels of doubt clouded her mind, whispering that a mixed blood wasn't worthy of such an honor. A few weeks ago, she would've listened to those insecurities, letting them fester and grow. But something had happened since she'd left her father and Brookshire. She'd learned something about herself. A strength she never realized lived within her. She was no longer an insecure, timid girl willing to be a victim, but a fighter with the tenacity to protect herself when cornered. Either by arrows battling Tiwan warriors or her fists fending off Sampson—whatever the injustice, she would fight.

No one, not even a mixed blood, deserved the treatment she had endured yesterday. And with this realization, a sense of peace filled her with acceptance of who she was—a woman with an inner power fed not only by courage, but surprisingly, by compassion too. And this newly discovered understanding told her that Sampson shouldn't die by Marek's blade.

She sat up and clasped both of his hands, bringing them into her lap. She intertwined her fingers within his and marveled at how hands that displayed such strength could be so gentle.

"Will you please not kill him?"

Although she remained focused on their interlocked hands, his entire body stiffened. After a long moment, his curt response buffeted her like a cold wind.

"As king, I choose how to handle those who've sworn allegiance to me."

She glanced up to confront the uncompromising clench in Marek's jaw. She almost wilted at his determination, but somehow continued. "I can't have his blood on my hands."

Marek shook his head. "And you won't. His blood will be on mine."

"But he was your best friend. You grew up together. If you kill him, I fear it will leave a wound upon my soul that will never heal." She squeezed his hands, hoping he could feel the passion of her request, and stared into his hardened eyes, pleading for him to reconsider.

He met her gaze with an iron will. But when she refused to back down, he yielded, exposing the anguish eating him. She gasped at the vulnerability he shared, which made her more determined that he not kill Sampson. He fought to stay composed, but glanced away.

"I don't know if I can let him live knowing what he did to you." He stammered. "Knowing that he touched you..." His voice trembled, raw with emotion.

She pressed her hand against his cheek and forced him to look at her. "He didn't do anything that won't heal in time. I'm still yours. That hasn't changed."

He sighed, wavering.

"Please, Marek. Please, do this for me."

He reached for her hand and kissed the back of it. "I can't promise you, but I'll consider it."

She smiled and threw her arms around his neck. "Thank you," she whispered, enjoying the comfort of his strong arms wrapping around her.

CHAPTER 32

······························

JUDGMENT DAY

Marek stepped out the door into the early morning sunshine. Summer was but a memory as the harvest season took center stage with brilliant yellow, brown, and orange colors transforming the countryside. He had a special fondness for this time of year as plants and animals hunkered down, anticipating the season of rejuvenation. The cooler weather energized him. Often he used this time to enlist his men in strenuous training regimens, repair buildings, and improve Stirrlan in some way before the snows lured life into a sleepy listlessness.

Today, however, his usual excitement eluded him as he inhaled a deep breath. The crisp air chilled his blood and dulled his spirit. His blades lay cold and heavy against his body, feeling burdensome and oppressive. He moved with a fluid confidence, coiled and ready to unleash his anger on a man he once considered a brother.

He had lain awake most of the night watching Carina sleep, marveling at the smallest details—the flutter of her eyes as she dreamed, the soft curl of her eyelashes, her lips mumbling his name when he stroked her hair, and the gentle beat of her heart. At first, he stared in fascination. Then, he noticed her darkening bruises and the rage inside him stretched. And when a movement caused her pain forcing a small moan to slip from her mouth, the rage unsheathed its talons. By the time the sun threatened to burst above the horizon, he could barely contain his anger. And the more he thought about Sampson touching her, the more the rage blazed through his bloodstream, finally driving him from Carina's side.

The housing quarters for unmated soldiers were to the west of the main house. Sampson had a cottage next to the barracks. Marek's feet crunched on the gravel as he rounded a corner of the castle. The pop and snap of the pebbles beneath his boots reminded him of bones breaking in battle. He flexed his fingers, anticipating his fist connecting with Sampson's jaw. He had told Carina that he would consider leniency, but he'd made no guarantee as to the quality of Sampson's life if the man lived.

Carina's image scattered the violent thoughts swirling inside his mind. He still couldn't figure out how she'd convinced him to consider sparing Sampson's life. She had just seemed so vulnerable and grief-stricken that he would've promised anything to ease her pain.

He smiled despite the situation. He might be in trouble if Carina ever realized the power she wielded when she gazed at him with those brown, searching eyes. Not much of a king when his mistress could make him to do her bidding with just a few well placed glances. Somehow though, such control over him didn't sound like a bad thing.

A twig snapped an instant before Damon stepped from the shadows of a small stand of poplar trees, their leaves still green despite the cooler temperatures. Dark circles rimmed his eyes and he stifled a yawn as he approached.

"You've watched him all night?" Marek asked.

"Aye."

Marek appraised Damon. Damon had always fought with an unwavering sword, ready to step into the toughest battle. His quiet manner had a calming effect on younger, inexperienced soldiers, and he was always eager to teach what he knew to those willing to listen. As if looking at Damon for the first time, Marek realized he'd underestimated this man. In his attempt to step from his father's shadow, he'd ignored someone who could've been—and still could be—so much more than just a soldier.

He gripped Damon's shoulder. "I'm sorry I cannot command you to go find your wife's bed...at least not yet." He ran a hand through his hair before explaining. "I'm afraid I might've made Carina a promise that will be hard to keep."

Damon nodded. "Women can have that power."

Marek's lips curved upward in an understanding smile. "Then let's get this over with so we can return to them." He strode down the gravel path with his hand resting on the hilt of his sword. Damon fell into step behind him.

A young soldier emerged from the barracks just as Marek approached Sampson's cottage. The lad looked crisp, well rested, and ready for the day. Marek recognized him as the blacksmith's son.

"Stefen," Marek yelled, and smiled when the startled boy stood at attention.

"Go saddle Reeza and bring her here."

Stefen saluted and clicked his heels before racing toward the barns.

"Am I going somewhere?"

Just hearing Sampson's voice turned Marek's blood cold. He watched Sampson step off the porch, and noticed the long scratches running from Sampson's left eye down the entire length of his face. Although Marek had seen the marks yesterday, Sampson's accusations about Carina had blinded him from

229

recognizing the meaning of those jagged wounds. Even though his chest swelled with pride because Carina had fought hard, the dark rage freed its cage and burst forth with such hunger that his fingers twitched at the thought of driving his blade deep into Sampson's gut. He clenched his teeth, gripping the rage on a tight leash.

If not for Carina, Marek would've surrendered to the rage and Sampson's blood would be pooling beside his severed head. But because of her—knowing he still had to go back, look into her eyes and tell her what happened—he forcefully held it simmering underneath his skin. Reluctantly, he removed his hand from the calming comfort of his steel.

"I have questions about yesterday." As king, his voice remained controlled, but the man inside struggled to contain a rising inferno.

"Don't worry, Sire. We'll search the town this morning and find the coward. I promise you." Sampson nodded, folding his arms across his chest.

Marek fisted his hands while the muscles in his arms bunched from self-imposed restraint. "What did Carina tell you yesterday when you found her?"

Sampson waved a hand in the air as if batting away an insect. "Oh, she tried to deny it."

"And you didn't believe her?" Somehow he rediscovered his claymore. The cool, smoothness as his fingers wrapped around the hilt encouraged the rage.

Sampson frowned, either from not understanding Marek's question or from a realization that he might be in trouble. When he answered, some of his blustery confidence had dissipated. "No, I didn't believe her. She'd obviously just bedded a man."

"But what led you to that conclusion?" With two broad steps, Marek stood in front of Sampson.

"She couldn't even button her shirt," Sampson blurted.

"Did Carina tell you that she'd been swimming?"

Sampson's face burned red with anger. "Of course she did. She got caught and would've said anything." Sampson shifted from one foot to the other.

Noting Sampson's discomfort, a strange quiet settled over him. Rage coursed through his veins, but he channeled it and used its energy to provide the restraint he needed to avoid killing the man standing before him.

Aware of Damon standing silent and watchful, Marek had no doubt Damon would come to his aid, if necessary. "Yet when Damon returned on DarkStar and they found nothing, you still didn't believe her?" He took another step forward, forcing Sampson to stand motionless with just a warning glare.

Fear flashed in Sampson's eyes and Marek's body rippled with satisfaction. Sampson tried to diffuse the situation by placing his hand on Marek's shoulder, and Marek resisted the urge to break every finger on that hand.

"Marek..." Sampson searched for the words to say and then spoke with a sincerity Marek rarely heard from him. "My brother, everything I've ever done has been to protect you and Stirrlan. Carina is a mixed blood and impure. She's not worthy of you. I was simply going to prove her taint...to spare you the pain and disappointment."

Marek shook his head. *Could Sampson really believe that his actions were for the good of Stirrlan...and him?* With a snap, the rage slipped its leash, escaping containment and boiling over his barriers. Marek grabbed Sampson's hand and in a smooth movement, twisted Sampson's wrist to force his palm up before pressing Sampson's fingers back toward his arm.

"Sire?" Sampson grimaced as Marek applied more pressure, forcing Sampson to his knees.

Sampson gritted his teeth. "Please, Marek...let me go."

Marek leaned forward, administering additional force. The vision of Sampson on top of Carina, hitting her and ripping her clothes, burned in his mind. Revenge simmered in his throat, tasting sweet and sensual. He glared at his friend who was a friend no more. If Damon hadn't intervened, Sampson would've forcibly taken Carina, *his* Carina. Sampson betrayed him and the disloyalty burned deep.

Stefen approached with Reeza who roared when she saw her rider in pain. Marek might've been worried if he'd been anyone else, but as FireStrike's bonded rider, Reeza wouldn't attack him. So Marek surrendered to the rage and with a push, broke Sampson's wrist before releasing him.

Sampson screamed and cradled his dangling wrist into his chest while draping his other arm protectively over it. He rocked back and forth, his body curled over his injured limb.

Sensing Marek's emotions, FireStrike dove from the sky to land with a thud next to the men. He lowered his head and growled at Reeza, ensuring his position as Alpha.

The rage inside Marek laughed at Sampson's pain, scorching Marek's blood and demanding more. Carina was *his*. No man had the right to touch her. He drew his sword, leveling the tip against the hollow of Sampson's throat. The rage rejoiced when Sampson raised his head, his eyes pleading for mercy.

Marek pushed the blade forward, just a mere movement, unnoticeable except for the small rivulet of blood that bubbled up and ran down Sampson's neck. Marek's eyes darkened at the sight of the life-giving fluid and his heart pounded as adrenaline surged through him. The sword in his hand felt like an old friend, an extension of himself. *End it*, he thought. Just a simple, forceful thrust and Carina would be avenged.

Thinking of Carina saved Sampson from the final lunge, and the rage howled in frustration. He hesitated, remembering Carina asking for mercy on Sampson's behalf. She should be demanding revenge, not compassion. Something inside him crumbled, and the rage whimpered. His beautiful Carina would be his salvation and Sampson's savior.

Marek sheathed his sword, the rage vanquished. "Sampson, I banish you from my lands. You're never to return to Stirrlan. And you should know, Carina asked me to spare your life." Marek shook his head in disbelief. "If not for her, your life would be forfeit. She might be mixed, but I'm the one who doesn't deserve her. My only solace is that I have my entire life to prove myself worthy…starting with you. Now, get on Reeza and understand that if I ever see you again, my blade won't be forgiving."

Sampson rose on unsteady legs. Beads of sweat dotted his pale face. He staggered onto Reeza before looking at Marek, his lips white from pain. "Sire, I'm sorry it came to this, but you must understand my purpose in life has always been to protect you. She's hiding something. I can feel it. And if you're not careful, she'll be your downfall."

Marek watched with an unsympathetic heart as Sampson encouraged Reeza into the air. FireStrike raised his head and wailed as Reeza left his band. Marek stroked FireStrike's neck. "I'm sorry, my friend," he murmured before turning to the men behind him.

Stefen stood with his mouth open, stunned at what he'd just witnessed. But the appreciation in Damon's eyes filled Marek with peace, like he'd passed a test. As if to confirm his thoughts, Damon spoke.

"To spare a man's life when it is so undeserving of mercy is the mark of a true king—a king worthy of the crown and allegiance from his subjects."

Marek shrugged, feeling a mixed sense of pride and remorse. Pride in that he could face Carina's inquisitive eyes without regret, and in his ability to control the rage within him. Remorse at the pain Sampson had inflicted on Carina, the loss of a trusted friend, and for an unease needling him for letting Sampson go. Marek straightened. If his decision to free Sampson proved wrong, he'd face the consequences when the time came.

Fatigue blanketed his shoulders as the last bit of anger caught a ride on his ebbing adrenaline and drained from his body. Carina and her soft skin lying in her nightgown popped into his mind.

He walked over and clasped Damon's shoulder. "My father always held you in high esteem and I've come to realize that in my foolish attempt to rise above my father, I haven't given you the responsibility you deserve. From now on, you are captain and guardian over Carina."

Damon's eyes widened before narrowing with understanding. "I won't fail you," he said with a bow.

"You never have." Marek released Damon, and with determined steps, headed for the castle and the beautiful woman waiting inside. His stride lengthened, ensuring a bit of distance from the two men before he allowed a small smile at the thought of Stefen—the poor boy still had yet to close his mouth.

....

CHAPTER 33

THE MAKING OF A MISTRESS

Carina settled into the patterns of Stirrlan life as the weather changed and the first snow brushed the ground. Her bruises faded and Sampson's attack dwindled to a bad memory. She spent most of her time with Marek as winter's breath blew across the land. During the days, they rode on Critonback. Sometimes she flew on Mira, but usually she rode with Marek enjoying the warmth and strength of his arms as his body surrounded her.

Although she adored his laugh, a rumble that began deep in his chest and traveled through his body to light up his eyes, she rapidly learned to appreciate his mouth. At first, his lips would remain soft and teasing until the desire between them escalated into a forceful and demanding fervor. She would lose herself within the passion, but ultimately panic and pull away—her body on fire.

Embarrassed and frustrated, she couldn't explain her hesitancy. After Sampson's attack, Marek had assured her that nothing would happen until she came to him willingly. Although grateful for his understanding, guilt dampened her spirit over the restraint he was exercising on her behalf.

When they were wrapped up together, as his hands roved over her body and his mouth drove her into a crazed state, she wanted to surrender to the sensations he stirred within her. But her well-fortified defenses would resist, driving her from his arms. She supposed fear of not knowing what to expect fostered her insecurity—some mistress she was turning out to be. But displaying a patience that endeared her more, he would draw her into his chest, hold her tight, and whisper things—private things—things she'd never heard before that would make her blush until they were both laughing.

The methodic swoosh of FireStrike's wings had pulled her thoughts inward, but a gentle squeeze changed her focus to the man holding her. Marek now commanded her attention. They were going somewhere special, a secret place he'd told her. They flew with their backs to the setting sun.

"My sweet lemming," he murmured, nuzzling her neck and sending glorious spirals of pleasure ping-ponging throughout her body. "You've been quiet and that worries me."

"Why?" she asked, trailing her hand down his banded forearm to entwine her fingers within his.

"Because that means you're thinking, and a thinking woman is usually something to fear."

She giggled at Marek's husky laughter, and reached up with her other hand to stroke his cheek, enjoying the stubbly feel of his day old beard. "Then you should be *very* afraid."

"What have you been thinking?" He encouraged on a whispered breath in her ear.

Although she couldn't control her erratic pulse, she vowed to remain silent against his delicious assault on her body as he attempted to coax her into revealing her thoughts. "Tell me where we're going first," she teased.

Marek smiled against her neck. His hand traveled up to hers still cupping his cheek. Using his fingertips, he traced a faint track down her arm. She shivered. She really needed to work on her willpower.

He nibbled her ear then bit down. "Tell me," he murmured between clamped teeth.

She sucked in a breath. Her hand clutched his arm. How could this man wield such power, tempting her with just his touch? Uncontrollable quivers cascaded inside her like mini earthquakes.

She shook her head and somehow found her voice, a breathy wisp of sound. "You first."

His low, soft chuckle speared her fluttering heart. "You're *so* tough," he scoffed. "But no matter, we're here." With a slight twist of his hand holding the reins, FireStrike descended.

Three opal pools glistened in the final rays of the falling sun. Steam danced along the surface and swirled into wispy funnels as FireStrike's wing beats changed the air flow. Rounded boulders surrounded the pools, isolating the water from the rest of the world. When FireStrike landed, Marek held out his hand for her as she slid out of the saddle then jumped down behind her.

Luna, a white orb in the sky, and her son peeking above the horizon, competed with the last stubborn shafts of light shooting upward from the sunset, illuminating the land in an eerie twilight.

"What is this place?" she asked in an awed whisper.

Marek grabbed her hand and led her to the largest pool. He pulled her into his chest and stared at the darkening sky. "The pools are called Azriel's Tears. According to legend, Azriel was a fledgling god when he lost his heart to a mortal maiden. She was but a child when he first spotted her running in the fields, her blond hair flowing behind her like silk. It's forbidden for a god to interact with mortals, so he watched and protected her from a distance.

She grew into a beautiful woman, full of life and laughter and much desired by the men of the village. But she refused them all. For unbeknownst to Azriel, the maiden had always sensed him even though he'd never made his presence known. She'd grown to love the voice that sang to her at night and soothed her fears on a summer breeze. Although she'd never met Azriel, she waited for him knowing someday he would come for her.

Azriel loved the maiden, but the only way he could be with her was to become mortal. It's hard for a god to give up power and immortality."

****

Carina rested her head on Marek's shoulder while he stroked her hair. Lost in the story, his voice surrounded her, reverberating in his chest and murmuring in her ear.

"Time is different for the Gods. Years may pass for us, but it's only a blink of an eye for a god. So, when Azriel finally chose to relinquish his power to become a man, he was too late."

She pulled away and gazed into Marek's somber face. "What do you mean?"

Marek's thin smile crinkled the small lines around his eyes. "He waited too long. She lived a full life, but lived it alone waiting for a man she never knew to come to her. Bound to him by a love she didn't understand, she refused to take another, never abandoning him even as she took her last breath.

Azriel lost his mind when he learned of her death. Without his young maiden to give him purpose, he scattered himself into the heavens hoping to find her in his next life. His tears now dot the world, leaving large pools that never cool even on the coldest nights."

She stared at Marek with teary eyes. "That's very sad."

Marek cupped her face in his hands, stroking her cheeks with his thumbs. "It's just a tale," he murmured. "I brought you here, not to feel sad about a story, but to enjoy the warmth of the pools. The water can be quite invigorating."

She wasn't sure what he meant, but the crooked grin and glint in his eyes fostered her cheeks to heat up, causing him to roar with laughter. He crushed her into his chest, holding her tight. "You do make me happy."

For some reason, the story of Azriel and the maiden replayed uneasily in her mind. Although Azriel loved his maiden, he waited too long to find his courage and they both died alone.

Her hands drifted around Marek's waist and she buried her face in the hollow of his neck, enjoying his smell and the wall of muscle surrounding her. She could spend the rest of her life wrapped in his arms, safe from the world.

She planted her chin on his shoulder. To her surprise, he was staring at her. The grey flecks in his eyes sparkled, dancing with a quizzical vitality of their own.

"What are you thinking?" he whispered.

With a slight shrug, she answered. "That I don't want us to be like Azriel and the maiden."

Marek frowned and his eyes narrowed. She squirmed under his gaze. "That will not happen, Carina McKay," he scolded gently.

"But how do you know?"

"Because I won't allow it," he murmured, dipping his head to kiss her. His lips brushed hers and passion blazed through her like kindling to fire. She smashed her body against his and reached up his broad back to hold him tight. His instant response fueled the flames licking across her skin.

His tongue darted inside her mouth and she met him with her own. His erection pressing against her intensified the dull ache throbbing low in her belly. Her body quivered, instinctively wanting him with every fiber of her being. She indulged in the luxury of a traveling hand and slipped it underneath his shirt, tracing her fingers over the planes of his chest and the ridges of his smooth, defined abs. He gasped when she brushed down the front of his pants, and she smiled.

With an unexplainable collapse, the walls she'd always hidden behind crumbled, exposing her to the raw emotions flooding her body. Alive with feeling, his every caress encouraged her while his every kiss spoke to her on a level only she could hear. He seared her…scorched her…burned her.

Because of him, she surrendered to the passion she'd always shied away from, letting it devour her. Desire welled inside her fast and furious, a beast consuming her. She dug her fingers into his back before burying her hands in his hair to pull his mouth to hers, needing this man to quell the ache eating her alive.

His kisses overloaded her senses, leaving her breathless. Panting, she broke away and ducked her head into his shoulder, trying to catch her breath but refusing to let him go. The rise and fall of his chest as he struggled to calm himself intensified her hunger.

His hand swept the hair off her neck just before nibbling kisses traveled down it, cascading chills over her like sheets of water. She clung to him as the sensations from his touch ignited a desire she didn't know existed within her, pushing her to relinquish control of her mind and body to another.

She lifted his shirt until with a quick grab from behind, Marek pulled it over his head. Unable to resist, she ran her hands over his bared chest. After a brief, questioning glance, she floated her thumb across a nipple and marveled at its instant reaction. When his chest expanded with a sharp inhale of air, she stilled her exploration to gaze at him, resting her hand on his pectoral muscle. Although his jaw clenched in restraint, he couldn't subdue the desire blazing in his eyes that blasted through her like a lightning rod.

"Marek," she moaned dropping her forehead against his chest, knowing she wanted him, but not sure what to do about it.

He lifted her chin with a finger an instant before his lips touched hers. His mouth teased while his hands fed the insatiable need ravaging her. She melted into his overheated body, succumbing to the desire.

His mouth traveled down her jaw, the sweep of his whiskers against her cheek a contradiction to the soft caress of his lips. He unbuttoned her blouse and pushed it off her shoulders, her thin undergarment the only barrier between her swollen breasts and his searching hands. She gasped when he cupped a breast and squeezed her nipple until it swelled to an aching point, straining against the flimsy material. Seemingly irritated by the hindering fabric, he grabbed her undergarment and yanked it off her.

The chilly air on her bare body cooled her skin while the blood inside her boiled. He worked the buttons on her pants and suddenly she stood naked before him. She knew she should feel embarrassed, but the hunger drove her now swallowing up every other emotion until only Marek existed.

His hands slid down her hips and she shuddered. The heat radiating from him incinerated her. Even though her cheeks flushed hot, a stronger overpowering need to see him pushed her. She stepped into the small gap between them, and with shaky hands, began unbuttoning his pants. Her concentration faltered when his fingertips traced a sizzling path down her back. His gentle stroke counterbalanced his iron stomach and the corded muscles in his forearms, reminding her that the man embracing her was a warrior who happened to be a king among men. How did she deserve such a gift?

She paused at the last button. His hard shaft threatened to steal her courage. Unable to continue, she glanced up and disappeared into his blistering eyes. He reached for his pants. She started to pull away but he interlaced his fingers within hers and guided her, so together they slid his pants over his rock-hard erection and down his legs. She stared unashamed, yet overwhelmed. She'd never seen a man naked before and wished she had the nerve to touch what she wanted with each clenching pulse of her body.

Marek pulled her into his chest and suffocated her with kisses until she clung to him out of desperation, her legs unable to hold her. She groaned as every cell in her body cried out for him to take her.

****

Somehow, he stepped out of Carina's arms even though his body screamed in frustration. She stared at him with puzzled eyes, her lips swollen from his kisses. He searched her face, but saw no fear. For the first time, he'd been the one to pull away, not Carina who had demanded more from his every kiss, who trembled at his touch, and who was driving him crazy.

He grabbed her hand and in a scrape of a voice, murmured, "Come, swim with me."

Her eyebrows furrowed. "I've nothing to swim in."

He grinned. "Me neither."

Even in the moonlight the beautiful blush on her cheeks melted his heart. Although still naïve with the innocence of youth, an unyielding strength burned inside her. She displayed a quiet courage, a resolve born of someone with an ageless wisdom. And tonight she would become his.

A gentle tug on her hand nudged her feet into motion until they were both walking toward the water. The moonlight dancing off the pools reflected in her eyes, radiating back at him in a shimmering silhouette. He paused and pulled her close, framing her face with his hands before kissing one eye and then the other, wondering in the beauty of her.

She shivered as his fingers skimmed down her arms. Entwining his hands within hers, he backed into the water so he could watch her every move. Although hesitant, she followed him. He wanted to be gentle, to make her first time memorable, but the sway of her hips as she tiptoed into the pool was going to make it difficult.

She glided into the path of the moonbeams bouncing off the water. The rays illuminated her body in a breathtaking iridescent light as her legs disappeared under the surface. With the soft glow reflecting off her skin, her hair mussed from his hands, and her beautiful, red lips—redder from kissing him—she looked like a goddess.

He guided her deeper until her breasts teased the surface, not completely above but not submerged either. Transfixed, his eyes devoured her. She stepped up to him and his teeth grazed down her neck to the hollow of her throat. He smiled at her rapid pulse, and ran his hands down her thighs before lifting her to straddle him. He held his breath when she rubbed against his cock, straining his already weakened willpower. Even in the water, he could feel her slick heat and it took all his strength not to enter her.

He wrapped her legs around his waist and gently pushed her back into the warm pool. She spread her arms wide, her upper body floating in the ripples, and closed her eyes. Her hair danced with the movement of the current and again he thought her a goddess.

Even as he bent over her, capturing a nipple in his mouth and hearing her whimpered response, a thought burst into his mind. Out of nowhere, he couldn't shake the feeling that Carina's fate had been predetermined at birth, and he was meant to protect and guide her. His chest tightened at the importance of this task and he trembled, humbled by the knowledge that he'd been the one chosen for such an honor. He prayed he would be worthy and his blades would be swift and strong when the time came to defend

243

her. But these thoughts were fleeting as Carina dug her fingers into his hair and pulled him into her chest.

His hand covered her other breast, the nipple hard and rigid, demanding the attention he readily gave it. She started rubbing against him, moving her hips up and down his thick column. Panting, he buried his head in her chest. His arms shook as he fought to maintain control when every instinct in his body urged him to drive into her in one long, deep thrust.

Grabbing his forearms, she pulled her upper body out of the water, pressing her taut nipples against his chest. Water trailed down the sides of her face. Her hands roamed along his arms and across his shoulders before her fingers settled in his hair, her palms against his jaw.

Her moans tantalized him while her body clamped around him tormented his throbbing need for her. Until Carina, he'd been devoid of life—living, but only walking through the days—not seeing the world around him. Yet with her every touch, she reawakened something inside him, a part of his spirit he'd somehow lost.

She showered kisses down his face. Insistent and pleading, she begged for him to ease the ache, and he obliged by lifting her and resting his tip just inside her heat. As he tortured himself by watching her mouth part in anticipation, he finally understood what she was offering. His beautiful Carina would breathe life back into his soul. She would help him see the world again, a world that had only regained its color because of the goddess he held in his arms.

He lowered her. Her satin walls grabbed him, encouraging him to fully merge with her. When he felt resistance, he paused knowing her first time would be painful. She opened her eyes and stared at him, sensing his hesitation.

"Marek," she whispered. Her eyes, glazed with passion, yet the trusting eyes of someone experiencing the beauty of what was about to happen for the first time, crushed his heart and a flare of protectiveness flooded his veins.

"Carina." He rasped her name, his desire so great. "The first time might hurt, we—" He had intended to say they should go slow, but her lips plundered his mouth, unrelenting and insistent. He lost all thought, wrapping his arms around her and pinning her lithe body against his chest, losing himself in the welcoming marvel of her mouth.

In a sudden motion, she used him for leverage by tightening her legs and lifting her body to plunge down hard onto him. He tore through her barrier in one smooth motion until he was buried deep inside her. She cried out and burrowed her head in the crook of his neck. He groaned, clamping his teeth in restraint as she cradled him in a silken cocoon. The wonderful velvet steel of her body beckoned him, forcing him to use every ounce of self-discipline to keep from driving into her. She was in pain. His focus had to remain on her.

She rested against him, breathing heavy. He stroked her back, tracing his fingertips along her smooth skin. When she shivered, he smiled.

He murmured in her ear. "Are you okay?"

She lifted her head and gazed at him with wide eyes. "Yes," she stammered, her voice washing over him like a whispered caress. "I guess I lost control," she mumbled with a sheepish smile. Not even the soft moonlight could hide the rush of red filling her cheeks.

A veil lifted from his heart. He laughed and pulled her to his mouth, kissing her until they were breathless. When he spoke, he refused to remove his mouth from hers, murmuring against her lips. "Then we should finish what we started, luv." His hands grabbed her hips and coached her by sliding her up and down the length of his pulsing cock.

She moaned in the back of her throat and tightened her legs, following his direction and guidance. With a final shudder, he surrendered, closing his eyes to the world and losing himself to the sensations Carina commanded with every thrust of her body.

Aye, a goddess indeed.

CHAPTER 34

....

MORNING AFTER

Carina awoke the next morning to an empty bed. The sun streaming in from the windows bathed her in warmth. She rolled onto Marek's pillow. Just the faint smell of him rekindled a flood of memories. Although a little overwhelmed by what had happened, a lazy contentment filled her with peace.

She yawned and arched her back in a relaxed stretch, but a twinge of discomfort fluttered low in her belly. Marek had told her that any soreness would pass. He'd also promised next time would be better, but she doubted that since their first time was burned in her mind forever.

She closed her eyes. Last night, she couldn't control the desire Marek had awakened from some hidden depth within her, and never imagined wanting someone so much that her body ached for him. Marek brought those feelings to the surface, exposing them in a raw, basic emotion. She blushed as images replayed in her mind. And even though tender, a dull longing throbbed in her core at the thought of him inside her again.

Her stomach growled. She roused herself out of bed, splashed water on her face, and dressed. With a quick pull on the door, she hurried down the circular staircase, her purpose twofold—to eat breakfast and find Marek, but not necessarily in that order.

When she reached the bottom floor the unmistakable rumble of Marek's voice booming from the foyer greeted her. As if they were connected by an unseen tether that snapped taut whenever he was near, she turned away from the kitchen to find him. She rounded a corner in time to witness a group of men leaving through the main door. Marek was shaking hands with someone she didn't recognize. Although shorter than Marek, the man still looked intimidating with thick arms, a barrel chest, and long red hair that flowed over his shoulders like a panthera's mane.

Feeling self-conscious, she almost slipped back around the corner, but Marek glanced up. His eyes raked over her with an unfettered heat that caused her heart to somersault. The red-haired man followed Marek's gaze and smiled before exiting with the others, leaving the foyer empty except for Marek, Damon, Caden…and her.

Not sure what to do, she stayed rooted in place, a silent shadow watching Marek talk to the remaining men. With hard eyes and grim faces, their body postures were of warriors about to go into battle, and a whisper of concern chased through her mind.

Caden said something and Marek nodded. After Marek had formally spared Caden, the fair-skinned Tiwan had surprised everyone by swearing a loyalty oath to Marek.

Marek finished speaking and both men disappeared through the door, leaving it open behind them. An open door beckoned for another to follow and Carina doubted the invitation was meant for her.

Even from across the room, she noticed Marek's forehead etched with worry. The noise from her footsteps echoing off the walls as she approached seemed to disturb a lingering tension, like a trapped animal searching for a way to escape.

"What's wrong?" she asked.

Marek scrubbed his hands over his face before wrapping his arms around her. Normally, she would've enjoyed their closeness, but now the embrace combined with his silence stirred a growing fear.

"Marek?" The rise and fall of his chest as he sighed only intensified her anxiety.

"This is not how I wanted things to be."

"Just tell me," she insisted, the not knowing unbearable.

"The man with the red hair was King RiJec Gaiwane. His lands were attacked by Outlanders yesterday, two villages slaughtered. His trackers are following the marauders and he wants my assistance."

She stared into his somber face. A muscle ticked in his jaw and his narrowed eyes chilled her heart. She glanced at the floor and whispered, "So, you're leaving."

When she tried to slip away, he gathered her back into his chest. "Aye, I must. He's a neighboring king. We've sworn an allegiance to each other. Please, understand this."

Of course, she knew he had to go. She expected nothing less. But how could she let him leave knowing he'd be in danger. She lifted her head and fixed her eyes on his. "Then, I'm going with you."

From the frown on his face, she knew his answer before he spoke and anger flared in her belly. "Why not?" she demanded. "I'm just as good as your archers...if not better."

He stepped away. "No, Carina. I won't discuss this further."

"But I'm not finished," she persisted, blocking his retreat when he would've left the hall.

The grey flecks in his eyes darkened, but she refused to back down. "I can help."

"No." He spun for the door.

An irrational panic rose inside her, choking the air from her lungs. She reached for him. "Please, let me go with you."

He stopped when her hand grabbed his arm, but didn't look at her. When he finally turned, her boldness wavered. The set jaw and clamped lips told her that he was still going to refuse her, but he couldn't hide the sadness in his eyes.

"Carina," he whispered on a defeated breath. As if he needed to touch her, he buried his hands in the curls of her hair. She glanced away, unwilling to let go of her anger. She could ride a Criton and shoot an arrow with as much accuracy as any man, so his reluctance to even consider her offer chafed her pride. She'd proven herself in battle. She'd be an asset, not a hindrance.

Marek chuckled, and forced her head up to place his forehead against hers. "My stubborn girl," he whispered. "You're too important to me. I won't put you in danger."

"But it's okay to put *yourself* in danger?" Her hands slid up his chest as her body gathered strength. She tried to turn when his lips brushed against her cheek, but he held her. And when his mouth found hers, she shoved hard against him. He countered by grabbing the back of her neck. His other arm encircled her waist and locked her body against his.

Anger blistered through her veins, but his kiss remained soft. "Shh, Carina," he murmured against her mouth. "Be still."

His request dampened her resolve. Despite herself, her body shivered. She faltered. Her mind wanted to stay mad, but her body betrayed her and surrendered to the longing he could bring forth from deep within her.

"Don't make this more difficult for me and let us not part on an argument."

His voice seeped through her skin. He smelled of fresh pine and leather. Pressed against his chest with his hands splayed along her back, her anger evaporated. She opened her mouth and melted into his body. Her arms swept around his waist, clutching him tight. She could feel the desperation in his kiss and her body reacted with a need of its own.

He broke the kiss and rested his cheek against hers, breathing heavy. "You make it hard to leave."

"Then don't go."

"You know I must."

"Yes…I do." With a courage she didn't feel, she stepped from his arms. "Then go so you can come back to me."

The whoosh of leathery wings as Critons landed outside, and FireStrike's distinctive roar demanding obedience from his band, drew her attention to the open door. The iron fortified, hardwood entrance reminded her of a gaping maw about to swallow the only person she couldn't live without.

"Caden is coming with me because RiJec's men have tracked the Outlanders into the Bridal Lands and Caden can enlist his tribe to help. But Damon is staying here as captain of your guard." Marek lifted her chin with his finger. His eyebrows furrowed with the importance of his command. "Listen to Damon, and don't get into trouble." After a quick kiss on her forehead, he strode for the door but paused at the opening to look at her. His tortured gaze captured her soul and stole the breath from her lungs.

"I will be back, Carina McKay," he vowed, then stepped through the doorway. In a fluid motion, he jumped onto FireStrike. A few words later, the Critons took to the air with FireStrike and Marek leading the way.

She watched until she could no longer see them then closed the door to the world that had just snatched the man who had seduced her heart.

251

....

CHAPTER 35

DREAMS

Almost two weeks to the day after Marek left, Carina had her first nightmare. She hadn't been sleeping well to begin with, her mind simply refused to shut down. But the nightmare was worse than anything she could conjure up during wakeful, restless mental wanderings.

The nightmare became a regular interloper. They were on a hilltop on a beautiful, sunny day. Out of nowhere a storm developed, darkening the skies and swirling dust into the air. Black thunderclouds tumbled above the Dorrado landscape. Without warning and devoid of mercy, demons poured from the heavens. Swooping and diving, they attacked from everywhere, yet came from nowhere.

Lightning splashed across the sky illuminating his swords and chest armor in brief, intense flashes of light. Silhouetted against the roiling thunderheads, Marek protected her from the endless onslaught. She knelt beside him as his blades whirled in a continuous, unyielding cadence. To observe him was to see grace, skill, and a sheer masculine strength that filled her with awe.

As he fought the flying demons that always stayed beyond the reach of his steel, her heart would swell with such pride and admiration for the man who would be her warrior, her king...her lover that she would willingly forfeit her life to ensure his survival. But the sky would unleash a sudden blinding light, engulfing him. In agony, he'd crumble to the ground. As she screamed his name, his pain-filled eyes would find her and shatter her heart into a million jagged pieces before he burst into flame. Again and again the dream played out in her mind, night after endless night.

During the days, she drifted without purpose as lack of sleep and worry for Marek battered her body like a wave crashing down upon her. She lost weight, her energetic appetite gone. She tried to distract herself by attending a few formal functions, but the queen mother wasn't hospitable, which the Ladies of the Court took as an example to follow.

She could only find solace by taking to the skies on Mira. She'd get up in the morning, call Mira down from one of the cave dwellings, and spend the rest of the day flying, letting her mind drift with the wind.

Now, several weeks later, she sat on top of the tallest mountain along Marek's western border. A constant wind blew in her face causing her skin to pebble from the chill. She hugged her knees in a poor attempt to console the hollow emptiness inside her. Desolation, her constant companion, hung from her shoulders like a shroud.

Mira's impatient snort drew her attention. She tucked away her misery to check on her beloved creature. Mira stood next to a spindly tree, the sole living resident on the mountaintop.

She smiled at Mira's transformation. Her emerald skin shimmered in the late afternoon sun and her green eyes glistened with intelligence. She pawed the ground, her four claws digging divots into the only patch of dirt where the tree could take root, and snorted again.

Carina's lips curved up in a small smile. "I get it. You're ready to go."

Mira jumped into the air before Carina's feet were secured in the stirrups and pumped her strong wings to propel them skyward. She banked toward Stirrlan without guidance, rising until she caught a wind current to increase her speed.

They were gliding down the backside of a smaller mountain range when something in the distance captured Carina's attention. A glimmer of red sparkling in the fading sunlight before it disappeared over the horizon. She gasped as her cobwebbed heart sputtered to life, beating for the first time in weeks.

CHAPTER 36

RETURN

Carina landed Mira in a lower pasture near the castle proper. She rubbed Mira's nose before unbuckling the saddle and slipping the bridle from Mira's head. "Forgive me, but I must hurry," she mumbled. Abandoning the saddle and reins where they had fallen, Carina sprinted up the hill.

Dust hung in the spring air from the trampling feet of excited people and Critons, mixing with the sweet scent of wet leather and orange blossoms. She tried to organize her thoughts while dodging high-strung Critons and barking warrigals. For weeks, she'd rehearsed what she would say and how she would behave for Marek's homecoming, but she'd missed her opportunity. Why had she picked today to ride so far from Stirrlan?

She pushed past soldiers who were hugging their wives and sidestepped the horde of children who were jumping and behaving...well...like children. Sweat trickled down her back as she darted around people and animals. She should act more civilized and slow down, but the crowd thinned before she could adjust her behavior. Sliding to a stop, she scanned the diminishing throng.

Her heart stumbled. She batted away the tears that tumbled down her cheeks. Her body quaked as tremors threatened to toss her to the ground. He hadn't returned, her worst nightmare proven true. The world lost focus. Her body disconnected from her emotions to protect itself from the pain searing a hole through her heart. How could she survive without him?

She turned away from the dwindling group, already cutting herself off from the world when a stable boy holding the reins of a tawny Criton blocked her path. As they walked past, her breath caught in her chest. In the opening the Criton had just vacated, Marek stood. His eyes ensnared her. Nareen hovered beside him and a rush of jealousy chased through her veins. *She* should've been the one to greet him, not Nareen.

She walked toward him, but her pace was too slow. So, she ran. Her mind whirled. What should she do when she reached him—a low bow, hold out her hand for approval, a simple greeting? But when Marek smiled, she forgot about etiquette. Whatever royal control she was supposed to exhibit shed from her like a thin veil. She raced to him, her feet churning up small puffs of dust. And she didn't stop and bow when she approached, but jumped into his waiting arms. She held him tight, burying her head in his shoulder and digging her hands into his hair.

"Carina," he murmured.

Like a tonic, his voice healed her soul and breathed life back into her body. She lost control, sobbing against his neck as weeks of pent up feelings tumbled out of her in jumbled waves.

"My dear one, why are you crying?"

He smelled of Criton and leather as she hugged him, rejoicing in the strength of his embrace. When he had left, her loneliness had grown into an intolerable beast, sucking away her life force until she had become a shell of a person. As she clung to him, she vowed she'd never endure such heartbreak again because Marek would never leave her again. Whatever their journey in life, they'd do it together regardless of the danger or consequence.

Gently, he pried apart her death grip hold and lowered her to the ground. His hands cradled her face, his brows creased with worry. She skimmed her fingers along his jaw. "You were gone so long," she stuttered.

With a low moan, Marek wrapped his arms around her and buried his head in her hair. "I know. I'm sorry."

"I was going mad," she hiccupped. "I saw you dead. I'd wake up reaching for you."

Carina's pain speared his chest as if he'd been impaled by a harpoon cannon. He tilted her head and rested his forehead against hers. "I'm here now."

Tension vibrated off her shoulders. He had sensed her distress as soon as she jumped into his arms, disregarding all sense of protocol and risking disgrace. His heart tightened. He should've been here to watch over her.

She swiped at the tears leaving tracks down her dirt-smudged face, and inhaled gulps of air trying to compose herself. But it was too late for him. His control slipped through his hands like water. Dipping his head, he brushed his lips across hers just to taste her. Her immediate response inflamed him. Ignoring their public display and his mother's hiss of disgust, the kiss deepened. Her body molded to his. She slid her arms inside his riding duster and secured him around the waist.

Exhaustion plagued his body from the grueling pace he'd demanded to get home, but Carina's caress and the sweet smell of her revitalized him. The world disappeared, his focus narrowing to the girl in his arms. She was the craving. Only her touch, whispered laugh, and body could save him. A sudden need to claim her overrode coherent thought. He forced his lips from hers and wrapped an arm protectively around her before bending to whisper in her ear. "Come with me."

She nodded, but kept her head buried in his shoulder as he led her into the castle, leaving the door open for servants to close. When they reached the staircase for the master suites, he swept her into his arms. She linked her arms around his neck and murmured his name.

He wanted to go slow so they could get reacquainted, but holding her was too much. He was kissing her by the time he burst into the bedchamber, kicking the door shut behind them. She responded with an eagerness that fueled the desire racing through his blood.

He set her down beside the bed, his hands and mouth never leaving her body. She pressed against him, but he couldn't get enough of her. His lips whispered down her face. She moaned and bent her head, giving him access to the elegant curve of her throat. He shrugged out of his duster and resumed his exploration. He was a man parched with need and Carina was the cool water who would replenish his body and soul.

She shivered when his hands traveled underneath her riding tunic, and gasped when he nibbled an earlobe. She pulled his shirt out of his pants to touch his skin. Her hands glided up to his shoulders before her fingernails raked down his back, the pleasure-pain sensation driving him crazy. His cock swelled and throbbed. His teeth grazed along her jaw until he found her mouth and his tongue darted inside. He ravaged her with a savage, uncontrollable hardness, taking her breath into his lungs before replenishing her with his own.

With a teasing smile, her fingers skimmed up the sides of his body. He fisted his hands and struggled to remain still so she could remove his shirt. He trembled when her fingers breezed across his chest and stomach.

Although strangely pleased that he could endure the torment of Carina's curiosity, even a god couldn't withstand the need he held at bay. He savored the sensations from her touch, but his pulsing cock acted as a painful reminder of the desperation taking control of his body. So, when she glided a hand across his nipples, the time for tolerance was over.

He grabbed her riding tunic and yanked it over her head. Smothering kisses down her chest, he released the clasps to her undergarment and let it fall to the floor. She unbuckled his belt while he slid her pants down her hips and stepped out of his leathers. Desire, and a bit of fear, burned in her dark eyes. His thumb swept across her swollen lips before caressing down her jaw. Immersing his hand in her jumbled hair, he lowered his head until his mouth almost touched hers.

"You're beautiful," he murmured. Lifting her into his arms, he placed her on the bed and lay beside her. His mouth captured a breast and sucked while his hand squeezed the other. She moaned and arched her back, digging her fingers into his hair. Her body reacted to his touch with an enthusiasm that shot straight to his groin as if the Gods had made her especially for him. His tongue rolled over a nipple and she whimpered. Her rapid heartbeat heightened his desire and he plundered her parted lips.

She reciprocated by wrapping her arms around his neck and plunging her tongue into his mouth. He slipped two fingers inside her and she cried out, bucking against him with her hips. His cock surged. Gods, how he wanted her. His lips foraged down the front of her while his fingers moved inside her. She was slick and ready. Her every moan and gasp beckoned him to lose himself within the silky heat of her body. He clenched his teeth as hot blood lengthened his already engorged shaft.

Her hair cascading on the pillow around her, reminded him of the seductive nymphs of legend whose beauty would drive men insane. With her eyes closed, her eyelashes acted like small fans against her skin. Her breathing came in short, panting gasps. One hand, across the small of his back, held him tight while her other hand dug into the sheets until a twisted bunch of linen lay trapped within her fist. Her hips moved in rhythm with his fingers. He stared at her in wonder, memorizing her forever in his mind.

****

Liquid fire sizzled through her veins. His hands and lips were the spark, igniting her body wherever he touched. She was losing herself within his caress, his kiss...within the very essence of the man who could make her heart stumble with a sideways glance. And when his mouth covered hers, she returned his kiss with greedy lips until she had to break away to gulp air. But that didn't stop him.

He moved to her jaw then to her ear. His hand traced along her thigh and slid over the curls between her legs. She gasped when his fingers entered her causing the ache building in her belly to explode. The yearning for him magnified the more his fingers moved inside her.

He brushed his lips across hers. "This time will be different," he whispered with a sheepish smile.

Did he blush? As she gazed into his blazing eyes, her warrior king seemed hesitant. Concern, that simple display of compassion, pushed her over the edge. No one had ever shown such care for her wellbeing until Marek, who even now struggled to control his desire. She could no longer deny what her heart knew. She loved him. Her love was absolute. A part of her soul now belonged to another. A secret piece of her beating heart she treasured most, given away. She was the maiden and he, her champion, who unlike Azriel had the courage to claim her.

Basic emotions dominated her, coursing through her body in wild, uncontainable beats. She cried out when his teeth grazed across a sensitized nipple before seizing the other one. His mouth nibbled and sucked while his fingers and hands manipulated her body like a puppet. She pleaded for him to stop his unrelenting assault that had her teetering on the precipice, and satisfy the longing ravaging her body. She bucked and thrashed underneath him.

"Marek, I need you inside me..." she trailed off, lost to the passion consuming her. He covered her, the hard thickness of his shaft pressing against her. She spread her legs, begging him to stop the ache. He pushed his tip inside her and paused.

She grabbed his shoulders and opened her eyes. His rugged beauty stole the breath from her lungs. "Please..." she implored. *"Please."* The desire he'd nurtured within her burned out of control. And the longer he denied her, the more the flames scorched her.

He leaned forward and tracked kisses down her jaw. His breath tickled when he murmured in her ear. "As you wish."

In a fluid movement, he thrust deep inside her. She screamed, welcoming his thickness. He plunged inside her again and again. She wrapped her legs around his waist giving him deeper access, and dug her fingernails into his shoulders. The pressure inside her grew, swelling and expanding until every cell within her shouted for release, but she refused to let go. She flung her arms wide and seized the headboard, pushing against the iron bars in rhythm with Marek's thrusts, propelling him deeper.

She opened her eyes at the intensity of emotion racing through her. Unable to contain the rising force, she yielded to the wave crashing over her, racking her body with spasms. She rode the sensations ripping through her as Marek drove into her until he tensed and cried out. His body trembled. He collapsed on top of her and dropped his head to her shoulder, his breath hot against her neck.

She held him as the rise and fall of his chest slowed. Stroking his broad back with lazy fingers, she listened to their breathing return to normal while little tremors rippled through her. If she died this very moment, her last prayer would be to thank the Gods for giving her Marek.

He adjusted his weight and stroked her cheek before bending over to kiss it. "Carina," he whispered. The timbre of his voice shot through her like a brilliant star, blinding her even though her eyes remained closed. His teeth scraped along her jaw. "Carina," he murmured against her skin.

Unable to resist, she opened her eyes. The corners of his mouth twitched upward, and she smiled at his self-satisfied grin. Sleep lurked at the edge of her mind and her eyes flickered closed. For a day that had started out with such sadness, the wonderful turn of events left her exhausted as weeks of not sleeping caught up with her. She wanted to fall to sleep wrapped in Marek's arms, but could sense his penetrating gaze, waiting for her to speak.

She lifted her heavy lids and cupped his face with her hands. He turned his head and kissed her palm broadcasting small shivers down her arm. Her tongue felt thick and heavy, but somehow she whispered his name. He leaned forward, his head only inches from hers. Oh, how she loved him this close. She stared at the amazing man covering her.

"My Marek," she murmured again.

"Aye, luv." An undercurrent of concern threaded through his voice.

"We *must* do that again." She sighed and dropped her arms to the bed. Her eyes fluttered closed and a peaceful quiet settled over her.

Marek's laughter filled her heart as he grabbed her and rolled so she rested on top of him. She nuzzled into his shoulder while his muscular arms insulated her in a shelter of contentment.

CHAPTER 37

CALL OF THE CRITON

As if he'd never left, Marek took to the air on FireStrike as the sun rose with Carina cradled between his legs. They traveled far and fast so he could re-familiarize himself with the terrain. Although the season of rebirth was upon the Mother Source, a chill hung in the morning air. But Carina seemed warm enough snuggled against his chest. Saffron had hated Criton riding, so having Carina share his passion was an unexpected pleasure. As they flew over his land, peace bathed his heart in a warm glow.

Somehow, Carina had become part of his existence. Just like the air he breathed, he could no longer imagine a life without her. Her laughter brightened his soul. He buried his face in her hair, smiling at his sudden revelation. She'd been created for him, and he for her. He couldn't turn back even if he wanted to. She'd imprinted herself in his mind and burned her spirit into his heart. He'd never known such happiness.

As he wrapped an arm around her, he realized how empty his life had been before her. Carina had shown him what it was like to enjoy the company of someone so much it hurt to be apart. Her quarters were no longer necessary. He'd have the servants move her belongings into his chambers.

He spotted the mountain marking the edge of his northern border and guided FireStrike toward it. Steep, vertical sides contrasted with the trees and grass peppering the top of the flat peak. After FireStrike landed, he jumped off and reached for Carina. Holding her hand, he led her to the ledge overlooking a meadow with a wide, meandering stream.

"You can see forever," Carina whispered.

He stood behind her, enjoying her weight as she leaned against him, and pointed toward the morning sun. "Aye, if you look in this direction, you can see the lands of Saffron's father." He turned her ninety degrees. "And if you look over here, you can see the forest marking the border of King Gaiwane's lands. This is an excellent strategic viewing spot."

Carina laughed. "It's also a wonderful place to enjoy the beauty of the land."

He wrapped his arms around her and dipped his head to whisper, "Aye, that too."

****

She shivered at Marek's voice rumbling in her ear, and smiled. Her traitorous body would always give her away. She wanted to focus on the sensations zinging around inside her, but FireStrike bumping them from behind distracted her.

Marek released her to stroke FireStrike's sleek neck. "Don't worry, my friend. I won't forget about you." The Criton lowered his head, begging for attention, and Marek scratched behind his ear.

She watched the interaction between man and beast. Marek had wrapped his arm underneath FireStrike's neck while FireStrike stood over him, and both scanned the meadow below. An overwhelming sense of rightness enveloped her. Out of all the

Critons and men traveling this world, they'd found each other without the help of the Caller. What an amazing feat. Her heart swelled and tears threatened. Why was she so emotional? As if on cue, both turned to stare at her. She giggled at Marek's toothy grin.

Although the nightmares had ended, the image of Marek bursting into flames would still resurface in her mind during the quiet, tranquility of night. She'd lie in bed, her lungs constricted to the point she couldn't breathe as the flames consumed him. She tried to turn off her mind's eye, but the flames were unrelenting. Each time she witnessed his death a burning tendril would lash out and strike her too, vaporizing her heart. Once the flames finished tormenting her and the vision died to just smoldering embers, she'd draw comfort in the heavy weight of Marek's arm draped over her and the steel wall of his chest pressed against her back until the steady rhythm of his breathing lulled her to sleep.

At first, she cowered from the flames, praying for them to disappear. But their cruel persistence had ignited a spark within her and each night that ember grew until she no longer feared the fire. Burrowing into Marek's body, she'd curse the flames and dare the living inferno to try its best.

She shuddered, shaking her head to clear her thoughts from the ominous path they had traveled as Marek stepped from under FireStrike's neck. He pulled the bridle over FireStrike's head and uncinched the saddle before trailing his hand along the Criton's body to the pack on his hindquarters. With two pulls of a string, the pack dropped into Marek's hands. Holding the pack with one hand, he slapped FireStrike's rump with the other and the magnificent beast jumped off the edge. The breath rushed out of her lungs as she watched the spectacular, red Criton soar toward the meadow below.

Marek reached out with his free arm and hauled her close. "He'll be happier exploring instead of staying up here with us."

"And just what are we going to do?" she asked turning to face him, linking her arms around his waist. Aware they were alone, she nuzzled his neck. With ill-behaved fingers, she slipped her hands underneath his shirt to enjoy unhindered access to the muscular curves of his back. She smiled at his intake of air.

"Careful luv," he growled. "Or I'm going to jump to the second part of my plan first." His green eyes sparkled with a mischievous glint.

Her heart sputtered. "What do you have in mind?"

Instead of answering, he ducked his head and kissed her. His kiss deepened and she responded with a hungry eagerness until he broke away leaving her breathless. Grabbing her hand, they walked to a patch of grass where he pulled a blanket from the pack and spread it out before plopping down in the center of it. Resting his elbows on his knees, he patted the empty space between his legs. "Come, sit here." He smiled.

She hesitated. Except for a few obstinate rays, a threatening storm cloud obscured the sun. By sitting, Marek had interrupted the path of one of the shafts of light. Immersed in a soft glow, his eyes shimmered in the yellow radiance. She stopped breathing. A slow ache filled her chest. He was the most beautiful man she'd ever seen, and part of him belonged to her.

He reached out, beckoning her with his fingers. "Come, sweet one."

His velvet voice caressed her skin. She accepted his hand and settled herself between his legs. Relishing the strength of him all around her, her concentration stumbled as he pulled her against his chest. "Tell me what you have planned?" she asked, noting her breathy voice. She really needed to work on her self-control.

"Well, I thought we'd try an experiment."

She detected his uncertainty and twisted to scan his face. "What experiment?" she asked with an arched eyebrow.

He brushed a hand through his windblown hair. "I want you to call the Critons," he blurted with a tentative smile.

Her mouth dropped. How could he ask this of her when he knew her place in the scheme of royalty? She was a *nobody*. Just asking her to do this dredged up painful memories.

She shook her head and pulled away, but Marek's long, sinewy arms ensnared her. He stroked the side of her face before wrapping his hand in her hair and forcing her head to his shoulder. His breathing remained steady as he waited for her to relax into him.

"Carina, I know about your heritage. But I've never seen someone so carefree around Critons, and more importantly, how attracted they are to you."

Her eyebrows furrowed. Was he teasing her? She lifted her chin to look at him, but his face displayed warmth and reassurance.

"I don't understand."

He smiled. "Oh, my dear one," he murmured, kissing the top of her head. "Haven't you noticed that more Critons live on my land since your arrival? And more come each day. I imagine it won't be long before we start drawing attention."

"Is that good?"

Marek shrugged. "More Critons, aye, that's definitely good. More attention, well, that remains to be seen." With lazy strokes, he rubbed her arms up and down. She assumed he meant for his touch to be comforting, but it had the opposite effect and her pulse quickened.

"I know this seems like a useless endeavor to you, but maybe mixed bloods can have the gift too?"

She rolled her eyes. "There's never been a mixed blood Caller."

Marek sighed. "Not documented. But maybe that's why some kingdoms have more Critons residing on their lands...because someone living there attracts them."

She glared at Marek.

He frowned. "Will you at least try?"

"I don't even know how to call Critons."

"That's why you're going to *try*," he persisted. "Just lean into me and clear your mind. When you're relaxed, think about calling them to you."

She narrowed her eyes, filleting him with her best dubious look. She hoped the doubt splashed across her face and defiant tilt of her chin accurately depicted her disapproval for becoming an unwilling participant in this nonsense.

He chuckled and squeezed her. "Just try," he whispered in her ear. "If you do this for me, I'll do something for you."

Her heart fluttered as very unladylike thoughts invaded her mind. "You promise?"

Marek threw his head back and laughed. She really loved his laugh.

"Aye, *whatever* you want."

"Very well." She sniffed, and settled into his massive chest. Because she didn't know what else to do, she initiated the relaxation and visualization techniques Master Dupree had taught her. Closing her eyes, she focused on her breathing and filled her lungs with deep, cleansing breaths. She exhaled and relaxed her body, part by part, starting with her toes and working upward.

With her eyes shut, she opened her other senses to recreate a picture of her surroundings within her mind. She smelled the vague hint of rain imbedded in the air and heard the grass bending in the breeze. The darkening sky as thunderheads rolled across the heavens didn't concern her because Marek's body protected her.

Her breathing slowed to long, regular breaths as if sleeping. With a painful abruptness, her senses exploded into a state of hyper-awareness like the Mother Source had reached out and in a selfless act of sharing exposed her to the Mother's immense power.

Carina could see everything around her as if her eyes were open. If she concentrated, she could experience the world through the Great Mother—the nematodes tunneling deep within the rich soil, the joyous voices of the trees singing to the sun, the water in the valley far below tumbling and playing over the rocks as it journeyed across the land.

Her mind could touch the world with a simple thought. From outside her body, she stared at her physical being sitting between Marek's legs as he caressed her. They were so small in a world of vastness. She was life and death, all that was and would be. She had called and the Mother Source had answered, giving her access to the beauty and power of everything the Great Mother had to offer.

She smiled at the wondrous gift as power flowed into her. When every cell in her body throbbed with endless energy to the point she wanted to cry from the joy of life consuming her, she took another deep breath and marveled in her connection until a soft whisper told her to let go. Reluctant to dissolve the joining, but knowing she must, she threw her thoughts to the wind as if tossing a net across the water to catch fish and shouted the words, *come to me,* in her mind. A surge traveled down her arms and vanished through her fingertips jerking her out of the trance.

She pressed her fingers together wondering about the numbing sensation at the tips when Marek grabbed her hands and brought them to his mouth. With deliberate slowness, he kissed each finger. She watched in fascination as his lips nurtured each tip.

"Thank you," he murmured without skipping the attention he was lavishing on her fingers. "Now, was there something in particular you wanted me to do?" His voice sounded innocent, but the gleam in his eyes spoke otherwise.

Heat rose in her cheeks as she remembered to breathe. When he got to the last finger and gazed at her expectantly, she forgot about her glorious daydream.

"Well, um…" She cursed the flush warming her cheeks. "I suppose you could continue with what you were doing."

In a flash, she was lying on the ground with Marek towering over her. His eyes blazed and her heart skipped beats. His voice barely contained what his eyes proclaimed. "Is there a particular place where I should begin?"

Her eyes widened, and she nodded.

"Then tell me, so I can repay my enormous debt to you?" He leaned close, encompassing her entire field of vision. Not trusting her voice, she pointed to her mouth.

Marek chuckled low, bending over her. "Aye, that's an excellent place to start."

His lips brushed against hers, just a taste, before he kissed her with such unabashed intensity she succumbed, riding the sensations and passion flooding through her veins caused by the mere touch of the man who could command her total submission with just a whisper.

CHAPTER 38

....

BRANDING

A low warning hiss from FireStrike startled Marek awake. He untangled himself from Carina who groaned in disapproval when his arm slipped out from underneath her. Although he would've preferred coaxing her awake in a more enjoyable manner, his Criton ripping gashes into the Great Mother with his front claws demanded his attention.

He stepped into his pants and walked over to his winged companion, resting a reassuring hand on the Criton's neck. FireStrike snorted and postured by extending his wings as he stared at the northern skyline. Another growl rumbled from the back of his throat.

"What do you see?" Marek followed FireStrike's gaze, scanning into the distance. Although the skies were clear and the meadow empty, the hair on the back of Marek's neck rose. He knew his Criton well enough to realize something was wrong. They were at the edge of his border, still within his lands, but probably out too far to have traveled alone with Carina. His desire to spend time with her might've just put their lives in jeopardy.

He hustled over to Carina. Immersed within the blanket, only a foot and a few coils of hair braved exposure. In a short amount of time, she'd become the center of his life. The invisible pull toward her, an attraction he'd never experienced with any other woman, intrigued him. She'd come from nowhere and enchanted him. His precious Carina had captured him in an unbreakable hold that he'd gladly carry for the rest of his life—for as long as she would have him.

He strapped on his claymore and welcomed the silence, letting the cool air revitalize his body. But the peaceful serenity erupted into chaos when FireStrike's earsplitting roar flooded his ears a millisecond before the mountaintop burst into flame around him.

The deafening sound jerked Carina awake. Heat prickled her skin. She lay frozen, her heart plummeting into her stomach. She recognized the scene unfolding, it had replayed in her mind, night after night.

Critons filled the sky. They screamed and strafed the bluff before rising to dive at them again. A large, yellow female with red streaks on her wings dropped from the heavens, blocking the sun to spew fire at Marek. Reacting with warrior reflexes, he dove behind a boulder and huddled close to the rock while flames surged around him.

FireStrike bellowed in defiance as riderless Critons lashed at him with their teeth and claws whenever he tried to take flight. The ground trembled from FireStrike's flame shooting skyward as he kept the brunt of the Critons at bay.

The yellow Criton screamed. Her gold eyes focused on Marek. She maneuvered around the rock to corner him, her wings flapping in strong, powerful strokes.

Marek jumped away from the boulder. His eyes blazed. "Run Carina," he yelled while drawing his sword.

Although Carina admired Marek's courage, she knew he had no intention of attacking the Criton. He was the distraction so she could escape. Paralyzed with fear, she watched her nightmare break out of the dream realm to unravel before her in vivid color. The overheated air undulated with a life of its own. The acidic odor from the yellow Criton's flame scorched her lungs. Her body shook and her mind shattered.

Marek had transformed into a wild beast with crazed eyes and lips curled into a snarl. His bare chest, rising and falling from the adrenaline pumping through him, glistened with sweat. He was magnificent, standing in front of the yellow Criton with his sword raised overhead. If the Criton got close enough, he'd use his claymore as a spear in an attempt to penetrate the strong muscle surrounding her chest cavity.

"Carina!"

She jumped at his shout. His face twisted in fury.

"Run!"

His speckled eyes locked onto hers and held her spellbound as if inhaling her essence into his soul. A sob escaped her, and tears ran unchecked down her face. Sadness and regret glimmered in his eyes. But what ripped her apart, what devastated her, was acceptance. Acceptance for the sacrifice he was about to make on her behalf. She'd spent her life trying to find her way, to discover her place in the world, and when she finally realized her path the Gods were about to snatch it from her.

She stood on shaky legs. None of the Critons, including the yellow female, seemed interested in her. A strange calm settled over her because now she understood what had to be done. The flames in her dreams had coached her well, hardening and fortifying her. She inhaled the heated air, breathing it deep into her lungs, and summoned her courage.

The yellow Criton had Marek cornered. The steady flap of her wings kept her stationary in front of him. She raised her head skyward and bellowed in triumph with her victory near. An immediate cacophony of responding Critons permeated the air. Carina covered her ears, grimacing from the noise.

No longer able to protect Marek, FireStrike lay gasping for breath. Blood streamed down his body from gaping lacerations. Critons surrounded him, their heads low, ready to finish the attack.

As if mocking Marek, the yellow Criton lowered her head and opened her mouth to display rows of sharp teeth.

Marek extended his arm, preparing to throw his sword. Even in this desperate hour, Carina marveled at his powerful chest and the rippled muscles lining his abdomen.

Arid blasts of air slammed into Carina's body from the heat emanating inside the Criton's mouth. Wisps of smoke escaped between the gaps in the animal's teeth. The angry Criton roared, exposing the flames at the back of her throat. Although death by Criton fire was considered honorable, only sadness gripped Carina's heart as she stepped in front of the man she loved.

"What in Haden are you *doing*?" Marek pulled her into his chest, shielding her with his body.

"I'm not leaving you," she whispered with quiet determination.

Marek's eyes slashed through her. A muscle ticked along his jaw. His strong hands gripped her arms in a painful hold, but she didn't waver. She stood tall and lifted her chin, daring him to challenge her.

He stared at her a moment before his resolve crumbled. Brushing his thumb across her cheek, he buried his fingers in her hair. She leaned into his hand as unexpected tears bubbled over her eyelids and tumbled down her face.

He kissed her forehead. "I told you to run," he murmured without conviction.

She wrapped her arms around his waist, his closeness comforting her. This was her defining moment. The flames had prepared her. She knew her fate, and for him, would accept her destiny with grace. She kissed the hollow pulse point in his neck, welcoming his strong heartbeat against her lips.

"The Criton isn't after me," she whispered. "I'll distract her so you can run."

Marek didn't flinch. His voice remained steadfast. "You'll not sacrifice yourself for me."

She swallowed the sobs in her throat and buried her head into the curve of his neck. She would sooner die alongside Marek than live without him.

The yellow Criton squealed.

Why hadn't the animal flamed them yet? And why had the Critons ignored her when they attacked? A sudden idea jabbed at the back of Carina's mind and with that kernel of thought, a glimmer of hope chased after it. The thought—a small, persistent pearl of awareness—grew as she fed it attention and ran through scenarios. Her back stiffened when she reached only one possible conclusion.

Could it be? Did she have the courage to make the challenge? Would it even matter? Or just bring about their end sooner? Her lips curved up.

Marek frowned at her small smile. "What are you thinking?"

"Remember what you told me that night at Azriel's Tears?"

Marek's brows furrowed in confusion, so she answered. "That a thinking woman is something to fear."

His dazzling smile rewarded her, supplying her with the final raw nerve she needed. Before he could stop her, she grabbed his hand and stepped around him to stand in the angry Criton's path. She interlaced her fingers within his and relished his hand tightening around hers.

The Criton snorted, spraying dirt upward in small, swirling eddies.

Carina stared into the amber eyes peering back at her. "This man is mine," she shouted. "He's mine and you will not take him from me."

The Criton's eyes narrowed. She lowered her head as if getting a better glimpse of the man whose hand Carina held. Air churned around them when she slowed her wing beats and dropped to the ground. Showing dominance, she stood erect on her hind legs with her wings spread wide.

"What's going on?" Marek moved up next to Carina, his sword at his side.

"I'm not sure," Carina whispered, not willing to voice her thoughts for fear that if she spoke them the ridiculousness of her idea would be proven true.

The yellow Criton planted her front feet on the ground and tucked her wings at her sides. She leaned forward and inhaled their scent, cocking her head sideways as if memorizing them before arching her powerful neck to gaze down at them.

From everywhere, Critons descended from the sky like falling stars. They formed a ring around them, pushing and shoving each other for space on the crowded mountaintop.

"In the name of the Gods..." Marek muttered, sheathing his sword.

Not giving in to her fear, Carina stood her ground with her feet spread apart. A soft ringing filled her ears. The humming grew into a constant, nagging hum. But she refused to show weakness by looking away. The noise clogged her mind, escalating in strength until it pounded in her head. The ground spun beneath her and she clutched Marek's arm to keep from falling.

Marek's worried voice called to her, but she couldn't answer because she'd fallen into the Criton's eyes, drifting weightless in darkness. A force pushed at her mind. Unrelenting and unwavering, the Criton demanded entry. Carina resisted, throwing her consciousness against the invading presence, but the Criton throbbed with ancient power.

A vast intelligence converged on her. The sudden influx of knowledge overloaded her mind and she screamed. Her legs buckled. Marek caught her and held her against his chest. The pressure increased into an insistent, inescapable crescendo, shredding her to pieces. Thoughts, not her own, saturated her mind. She arched her back and rode the agony reverberating through her. Using Marek as a lifeline, she pressed his hand against her temple. "She's in my head. Get her out of my head."

Carina floated in a plane of unconsciousness, losing a battle of wills against a Criton straining to take over her mind. Although she couldn't see him, Marek's nearness calmed her. For him, she would do this. For him, she'd surrender herself so she could return to him once more. She didn't understand how she knew this, but a simple, reassuring feeling encouraged her to let go.

She inhaled the heated air, and as much as it terrified her, released control of her mind. Light erupted in a brilliant flash as energy scorched every nerve ending in her body with an all-seeing wisdom. Her mind split in two, but she absorbed the pain with a calm acceptance.

"You are the Caller, my child," boomed a gravelly, multilayered voice.

Carina clenched her teeth as she merged with the great creature, their minds blending into one.

"I have waited years for you to call me. Now your time has arrived to fulfill your destiny."

Carina grimaced as the Criton's consciousness saturated her mind. Through their connection, she experienced the animal's immense despair as if it were her own. She extended herself to offer comfort and brushed against the limitless knowledge of the mighty animal. The information flooded Carina's mind faster than she could process and she withdrew to a distant corner within herself, cowering like a child. Even though her touch was small, she learned enough to recognize a normal connection shouldn't cause such pain.

"Yes, my mind has melded with many, but I am not meant for you." The Criton's voice echoed from everywhere around and within her. *"I am sorry for the discomfort, but there is no other way."*

Carina bit her bottom lip in restraint.

"My children have lost their way since the Caller's absence. They have grown unruly because they do not know the serenity of bonding with the missing half of their soul. They seek other paths to overcome the ache in their hearts, and I cry for them."

Carina listened as the intensity of the Criton's words pounded in her head, chipping away bits of her sanity with each word spoken. She didn't know how much longer she could keep the madness from consuming her.

"Although my children are strong and worthy Critons, they will no longer readily submit to a rider. But you are here, and have experienced the power of the Great Mother. Using the Mother's sight, you will see the strands of light connecting the souls of my children to their riders and guide them for the joining. Be forewarned, however, you can only show them the path. The ultimate decision to bond lies with each rider and Criton. Although joining is the nature of their destiny, free will always controls. One can fear the unknown and choose to deny the bond calling.

I am old and my strength wanes. The time has come for another to lead. Your courage gives me hope for our continued co-existence, my young Caller."

Just when Carina was sure her mind would explode the presence disappeared, taking the power and knowledge with it and leaving behind a cold emptiness in the vacated space.

****

Marek held Carina close as the yellow Criton lifted her head and roared. The thunderous cry from answering Critons shook the mountaintop. Carina's eyes fluttered open and he stared at her in disbelief. Her beautiful, brown eyes blazed with energy.

Carina moaned and tightened her already death grip hold on his hand. Desperation and remorse crawled through his veins. This was his fault. He'd asked her to call Critons on a whim, just to see what would happen. His recklessness had thrown her into an internal power struggle where he couldn't protect her.

Marek stared into the Criton's face. "Release her," he commanded. The Criton's shining eyes pulsed and he resisted the urge to glance away from the uncharacteristic glow.

A stinging sensation spread across his chest and down his arms like hundreds of fire rifas biting his skin. Caught within the hypnotic hold, an increasing pressure pushed behind his eyes. A heaviness descended upon his mind as fingers probed through his memories like slithering tentacles, prying for answers with meticulous scrutiny and without regard to the discomfort caused. "You must release her," he pleaded without force, his voice lost within the gold pools of light.

At first the exploring feelers were an inconsequential nuisance, like a sandfly buzzing about his face. But the strain compounded, doubling on itself until it became a thick, unbearable harmonic. He clamped his mouth shut and fought the urge to shout out in anguish.

A thought popped into his brain, clear and unmistakable. A thought not his own.

"You are the lifemate, the protector. Guard her well."

The Criton's eyes flashed and a blinding light enveloped him and Carina in a cocoon. Unable to withstand the surge of energy raging through him, he yelled to the heavens and held onto Carina by sheer will. A heartbeat later, the brightness vanished taking his strength with it.

Carina lay like a rag doll in his arms. After a quick check, relief flooded his body at her strong, steady pulse. He gathered her into his chest and carried her to the blanket on wobbly legs. Trying not to wake her, he laid her down and covered her with his duster before sitting beside her.

He fisted his hands and grimaced in pain. His eyebrows furrowed at the swollen, red mark on the palm of his left hand. An impression he couldn't decipher was emblazed on his skin. He reached for Carina's hand. She too, had the burn.

They'd been branded, but why? He was missing something obvious, but exhaustion clouded his mind. His remaining strength ebbed from his body on a quiet exhale. He glanced at the yellow Criton. She could easily kill them.

As he lay beside Carina and pulled her into his chest, he spared the Criton one last look. She seemed content with whatever she'd done to them. He even thought her head bobbed in a gesture akin to satisfaction. Air buffeted him as hundreds of Critons hurtled themselves skyward, leaving the mountaintop empty except for FireStrike who had hobbled over to stand protectively over them.

FireStrike's wounds must not be severe, he thought before succumbing to the fatigue riding his body.

....

CHAPTER 39

CALLER OF LIGHT

Marek's palm ached, but he ignored it and encouraged FireStrike to land in front of the castle. Carina rode sidesaddle with her head pillowed against his chest. Her breathing remained steady, but her responses were sluggish as if she couldn't wake from a deep sleep. He slid off FireStrike with Carina cradled in his arms.

Damon raced up, concern etched across his face. "What happened?"

"I'm not sure," Marek admitted. "Find the healer, and have someone tend to FireStrike."

"Straight away, Sire." Damon rushed off.

He was reaching for the door when Nareen flung it open. She blocked the entrance. Her hands rested on her hips, and anger hardened her face. "This public display of affection is very inappropriate."

Fire flashed through Marek's body. "Mother, remove yourself from my sight before I do something I regret."

Nareen's face turned ashen. After a whispered apology, she retreated into the castle.

He strode past Nareen and climbed the stairs two at a time. But the stairs he'd clambered up and down since childhood quickly transformed into giant stepping stones. By the time he reached the top floor, his lungs screamed for air and his legs trembled. He fought the urge to lean against a wall to catch his breath, and used his shoulder to push the chamber door open. He eased Carina into bed before wiping sweat from his brow, struggling to calm his racing heart.

Carina looked so pale. His fingers trailed across her cheek, willing her to awaken.

"Come back to me," he murmured. But she didn't heed his call. He was a king, a leader of his people, and a commander used to being obeyed. So, when she refused him, his body shook. Like Tiwan poison darts piercing his chest, his heart stumbled.

He grabbed her hands and interlaced her delicate fingers within his. Her small bones seemingly so fragile, yet capable of so much strength. His beautiful Carina, the magnificent woman who challenged a fire-breathing Criton to save him, lay motionless and cold in his bed.

He rushed to get a blanket. Although away from her for mere seconds, her body quaked by the time he returned. He covered her before caressing her face. "Shh, dear one. You're safe. We're safe."

Her eyes flew open and pierced him with an unseeing gaze before slipping shut again. "Marek," she whimpered.

"I'm here, luv." He kissed her forehead.

He was leaning over her when the healer burst through the door and pushed him out of the way.

Damon and Caden stood at the entrance, offering silent support. Marek was about to dismiss them when his eyes lost focus and the room spun under his feet. He reached for the wall to steady himself. *What in Haden's spit?*

Damon and Caden entered the room to assist, but he waved them away. When the dizziness subsided, he pushed off the wall to stand helplessly beside the bed.

Carina struggled with the healer. Her eyes stayed closed. Her chest labored in shallow, panting breaths. Her whisperings remained the incoherent ramblings of the delusional.

"What's wrong with her?" Marek asked.

The healer shook his head. "I don't know. What happened?"

"We were attacked by a large, yellow Criton."

"What?" Caden asked.

Marek mistook the incredulous look on Caden's face as disbelief and his blood boiled. "Aye," he snapped. "An enraged female would've killed me if Carina hadn't stepped between us. Then something happened—" Marek's legs buckled.

Caden grabbed Marek's arm while Damon seized the other.

"Sire, you should sit," Damon insisted.

Marek accepted their assistance into a chair. He too, was getting worse. He struggled to remember, but a fog had rolled across his mind zapping his ability to think. And the more he concentrated, the more the elusive threads of coherent thought danced deeper into the thick vapor.

Carina's mumblings rose. Only her voice could penetrate his confusion. He had to get to her, but his legs refused to work.

Out of nowhere, Caden knelt in front of him. "Forgive me, Sire, but I must know. What did the yellow Criton do?"

Marek stared at Caden. His body shuddered, but not from being cold. He concentrated on swimming through the haze so he could remember the only thread that mattered—Carina. "Her eyes glowed," he whispered. "And we were surrounded by light."

He closed his eyes at the memory. "I was so tired. When I woke, the Critons were gone and Carina wouldn't wake up." Just speaking rendered him breathless.

Caden reached for Marek's arm, but Damon drew his sword and pointed it at the Tiwan. "You will not touch the king."

Caden remained kneeling and raised his hands in a non-threatening gesture. "Damon, I know you're protecting your king, but if what I believe is true, then both Marek and Carina will die soon if we don't take action."

Damon's brown eyes narrowed. His face twisted with uncertainty. He glanced at the healer.

The healer shrugged. "Magic is at work here. I might be able to bleed it out of her, but she's already so weak, I fear bleeding would cause more harm than good."

"We must hurry," Caden urged.

Damon nodded, but kept his sword drawn as Caden grabbed Marek's right wrist. Frowning, Caden reached for Marek's left. Caden's hands shook when he noticed the marking.

Damon leaned forward to see the wound. "Looks like a burn."

"Carina's right hand also has the mark," Marek gasped. Breathing had become a battle, the simple inhale and exhale of air a crushing weight on his chest.

Caden bowed his head and placed both hands on Marek's knee. When he glanced up, tears rimmed his eyes. "Sire, you already have my loyalty, but henceforth, I pledge my tribe to your service."

Damon's eyes widened. "But the Tiwan Tribe has never sworn an allegiance to anyone."

"That's only because Tiwan Callers have always bonded to Tiwan men."

Damon shook his head. "What in Haden's breath are you talking about?"

"Carina is the Caller of Light and Marek, her bonded lifemate. Now, help me get the king to his bed so they can finish the bonding process."

When Damon hesitated, Marek nodded. "Do it, Damon…I must be with her."

As soon as Marek stretched out beside Carina, air that had been unobtainable moments before flooded his lungs. His heart stopped floundering and thumped in a strong rhythm, pumping blood through his body and feeding strength into his arms and legs. The fog in his mind dissipated. He slid an arm underneath Carina's head and pulled her against his side. His heart swelled and throbbed with a dull ache because of the beautiful woman he held. His cure and salvation, she breathed life back into his dying body.

His touch seemed to have a calming effect on Carina. She buried her head into the crook of his shoulder and draped an arm across his chest before settling into a deep sleep.

The healer placed a blanket over them and straightened on his large frame. He crossed an arm over his rounded belly and cupped his chin with a meaty hand. His brows furrowed in concentration. "Sire, I don't pretend to understand this. But unless you wish me to stay, I'll check on you later."

Stroking Carina's hair, Marek drifted on a plane of peaceful awareness and could have fallen asleep with everyone in the room. "Go," he murmured so as not to wake her. The healer bowed and left.

Both Caden and Damon turned for the door. Although Marek longed to close his eyes and let sleep wash over him, he needed answers. "Caden," he called quietly.

The men stopped. Damon looked at Marek for direction and Marek nodded, giving him permission to leave.

"I'll be outside if you need me, Sire." Damon bowed before disappearing from the room.

"What did the yellow Criton do to us?" Marek asked.

Caden's lean body moved with the fluid grace of his people as he walked over and settled into the chair Marek had just vacated.

"Although Callers cannot Critonbond, they can bond with a lifemate. The yellow Criton who attacked you was the Criton Matriarch, Naya. Carina must have claimed you and Naya found you worthy because she sealed your bond. You are now Carina's bonded lifemate.

Marek shook his head. Sleep pressed on his body and lurked at the edge of his mind, but he was alert enough to know Caden had to be wrong.

Caden persisted. "Sire, why did you choose Carina instead of her sister?"

He shrugged. Carina mumbled at his movement, but he silenced her with a kiss to her forehead. "I'm not sure. I just couldn't leave her."

Caden nodded. "Probably because the bond tie was already calling you, but you both didn't realize it."

"How can Carina be the Caller?"

"Because Carina's mother was Alaine, the previous Caller. Alaine was the most powerful Caller we've ever known due to her strong bond with her lifemate."

Marek frowned. "No, your words cannot be true. Carina's mother was a servant in King McKay's household."

Caden bowed his head and sadness filled his voice. "I don't understand why Alaine lied about her identity and why she didn't try to find her way back to us. I only know that Alaine's mate died in a battle against dark Criton riders and she disappeared. For two full cycles we searched for her, but finally decided that both she and her unborn child had been killed."

"How do you know Carina is Alaine's daughter?"

"Because she wears Alaine's medallion, the symbol of the Caller. And more importantly, because she called Naya," Caden answered with an awed reverence. "Untrained, yet she summoned the Criton Queen."

Sleep whispered in Marek's ear, encouraging him to slip into its embrace like a lover's kiss. The temptress called to him, ran soothing fingers down his body, and sang softly in his mind, commanding him into her care. He fought the desire. Until he knew what happened so he could protect Carina, he wouldn't surrender to the luxury of sleep.

"If she's the Caller, why did the Matriarch attack us?"

Caden leaned forward and placed his elbows on his knees, his long, blond hair shadowing his face. "The Matriarch would never attack the Caller. Something you did must have appeared threatening."

Caden raised his eyebrows, but Marek ignored his curiosity. When the Matriarch attacked, he'd been standing over Carina putting on his steel. Maybe Naya had misinterpreted his actions.

He glanced at his palm. Except for some tenderness, the pain had subsided. "And our hands?"

"Once Naya deemed you worthy, she used her power to mark you. Your brands are the same Criton heads that are on Carina's medallion. Once the swelling subsides, when you hold hands your Critons will intertwine just like the necklace."

Caden stared at Marek for a moment. "Sire, it is a great honor to be chosen as the Caller's lifemate. But, it can also be a great burden."

What burden? Marek thought, unable to voice his question. Sleep, the ever persistent seductress, refused to play fair and his body couldn't resist her call.

"Carina's necklace now can be detached into two separate Criton medallions. The pendants enhance your power and will remain separate and distinct until one of you dies, then they'll merge into one piece again."

"Why am I so tired?"

Caden stood, preparing to go. "Naya forced powerful magic on you in order to leave her mark. The fact you are tired is good because that means you and Carina have a strong bond. Your bodies need time to absorb her magic, which can only happen when you two are touching."

Caden paused at the door. "You would've died if you had stayed apart because alone your bonds cannot absorb that enormous amount of energy."

Marek wrapped both arms around Carina and closed his eyes. Caden's voice drifted over him.

"One thing is certain. Carina is not just the next Caller. She's an extremely powerful one."

Marek smiled. He wanted to tell Caden that she was so much more than just a powerful Caller, but had slipped into that relaxed just before sleep stage. Tiny sparks of heat shot through his body acting as a reminder of Naya's magic. Silence blanketed him in a soothing tenderness. Now he understood his purpose in life and knew exactly where he was supposed to be—holding the woman who had captured his heart and soul. With a soft exhale, he yielded to the sorceress murmuring in his ear and joined his lifemate in the dream realm.

CHAPTER 40

....

KINGS' ARRIVAL

Carina basked in the sun's rays, the warmth restoring and rejuvenating her body. Practically lying on top of Marek with her head buried under his neck and his arms wrapped around her, she couldn't imagine a better place to be. The light filtering into the room indicated they had slept a long time, but she didn't have the desire or energy to move.

From the shelter of Marek's arms, she remembered what happened. She'd never been so terrified, but not for herself. She shuddered at how close she'd come to losing the man she loved more than life. When she had stepped in front of Marek, her only thoughts were of protecting him. She smiled at her foolish, self-sacrificing courage. Not even the mighty Criton Queen had expected her to jump between them. She closed her eyes at the memory of Naya's voice booming inside her head and the pain cascading through her body. Naya had forged some mental connection between them, and in a strange way, a part of her now missed Naya's reassuring presence.

A deep sense of contentment washed through her knowing Marek was safe and asleep beside her. She inhaled his earthy smell and savored the soft rise and fall of his chest. He looked so peaceful with his long eyelashes pressed against his skin. She reached up to touch his face, but winced when a spasm shot through her right hand. She rolled off him to look at her injured appendage and gasped at the puffy red Criton staring back at her. The angle of the Criton's head reminded her of her mother's pendant and her hand drifted toward the necklace. With a groan, she bolted upright. A small sob escaped her lips when each hand cradled a separate piece of the pendant. Somehow, she'd broken the necklace—ruined it. Tears slipped down her cheeks.

She heard a rustling of sheets and found herself surrounded by a wall of muscle as Marek leaned into her. "What's wrong?"

She gazed into his concerned eyes—eyes that offered her sanctuary when she needed to disappear—but couldn't find her voice. So, she stared at him, holding the broken necklace.

****

Marek's lips twitched into a soft smile. With gentle thumbs, he wiped her tears away before framing her face with his hands. "Caden told me this would happen."

"What?"

His fingers roved through her jumbled hair then drifted to the back of her neck. He noticed the slight catch in her throat and the rosy flush in her cheeks. He loved how his touch could affect her. He unhooked the clasp to her necklace, but lingered to enjoy her fluttering pulse reverberating through his fingertips before focusing on the pendant.

With the medallion in two pieces, each Criton head cradled a separate eye crystal. He intertwined the heads so the crystals overlaid each other to become one, and then pulled them apart again, marveling at the intricacy.

"According to Caden, after the Matriarch marked us, the medallion was designed to separate. We are each supposed to wear one because they're magic."

Carina slid her hand down his arm and interlaced her fingers within his, trapping the two pieces between their marked palms. The sandwiched pendants throbbed with power.

"See?" Marek pulled her against his chest. "Do you feel it?"

"Yes." She gazed up at him. "I do."

"We're bonded," he whispered against her ear. She shivered, and images of his hands stroking other parts of her body filled his mind, the necklace forgotten. He brushed featherlight kisses down the beautiful curve of her neck and collarbone.

"What do you mean, bonded?"

Her breathy voice encouraged him. "You're the Caller and I'm your lifemate," he murmured, his lips never leaving her skin.

She twisted and stared at him with wide eyes. *"What?"*

He frowned, and leaned against the mahogany headboard. Obviously, he needed to explain what he knew before his perusal could continue. "You are the Caller of Light."

Her lips puckered. "I already know that part," she grumbled. "What about the bonded mate part?"

He arched an eyebrow. "And how do you already know that?" Unable to deny himself, one hand traveled to her breast.

She hesitated, but pushed him away. Curling her legs underneath her, she rested her knees against his thigh. "Because Naya told me," she explained as if to a child.

His hand settled on her knee, not his first choice of placement. "She spoke to you?"

Carina nodded. "In my head. I also heard her when we were in the Bridal Lands, but thought I was dreaming."

He exhaled, trying to wrap his mind around the enormity of the journey he was about to undertake. He wanted to think finding

293

Carina had been a coincidence, but knew better. His fate had been preordained, just like hers. They were meant to be lifemates, each a half to make a whole.

Her beautiful eyes stared at him, expecting his answer. But her lips captured his attention. They pouted because he hadn't yet told her what she wanted to hear. Oh, how he wanted to kiss those teasing lips. He shook his head in a feeble attempt to clear the picture of her naked body pinned beneath him from creeping into his mind.

"You claimed me when you challenged the Matriarch. Naya sealed that claim by marking our hands."

Carina's eyes dropped. She fiddled with the necklace. "You're bonded to me?"

"We're bonded to each other."

Her shoulders slumped. "I'm sorry."

His brows furrowed. Cupping her face, he lifted her chin. "Why do you say that?" She squirmed and tried to glance away, but he refused to release her.

"Because I'm mixed. And because Naya forced the bond on you."

"Is that it?"

Her eyes narrowed. He could almost see her mind churning as she decided whether to be angry or relieved. He needed to improve his odds. Without considering the enormity of what he was about to say, he blurted, "Caden said the Matriarch would only bond us if the feelings were mutual. Alaine was your mother, and you're actually a Tiwan of full royal blood. Alaine must have bedded King McKay in order to claim he was your father so you'd have a birthright."

The blood drained from her face, and he grimaced. Maybe he could've been a little more tactful, but he really needed to kiss her.

"My mother was Alaine, the Caller?"

"Aye." He smiled. Rubbing her cheek with his thumb, he fought the urge to drag her to him.

"And Naya bonded us because we feel the same about each other?"

He nodded. His eyes never leaving her full lips as a small smile curved them deliciously upward.

"Regin isn't my real father?"

He shook his head.

"And you want me just as much as I want you?"

"Aye." He could stand it no longer. He wrapped his fingers around the back of her neck and crushed her to his chest, kissing her firmly on the mouth.

She mumbled something against his lips, but he was done talking. "Later, Carina. We can discuss this later." He rolled so her body lay trapped underneath his, and buried his fingers in her thick hair. Pushing her shirt up, he squeezed her breast to a hard peak.

She moaned and wrapped a leg over his calf to secure him in place. Her fingernails grazed down his back igniting the blood in his veins. He plundered her mouth, biting her bottom lip and tasting her with his tongue. She returned his kiss with an urgency that multiplied his spiraling desire. Her touch and lips seduced him and his cock hardened in response. Fire shot to his groin in a savage, primitive need to claim her. He lost all sense of control as her body writhed beneath him.

A rapid knock on the door stopped the journey of his mouth to her breast, and stilled his hand from seeking entrance into her welcoming heat. She groaned in discontent, and he smiled. "Leave us," he shouted. He would deal with the fool who had disturbed them later.

"I'm sorry, Sire." Damon's muffled voice filtered into the room. "But King McKay and a King Remy are waiting for you in the receiving room.

Carina's body tensed. Concern flooded her chocolate eyes.

No one should have that power to cause her discomfort. "I'll be down in a moment," he snapped.

"Very good, Sire."

"What does he want?" she asked.

"Shhh." He nuzzled her neck one last time before climbing off the bed.

Carina pulled a sheet up in front of her as if hiding behind it would shield her. "What if Regin wants to take me back?"

He shook his head. "That won't happen. We have an agreement."

"But, I don't want to go back."

The anxiety in her voice pierced his heart. He sat on the bed beside her. Her bottom lip had disappeared between clamped teeth. He caressed her cheek with the back of his hand before digging his fingers into her tangled hair. She rested her head in his hand and a fierce protectiveness rose inside him. King McKay would never get her back.

Reluctant to leave, he brushed his lips across hers. He meant for his kiss to be reassuring, but passion burned just under the surface, hot and demanding. Carina's instant reaction as she grabbed his shirt and pressed her supple body against him fueled his burning blood. With a silent curse, he broke the kiss and rested his forehead against hers.

"Rest your mind, Carina. I won't let anything happen to you. No one will take you from me." He spoke with a quiet, but deadly conviction. When she nodded, he stood and left her warmth, smell, and body alone in his very large bed.

CHAPTER 41

....

TIME TO CHOOSE

Marek stormed down the hall, anger seething underneath his skin. And leaving Carina alone when he should be lying naked beside her just infuriated him more. What in Criton's breath was King McKay doing here? He could think of only one possible reason, and the rage he'd contained with Sampson once again crashed against its cage, screaming for release. The beginnings of a battle strategy formed in the back of his mind. If Regin planned on reclaiming Carina, he'd go to war to defend her. Regin was on very precarious ground.

He vaulted down the stairs and threw the receiving room doors open without regard for decorum. Marissa squeaked in surprise and bolted out of her chair at the sudden entrance. He scanned the long, narrow room. Light spilling in from the bank of windows along the western wall reflected across the ceiling in sparkling shimmers. In front of the stone fireplace, at the opposite end of the doors, a circular rug dominated the wood floor. Chairs and tables were scattered across the plush throw and situated in small groupings to foster conversation.

Both men stood at Marek's entrance. Regin puffed out his chest, but even at his full height, the top of his head didn't reach Marek's shoulder. Regin wore a red, velvet cloak with a fur-lined collar that billowed behind him as he strode over to clasp Marek's forearm in greeting. Regin smiled, but the smile did not reach his eyes.

"Welcome King McKay," Marek said in a clipped tone as he disengaged from Regin's grip. "I would've offered a proper welcome, but didn't realize you were coming."

If Regin noticed Marek's irritation, he ignored it and pointed to the man standing behind him. "Marek, this is my new son-in-law, King Villar Remy."

At the mention of his name, Villar nodded and summoned Marissa with an outstretched hand. Marissa hurried over to take his arm.

Marek assessed King Remy with a passing glance. Villar appeared to be the exact opposite of Regin. From his tall, lanky build to his calculating eyes and self-assured manner, Marek's instincts urged caution.

"Welcome King Remy," he said with a curt nod, but didn't extend his hand. Marek noticed Villar's eyes flash at the inadequate greeting. "And Marissa, congratulations on your marriage."

Marissa blushed and her eyes fluttered down. "Thank you."

Marek admired his restraint as the bonds of being Carina's protector hummed through his veins like wildfire, demanding justice for Marissa's betrayal. But now was not the time to confront her, and like a panthera stalking its prey, he could wait. Still, he had to ignore the mental image of his fingers closing around her delicate throat and squeezing until he choked a confession out of her. Marissa had acquired a formidable foe.

"So, I don't mean to sound abrupt, but what brings you?" He walked over to a high-backed chair and dropped into one before gesturing to the other chairs stationed around him. While the men settled into their seats, a servant placed a tray of pastries and a decanter of ale on a table before scurrying from the room.

Regin's eyes lit up. "How delightful." He grabbed a small candied delicacy with powdery sugar and popped it into his mouth before pouring ale into his goblet. "We're here to check on Carina," he mumbled with a mouthful of sweets.

"Really?" Marek struggled to control the rage. "You could've sent a runner."

Regin waved a chubby hand in dismissal. "I prefer to see how my daughters are doing in person. He leaned over his belly and pinned Marek with his best glare. "To make sure they're happy."

Marek dug his fingers into the armrest and ignored Regin's inference of mistreatment. With a sideways glance, he focused on King Remy. "And you Villar?"

Villar motioned to Marissa who stood behind him with her hands resting on his shoulder. "My adorable wife wanted to see her beloved sister and I couldn't deny her."

Marek glanced at Marissa who stared at the floor. In addition to Marissa's discomfort, she seemed different as if the fire within her had dampened. From her defeated look, he might've pitied her...once.

"So, where is my daughter?"

She's not your daughter, you pompous ass. Marek pressed his lips in a firm line and prayed his voice sounded sincere. "She's not feeling well."

"Oh my. I hope nothing serious."

Marek didn't have the opportunity to answer. Like a cool breeze soothing the rage within him, the receiving doors swung open and Carina stepped into the room. She paused just inside the entrance, surveying everyone with a quick glance. She opened her mouth as if to speak, but remained silent as her gaze settled on Marek. He could sense her anxiety. Drawn to her, he jumped from the chair and moved to stand protectively beside her.

Regin clapped his hands together and pushed out of his chair to waddle over to Carina. Pulling her from Marek's grasp, Regin hugged her like a lost loved one, and then stepped away to give her a thorough up-and-down appraisal. "My." He smiled. "You look beautiful."

****

Carina glanced at Marek. Apprehension curled up her spine. Never in her life had Father offered any sort of praise. Dread coursed through her, a dark foreboding chilling her heart.

"Thank you, Father," she murmured with a slight curtsy. Her eyes shifted to Marissa and the man Marissa stood next to. He was impeccably dressed in a black doublet with a single-breasted closure and gold trim. A short, black fencing cape covered his shoulders. He seemed pleasant enough, but something in his bulbous eyes and the way they darted back and forth, fueled a disquiet within her. He whispered something to Marissa who blushed before darting forward.

"Father is correct. You look like a proper mistress."

Marissa would never give a compliment without throwing a dagger behind it. Although she covered it in flattery, Marissa had just reminded everyone of her mixed heritage. Carina forced a smile.

"It's nice to see that you haven't changed. Should I use your proper title?" Carina glanced at the man whose smile caused the hair on the back of her neck to rise.

"She's Queen Remy now, my wife." Villar approached and extended his hand.

Carina placed her hand into his and dipped into a shallow curtsy. He pulled her up and raised her hand to his mouth. When Villar's dry, thin lips touched her skin, energy pulsed through her, singeing her nerves and leaving her feeling exposed. His black eyes bore into her as if trying to worm his way into her mind.

She eased her hand from his grasp, but the chill continued to spread through her body. The beginnings of a headache throbbed in her temple, matching her rapid heartbeat. She fisted her marked palm and quelled the urge to run.

As if on cue, Marek's muscular frame pressed against her back. His touch was like water to flame, cooling her body and quashing the intensity of emotion swirling through her. But warning bells reverberated in her ears, cautioning her that King Villar Remy was not as he appeared.

Unnerved, she looked away from Villar's piercing gaze. The land had not completed a full seasonal cycle yet, so the agreement between Father and Marek was still in effect. Did Father intend on breaking the arrangement? Her chest tightened at the idea of going back to Brookshire. She didn't even think of it as home anymore. She belonged in Stirrlan with Marek.

When in the company of royalty, etiquette dictated she remain quiet unless spoken to, but she'd never been one to follow protocol. "Father, why are you here?"

Regin spread his hands wide. "I've come to see how you are adjusting to your new life, my dear. But before we catch up, I need to discuss some important business with King Duncan. Maybe you could show your sister the palace in the meantime?"

Carina glanced at Marek who gave her a reassuring smile. Although ripping out her fingernails seemed more enjoyable than escorting Marissa, the words spilled out of her. "Of course."

Before she could move away, Marek's arm slipped around her waist. Her body shivered when he bent and whispered in her ear. "Don't worry, I'll find you later."

His lips brushed across her cheek causing a fire to ignite in her belly. Desire, swift and hot, wove through her. He released her, but his impact rippled through her like an unending wave. Remembering they weren't alone, her cheeks flamed. Except for Marissa, whose mouth hung open, no one else acknowledged the possessive display.

Marek's attention was meant to calm her, but it had the opposite effect. Although she doubted anyone noticed, the tension rolling off his shoulders vibrated through the air. She wanted to wrap her arms around his waist and hold him close, to shield him with her body and ease his distress. But for now, they seemed destined to play the part Father and Villar had scripted for them. So, when Marek stepped away and motioned for Villar and Father to sit, she turned to Marissa.

"Shall we go?"

"Yes." Marissa smiled, her eyes glittering.

As she led Marissa from the room, the image of a white-footed lemming being lured into a venomous urutu pit popped into her mind.

CHAPTER 42

··

HIDDEN MEANINGS

Since the queen mother had made it clear that the castle fell under her jurisdiction, Carina rushed through the indoor tour by sticking to the main hallways and avoiding the upper floors. Only when they were outside on neutral ground did she relax, grateful to have avoided Nareen altogether.

They strolled in silence, following a cobbled path toward the Criton barns. Carina inhaled the lilac and amaryllis infused spring air as a mild breeze ruffled her hair and whispered through the leaves. At first, the peace soothed her mind. But gradually the silence grew too silent. Instead of calming her, the quiet grated on her nerves.

By now Marissa should've been fully engrossed in the wondrous details of court life as queen and the unfortunate disappointment Carina must feel because of her status as mistress. With every murmured rustle of a leaf, every soft twitter from a tanager, every muted crunch of their feet on the pebbled path, the stillness taunted her. Unable to resist the challenge, Carina's curiosity overrode better judgment. Although she couldn't believe her ears, she opened the topic of conversation.

"So, how did you meet King Remy?"

"Oh, he started courting after King Duncan left," Marissa said with a shrug.

That was it? Nothing more? "So, what is it like being queen? Are Villar's holdings substantial?"

"Being queen is everything I've always imagined it to be," Marissa gushed while smoothing out the front of her velvet, green dress. "And Villar's holdings are more elaborate than King Duncan's." She waved her hand in the air to emphasize Marek's meager estate.

By her condescending manner, Carina could see the beginnings of the old Marissa peeking through her veil of silence. For the next few minutes, Marissa bragged about the holdings under Villar's control and the improvements he'd made in anticipation of additional Critons settling on his lands. But as Carina listened, she got the impression that Marissa was intentionally keeping the discussion light or inconsequential.

They had reached a small grove of poppy trees. A wood bench rested underneath the canopy, looking over a vast meadow. Although she would've continued walking to the barns, with a flourish Marissa plopped down on the bench, muttering something about the heat. She looked up at Carina and patted the empty space next to her. "Sit."

Carina hesitated, and ignored the unease brewing in her stomach. A small herd of gambels grazing in the meadow caught her attention as she dropped onto the bench. She very much wished she could be flying toward that herd on Critonback instead of sitting beside Marissa.

"You seem to have many Critons?"

Carina's mind snapped into focus. "Marek has been very fortunate." She shrugged, not willing to divulge the secret she kept hidden on the palm of her hand.

"Villar thought I was the Caller when he married me. But of course, I can't summon those dreadful beasts."

Carina stifled an involuntary gasp. "Why did he think that?"

Marissa stared at her with cold, calculating eyes as if studying her like a bug under a magnifying glass. "Because up until you left, our lands were known for their abundance of unbonded Critons." She raised an eyebrow? "Didn't you realize that?"

Carina shook her head as a rising panic clawed at the back of her mind. Self-preservation urged her to be careful. The air that had smelled so sweet moments before turned sour. She had to know the real reason for Father's arrival.

"Marissa, we've never been close." She overlooked Marissa's snort of confirmation. "So, why are you here?"

"Villar is disappointed I'm not the Caller."

"But he can't blame you for that."

"No, but he can blame Father who said I was. Villar gave Father a large amount of land in exchange for my hand. Now, he feels cheated and has threatened to go to war."

Carina's marked hand flew to her chest. "But you're his wife. Isn't the love you feel for each other enough?"

"He doesn't love me."

The icy bitterness in Marissa's voice chilled Carina's blood.

"So no, I'm not enough." Marissa fixed her stark, blue eyes on Carina. When Carina held her gaze, Marissa's bravado evaporated. Marissa's lower lip trembled and she brushed away a tear before glancing away.

Carina paused. She'd never seen Marissa cry before, at least not with authentic tears. But this time Marissa seemed to be in real pain. "Is there something you wish to discuss?" she asked.

Marissa bit her lip. With a fresh set of tears rimming her eyes, she placed a hand on Carina's arm. "Do you love your life here with Marek?"

Carina drew back, stunned. She never expected Marissa to ask such a question, let alone care about the answer. But Marissa was looking at her with such wide-eyed anticipation, she felt compelled to reply. "I do."

Marissa's face crumpled. "Oh."

Carina stared at Marissa's hand. The ostentatious rings on her fingers glittered in the sunlight. Her tailored dress and immaculate appearance embodied royalty. She was a perfect example of wealth and status, living a life Carina thought Marissa always dreamed about.

"You don't like being queen?"

Marissa lips turned down. She sighed and looked at the ground. "Oh, I love being queen," she mumbled. "It's just what I expected, except..." She folded her hands together and placed them on her lap.

Carina leaned forward, encouraging her to answer. "What?"

"He can be so...rough."

Carina shook her head, not understanding.

Marissa twisted an emerald ring on her finger. Her voice dropped to a whisper. "On our wedding night, he didn't even bother taking off my gown." She sniffed and dabbed at her eyes with a green handkerchief that appeared from a fold in her dress. "And I loved that gown, full of lace and beads. Afterwards, the dress was ruined." She glanced at Carina and blushed.

"I'm sorry, Marissa." Carina placed a reassuring hand on Marissa's shoulder. If Marek hadn't been gentle, her first time at the pools could've been full of regret.

" 'Tis nothing, really." Marissa smiled, composing herself. "But he's an animal when it comes to that and I find myself exhausted most of the time because he's eager to have children." A teasing smile pursed her lips. "Marek has taken you to his bed, yes?"

Dread filled Carina's gut. She had no intention of discussing private matters, and busied herself by brushing away some unseen speck of dirt from her blouse, trying to formulate an answer. "Well, um—"

"Oh, Carina, you're so modest," Marissa exclaimed. "Of course he has, you're his mistress after all. That's good, because you're experienced now." She settled into the bench, fluffing her dress like a hen ruffling her feathers, content with the knowledge she'd just gained.

The tiny hairs on the back of Carina's neck bristled. Somehow, she had divulged a vital bit of information without knowing it. She tilted her head and studied Marissa. Marissa glowed with her newly acquired wisdom.

"Marissa, we both know that you have no interest in me, unless it benefits you in some way. So, just tell me. Why are you here?"

Marissa glanced up through her eyelashes. Although mostly hidden beneath her brows, the glint in her eyes stilled Carina's heart. Anxiety crawled up her spine. She no longer wished to hear Marissa's response. But for once, Marissa answered.

"Father is a smart man. When the Critons started leaving, he realized you were the reason his lands were populated with so many of those filthy creatures. Father told this to Villar and together they've come to take you back." Marissa's lips twitched up at the edges. "You're to become Villar's mistress," she clucked.

"No!" Carina jumped to her feet. "Marek won't agree."

"Are you sure?" Marissa extended a hand out in front of her and studied her painted fingernails. The long, red nails reminded Carina of a griffon's claws, bloodied after ripping into dead carrion.

"I'm sure."

Marissa spoke with a confidence that fostered the growing knot in Carina's stomach. "If Marek refuses, then Father and Villar will declare war against him. Together they're a formidable team. And since Marek stands little chance of winning, I suspect he'd most likely die in battle. Could you live with yourself? If Marek dies?"

The air rushed from Carina's lungs. She stood frozen, unable to move. She must've had a horrified expression on her face because Marissa's tone softened when she glanced up to look at her.

"Oh Carina, it won't be so bad. But this is your fault, you know. We wouldn't be in this predicament if Marek had chosen me. Now, we must make the best out of what fate has handed us.

Marissa shrugged. "I suppose I love Villar, but since he can be so…" she paused, searching for the right word, "…demanding, it'll be nice to have you as a distraction so I can take care of the more important matters of the castle." She stood and brushed a hand down her dress. "As you attend to my husband, I will attend to affairs more befitting a queen."

Tears loomed in Carina's eyes, but she refused to cry in front of Marissa. She squared her shoulders and lifted her chin. Marissa underestimated her. She was no longer the submissive, little mixed blood girl cowering in a corner seeking acceptance. "How did you become so cruel?"

Marissa's face clouded. "You better respect your new queen, or I'll make your life very unpleasant."

Carina held her ground, refusing to apologize as years of torment at Marissa's hands surfaced. She'd always deferred to Marissa, hoping that if she was nice, she'd someday earn Marissa's love. But now as she looked into Marissa's powered face, Carina could only see a selfish, coldhearted person.

Relief washed through her, cleansing her of a dark insecurity she'd carried with her all her life. Marissa would never accept her and there was nothing she could do to change that simple fact. Her heart swelled when she realized that she didn't care anymore. Because she'd found Marek, someone to love, and who loved her in return. No matter how large the estate Marissa presided over as queen, or the expensive dresses she owned, or the quality of her possessions, Carina would always have so much more. Carina smiled, at peace with herself.

Marissa's eyes narrowed, squinting in uncertainty. "Why are you smiling?"

"I forgive you, Marissa. I forgive you for the way you treated me while growing up."

Marissa shook her head in confusion. "What are you muttering about?"

A whisper brushed across Carina's mind, distracting her. She scanned the surrounding area, but the presence disappeared as soon as it touched her. She would've dismissed it, except she recognized the feeling, as if Marek had reached across the distance between them and called to her. Panic gripped her heart. She spun and raced toward the castle.

Marissa's shrill voice pierced the air. "It's too late, Carina! There's nothing you can do!"

CHAPTER 43

....

TRUTH BE TOLD

Regin sauntered over to a bank of windows overlooking the grounds. "You have many unbonded Critons."

Marek stepped beside Regin, but kept King Remy within sight. Villar refilled his goblet and settled into his chair. Although Villar remained quiet, he appeared very interested in the conversation.

"My lands are accommodating for Critons."

"But they're more accommodating since Carina's arrival, yes?"

Marek lifted his shoulders in a casual shrug. "I haven't noticed."

Regin's lips twisted upward. "Well, it doesn't matter. I've come to take her home."

"We have an agreement."

Regin turned away from the windows to face Marek. "Of course. And you'll be compensated for any inconvenience. Now, have a servant pack Carina's belongings."

Marek's hand twitched, longing for his sword so he could run a blade through Regin's gut to end the man's useless blathering. "And if I refuse?"

Villar spoke in a matter-of-fact tone as if reciting a pledge. "We'll declare war. We'll burn your lands, kill your men, and drive you from your home. Then, we'll take Carina."

Marek assessed the man who had just threatened him. Villar swirled the ale in his goblet with a relaxed twist of his wrist. His body posture remained subdued as his long legs draped across the small table in front of him, his dark eyes revealing nothing. While Regin would appoint a champion to fight for him, Villar seemed capable of handling his own battles. Marek decided not to underestimate him.

"Then, we have a problem."

Like a sunburst, Carina stormed the room, her eyes wide with a quiet panic. Marek jumped between her and the other men, shielding her with his body.

Regin's face clouded. "Although, I find your decision regretful, Carina will do as she is told. Now daughter go pack your belongings. We leave within the hour."

Marek heard Carina's small gasp. She tried to step around him, but he kept her tucked behind his back.

"Father, please don't do this. I want to stay here with Marek."

Regin shook his head. His eyes narrowed to slits. "I decide what's best for you, and you *will* come home."

Except for Carina's breath puffing out in little, ragged pants, silence filled the room. With her body pressed close, she acted like a buffering wind keeping the brewing tempest inside him at bay. He'd learned to expect the unexpected from Carina, so when her hand touched the small of his back, he readied himself for the consequences of her actions. She peeked around his shoulder because he still wouldn't let her move away.

Her voice quaked. "So, I can become Villar's mistress?"

Rage slammed into the cage bars, an inferno blazing to life. His entire body tensed like a coiled urutu about to attack. He clamped

312

his teeth in restraint and clenched his fists, trying not to launch himself at Regin. Adrenaline strengthened his muscles and fortified his body, preparing him to do what was necessary to ensure no one touched her. Regin teetered on the edge of this life.

Regin raised his double chin. "If that's what I decide."

Villar unfurled from the chair in a slow, fluid movement just as Marissa entered the room. He beckoned Marissa to him before speaking. "Carina, your father and I have discussed your status as my mistress. My queen also assures me that you'd make a fine addition to the Remy household."

You are her protector. She's yours. The words ripped through Marek's mind, loud and demanding. A firestorm coursed through his veins. Only Carina's soothing influence kept him from ripping Villar's throat open. But even with her reassuring hand, his pulse quickened at the thought of Villar's blood pooling on the floor.

Somehow, Marek kept his voice steady, concealing what boiled inside him. "Carina is going nowhere. But you will depart immediately and won't stop until you are off my land. My riders will ensure you do as I've commanded." He nodded to a servant who scurried from the room.

Villar stepped forward, but hesitated when Marek bladed his body and wrapped an arm around Carina, pinning her at his side. Villar placed his goblet on a table and rested a hand on the hilt of his sword. "King McKay has the legal right to recall a daughter he's given as a mistress. No king will stand beside you when we return to burn your lands."

"She's not to remain my mistress."

"Marek, please—"

Marek silenced Carina by interlacing his fingers within hers and uniting the Critons on their marked palms. Warmth shot up his arm and radiated throughout his body. Carina's intake of air and wide-eyed expression confirmed she experienced the same rush of energy.

He kissed the back of her hand, and smiled when her lips parted in a silent gasp. A healthy blush flamed her cheeks.

He cleared his throat. A nervous apprehension burned in his belly for having to discuss such a private matter in front of an audience.

****

Marek smiled and the world around Carina stilled. She never thought she would fall in love, but the Gods had blessed her with a beautiful gift. They'd given her Marek—a man who could soothe her mind with a whisper and steel her heart with a touch. He couldn't meet her gaze as he rubbed her hands with his thumbs in a slow, lazy rhythm. His sudden uncertainty made him more endearing.

Damon and Caden burst into the room and stood on either side of the door—two pillars of raw strength harboring steel. They remained alert, waiting for Marek's command. Both men glanced at Carina, their eyes unwavering. Their presence reassured her just as Marek's next words knocked the air from her lungs.

"This is not how I wanted to ask you." He rolled his eyes toward the others in the room. "And you need to know I made my decision before yesterday."

She nodded, realizing he was referring to what happened on the mountain with Naya.

"From the moment I first saw you on Mira's back, diving down the cliff face and racing toward the forest floor, no one has ever bewitched me as you have. I'm drawn to you like no other." He paused and seemed at a loss for words.

Carina heard a loud hiss from Regin when Marek mentioned her Criton riding, but Father's presence was a distant buzz at the back of her mind. Marek commandeered her attention.

The sun filtering into the room caressed Marek's face, accentuating the flecks in his penetrating eyes, eyes that could spy upon her soul. She lost herself within his gaze. The room narrowed until only one man existed.

He caressed her cheek. "But, as I look back, I think the Gods sent me to find you, so together we could save each other." He pulled her close until their bodies touched and stroked her face before entwining his hand in her hair.

Her body flared at his touch, her core temperature jumping upward in large increments. Unable to resist, she brushed her thumb across his bottom lip. His mouth fascinated her. She smiled, remembering the pleasure those talented lips could elicit from her.

"Carina." He whispered her name like a hallowed word.

A longing rose within her, an ache only Marek could fulfill. She held onto rational thought by a sliver of thread. If he didn't get to the point soon, her overheated blood would scorch through the wispy string, the only thing keeping her from dragging him upstairs. A sly grin spread across his lips. *Could he read her mind?*

"Will you be my wife and queen for the entire world to witness?"

Her heart thumped two full beats then stopped altogether. A ringing in her ears made it difficult to concentrate.

Marek bent his head and whispered, "Carina, my love. Will you marry me?"

Chills ran down her body. "You want me to be your queen?"

His eyes sparkled. "No. I want you to be my wife first then my queen."

She shook her head, trying to clear her mind from an onslaught of emotion. She wanted nothing more, but wavered.

"Now, see here—" King McKay choked on his words when Damon's blade appeared at his throat.

"What about Nareen?" she blurted.

A soft smile crinkled his eyes. "I'll talk to Mother. She's not happy here. I should've released her years ago so she could go home."

Uncontrollable tremors racked her body. Fairytales didn't come true. She must be sleeping, lost in a wonderful dream. She opened her mouth then snapped it shut. Somewhere along her journey she'd given herself to this man. Everything she had to offer was his to take.

Worry deepened the lines around his eyes and his smile disappeared. Did she cause his concern? She didn't want to be the reason for his discomfort. He'd rescued her from a life of solitude and loneliness. This man standing before her was her savior, her world. Her lips curved into a small smile at the thought of becoming his wife.

Marek growled, and rested his forehead against hers. "Woman, you drive me crazy. Answer me."

She cupped his cheek with her hand. "Aye, Marek Duncan. I'll marry you."

Marek's grin lit up his entire face. He gathered her in his arms and swung her around, laughing. She wrapped her arms around his neck, and although tears played at the corners of her eyes, laughed with him. Before he stopped their wild spinning, his lips ravished her mouth, everyone in the room forgotten. When her wobbly legs touched the ground, only his embrace kept her from falling.

The hair on the back of her neck rose, warning her of the eyes stabbing into her back like twin blades. She turned to confront the man she would've loved as a father if only he could have offered her a tiny place in his heart.

Regin looked like a volcano about to spew fire. His white-knuckled fists trembled at his sides, and his lips were compressed into such a thin line, they were almost nonexistent. She used to shrivel at her father's aggressive posture, but now she kept her head high and her back stiff. She would never cower from this man again.

Marek's voice rumbled through her, a soothing presence standing at her back with his hands resting on her shoulders in a possessive display.

"King McKay, you no longer have authority over Carina. She's to become my wife and queen. And Villar, neighboring alliances *will* aid a king whose queen has been threatened."

Villar spoke with a calm assuredness. "But only if the union has been blessed by the father of the betrothed. And I doubt Regin intends to give his permission."

Carina lifted her chin. The words burned in the back of her throat, hot and eager to escape her lips. Her eyes raked over everyone in the room, demanding their attention. "Regin McKay isn't my father," she announced with a confidence that shattered the hushed silence.

Marissa gasped and flung her hand to her chest. Marissa's bottom lip trembled as she looked at Regin, anticipating his response. Carina didn't know if fear or excitement spurred her half sister's reaction.

The color drained from Regin's face. "How dare you make such an accusation," he stammered. "I should lay a strap to your back for your insolence."

The rumble building in Marek's chest reverberated through her body as the snarl escaped his mouth. She turned to restrain him, but Caden stepped in front of them before she could act. Caden raised the hilt of his blade partially out of the scabbard to expose the top half of the glimmering weapon. Carina had never seen such malice etched across the warrior's face.

"You will not speak to the daughter of Alaine Springborn in such a manner if you wish to keep your tongue attached inside your mouth."

317

Regin's jowls jiggled as he shook his head. "What in bloody Haden are you talking about?"

Marek's deep throated laugh burbled through his body and echoed across the room. "You're such a fool, Regin. You had the Caller under your nose for twenty-two years and never knew it."

King Remy edged forward, his black eyes shiny. "The Caller," he whispered.

Villar's closeness oozed across Carina's senses like a thick, slow-moving sludge. She resisted the urge to shrink away as her skin pebbled from a sudden chill.

Regin looked ill. A green tinge rimmed his mouth. His eyes were glazed and a noticeable wheeze accompanied his breathing. "But she's the daughter of a servant," he mumbled.

Metal clearing leather whooshed through the air a moment before Caden's blade caught the fading light spilling in from the windows. "She's a full blood royal princess of the Tiwan Tribe, and you'll show her respect."

Regin stared at Carina in disbelief. Carina supposed she should have felt vindicated in some way after all the years vying for his attention and love. But only pity encircled her heart for the aged man standing before her, and for wonderful memories that could have been, but never would be.

Marek called to Damon and Caden. Both men approached. Caden's sword glistened in the light while Damon's fingers encircled the hilt of his blade. "Ensure they are well beyond my border before you return."

"Aye, Sire." They answered in unison.

Regin shuffled toward the door. Carina expected him to say something, but he ignored her. A shiver slithered down her spine when Villar's eyes skimmed over her as he passed by. Marissa, never one to leave a room without speaking, broke the stillness.

"You always were a foolish girl."

318

"I'm sorry your life didn't turn out the way you wanted," Carina murmured. She hadn't meant for her remark to cause such a reaction, but Marissa's face paled and Villar's eyes darkened like a rising storm.

After the room emptied, Marek enfolded her in his arms and pulled her into his chest. She tipped her face against his shoulder and nuzzled underneath his chin. His strong heartbeat thrummed in her ear as she reached up to caress the back of his neck.

"Marek?"

"Aye, luv."

She smiled at his endearment. "Do you think they'll declare war against you?"

"Against us," he corrected. "Threatening to go to war is very different from starting one. But if they do, we'll be ready."

Together they stared out the window and watched the sun disappear below the horizon.

CHAPTER 44

CALL OF THE MATRIARCH

Carina stood with a foot propped on the bottom fence post, looking across a large pasture. Grazing ovine dotted the grassy landscape. Occasional bleats from a young kid who had strayed too far from its mother pierced the silence while the older animals settled down for the night.

With the constant arrival of unbonded Critons, Marek had started stocking his pastures again. But she barely noticed the ovine dotting the field like white powder-puffs. The beautiful sunset with its brilliant colors streaming through the sky captured her attention, like an artist had thrown his watercolors across the canvas, blurring the vibrant hues into a once in a lifetime creation. The breathtaking view bathed her in peace.

The day had been stressful at Stirrlan. Nareen had departed with her court. During their farewells when Carina had curtsied and wished Nareen a blessed day, the queen mother had returned the curtsy. Carina smiled. Maybe she could salvage their relationship after all.

A cooling breeze blew across her face, sweeping the hair off her neck and rustling the pasture grass in an undulating sea of motion. She hadn't been sleeping well. And now with the flurry of Nareen's departure over, she hoped to get more rest. But a growing unease dampened her optimism. The dreams were back. Only this time, except for a fleeting impression of someone calling to her and of time running out, she couldn't remember them.

Caden had told her that Naya communicated through dreams. According to Caden, she had to answer Naya's call by traveling to Crios to be welcomed as the next Caller of Light. But life had been so hectic for Marek, she'd downplayed her lack of sleep to avoid burdening him. She yawned and closed her eyes.

The sound of gravel crunching from behind forewarned of someone approaching. She knew whose boots those footsteps belonged to, and anticipated his touch. To her satisfaction, muscular arms wrapped around her, and she leaned into his chest. Resting her foot against his shin, she reached behind her to stroke his cheek. His mouth traveled along her neck, spurring tingling shivers to splinter and spiral throughout her body.

"You're still not sleeping?"

She frowned. He must've seen her traitorous yawn. "No," she admitted.

Marek sighed, and turned her so she faced him. His hands framed her cheeks while his probing eyes searched. She tried to glance away, but he held her. An eyebrow arched upward. "Naya?"

"I don't know." Wrapping an arm around his waist, she pressed into him. Her other arm traced up his back and gripped his shoulder. She inhaled his smell—a combination of leather and Criton—into her lungs. His arms tightened, locking her against his body. She clutched the back of his shirt, feeling safe and loved.

"I'll talk to Caden so we can plan our journey. Caden assures me that I can enter Crios since we're bonded." He kissed the top of her head. "Otherwise, I wouldn't let you go."

She leaned back to stare into his eyes. Those curious, sparkling flecks floated amid two endless, emerald pools. She loved his eyes the best. Although—with a blush she knew he noticed—she loved other parts of him as well. But his eyes held her, encouraged her, gave her strength; and most of all, displayed his love for her. Although afraid of traveling through the Realm of Light into Crios, she wouldn't be alone. And if her father did declare war, they'd brave the fight together.

With a sudden gasp, her thoughts scattered as Marek's lips roving down her neck made it impossible to think. She shuddered at his touch. Yes, she definitely loved more than just his eyes.

His strong arms swept her off her feet and carried her toward Stirrlan, the castle she now called home. She dug her fingers into his hair and surrendered her heart, mind, and soul to the man who had taught her not only how to live, but how to love and be loved.

The End

Also by TJ Shaw

Divergent Bloodline

While tracking down a killer, clues lead homicide detective, Viviane Taylor to suspect, Julian DeMatteo. From the get-go, DeMatteo unsettles and irritates her. He's a force she has never encountered, someone who excites her even though he is forbidden. Her instincts warn that he's hiding something and she is determined to uncover those secrets.

As king of the vampires, Julian DeMatteo protects the immortal clans. So, when the beautiful, bullheaded cop embroils herself within his world, he must choose between the woman who reminds him of the humanity he has lost or his loyalty to his people.

As confusing emotions awaken inside her, Viviane can either accept her fate as the one chosen to save the immortal race or lose her soul to darkness. With Julian's help, she fights an evil that would rip her apart in order to forge a new future with the homicide suspect who has stolen her heart.

A word about the author...

TJ grew up with the Robinsons and a robot who said "danger" a lot after her spaceship crashed on a distant planet. When the Enterprise rescued her, she quickly promoted to the captain's chair. But an unfortunate transporter glitch beamed her back to the days of Camelot where she rode with Sir Lancelot, and graciously accepted Excalibur from the Lady of the Lake. While tutoring with Merlin, a misspoken spell plunged her deep into the center of the earth, aligning her with Will and Holly in a valiant fight against the Sleestak.

Always a dreamer, TJ would relive her fantasies during the day and expand the scenes in her mind until she'd write them down. After five completed stories, she wondered if others might want to read her adventures. So, she exposed *Caller of Light* to the eyes of unknown readers. To her surprise, it placed (and won) in several competitions.

TJ hopes you enjoyed *Caller of Light*. She wonders if you had the courage to fly the air currents on Critonback, and whether the color of your bonded Criton is as vibrant as you had hoped.

Until the next adventure, as your imagination conjures up the dreams within you, she wishes you a safe journey. Because, if you believe, traveling to far off galaxies, swimming with mermen, and falling in love with aliens can be one helluva unforgettable ride.

Thank you for purchasing
Caller of Light.

For other stories filled with romance and different
realities from TJ Shaw, or for questions and
additional information, visit http://tjshaw.com/ and
sign up for TJ's newsletter.

And, if you enjoyed *Caller of Light,* please consider
leaving a review on a retail site or contacting TJ.

Printed in Great Britain
by Amazon